Collection of Short Stories and More

J. Gordon Monson

Published by J. Gordon Monson, 2023.

This is a work of fiction. Similarities to real people, places, or events are entirely coincidental.

COLLECTION OF SHORT STORIES AND MORE

First edition. April 29, 2023.

Copyright © 2023 J. Gordon Monson.

ISBN: 979-8223704003

Written by J. Gordon Monson.

The Collection of Short Stories
Subtitle:
Humorous short stories; Christian theme short stories; Poetry; One liners; and more
by J. Gordon Monson

Caution! Reader's Alert!

This book not a 'How To Book' but it has something for most everybody. It's not the Holy Bible, but most of the content, the stories, poems, and one liners, have some value for entertainment, humor, or deep thoughts, as well as, directions to many who are still searching for that something that still missing, or who are in need of answers and where you can go and look for them.

To the unbelievers who laugh at those neighbors who spend so much of their time and energy running to church, and even knocking on doors sharing their belief to others.

Those other people must have this something about them that appears like real lasting contentment and joy.

Or if you're thinking something like this. "My world seems to be spinning out of control and things around me are getting worse, even scary. Those neighbors seem to have that something that I'm still lacking. I go do all this fun stuff, but I still keep searching for more. What is it that I'm still missing?"

To the one who believes there is a God out there somewhere, but you haven't done one thing to go look for Him. You may say to yourself, "I just live my life, such as it is, without knowing where to go or what to do to make it better. But the world around me keeps going down with more and more problems without the adequate answers. What is it I'm I missing?"

To my fellow believers who just need another source of encouragement and a reminder of the hope we have in Jesus. My hope is that you find this book to be just that.

God's Words to each of us, "For His merciful kindness is great toward us, and the truth of the Lord endures forever. Praise the Lord!" Palms 117:2

Acknowledgements:

Acknowledgement goes to all who have encouraged me to combine all of these together in book format. This work includes a collection of Contemporary fiction and nonfiction short stories, some include a sprinkling of Christian truths. Then followed by several short poems and short literalisms, as well as, my '101 one-liners' all incorporated in this one manuscript.

My first acknowledgement is to Clarice, my sweet wife who is my life partner through all of the ups and downs that life has to offer. She has been, and continues to be, my Godly inspiration in how I live my life. Then to all of our grown children and grandchildren who keep us young and show us so much sincere love.

Another acknowledgement contains the source of all Holy Bible Scriptures included in many parts of this writing. These are taken from The Holy Bible, New King James version. These give us so much knowledge of how we should live our lives in a way to follow our Lord in every area of being. These are what we can install in our mind and our heart to pattern our life after the author and finisher of our faith. These words are God inspired and should continue to become and be used as our life manual.

Many of these scriptures are shown below and are also inserted throughout this entire manuscript.

Further acknowledgement goes to so many special people over many years. My parents, Henry C. Monson and Eleanor Dahl Monson; To my siblings, Dennis Eugene Monson, his wife Dorothy, their seven grown children and families; To JoAnne Monson Skramstad, her later husband, Thorvald Skramstad, their five grown children and families; To Ronald Monson, his wife, Pauline and their four grown children and families; To Gerald Monson, his wife, Florence and their three grown children and families; To Cheryl

Monson Jerome, her husband, Jerry and their three grown children and families.

Further to the many Godly pastors who ministered to me and my family over the years. To so many special extended family, first and second cousins, longtime friends and new friends who were instrumental, and are still an ongoing influence in all that I do, write and say. These people are too many to name separately in this writing, but are a big influence in all that follows in this and in all of my other past and current writings.

Further: A very special acknowledgement goes to my dear Cousin Lois Monson Hofmann. She is an author in her own regard. She has been my writing mentor and my coach for this writing. She has inspired me in so many ways to shorten my sentence structures, refine my use of punctuation, and in so many other ways. I am so thankful for all the help she had given me from afar, thanks to her willingness to help and for the modern technology of email, as well as, the use of moving information from point A to point B in a much slower method called snail mail.

Lois, it's been my joy to have you there to work with me on this project.

God Bless You

If My people which are called by My name shall humble themselves, and pray, and seek My face, and turn from their wicked ways; then I will hear from heaven, and will forgive their sins, and will heal their land. 2 Chronicles 7:14

"For I know the thoughts that I think toward you, says the Lord, thoughts of peace and not of evil, to give you a future and a hope. Then you will call upon Me and go and pray to Me, and I will listen to you. And you will seek Me and find Me, when you search for Me with all your heart." Jeremiah 29:11 – 13

But those that wait on the Lord shall renew their strength; they shall mount up with wings like eagles, they shall run and not be weary, they shall walk and not faint.

Isaiah 40:31

Table of Content

Part One Short Fictional Stories

Part two Short stories w/Christian Theme

Part three Short Stories Poems + One Liners

Chasing Butterflies

Grandma Willis would have made a great Marine Corp drill sergeant. She could bark out orders as well as the best of them. She may have been old and gray, but she didn't lack in the energy department. She could work from sun up until way after sun down Monday through Saturday. And she expected everyone else to do the same. She always said, "If you stop doing the things you're supposed to do, you shrivel up and die."

Grandma did believe that Sunday was designed as a day of rest, so she did back off on much of work she did then. She said, "Sunday God called a day of rest. So it's our day of rest too."

She and Grandpa lived on what they affectionately called 'God's Best Two Acres.' They had chickens, and sheep, and goats, and one cow, along with the biggest garden I'd ever seen in my life.

I loved them both, but Grandma was much harder to love than Grandpa. He was the most mild mannered, sweetest man I have ever known. He must have had something special guiding his ship to be able to put up with Grandma for all those years. I never heard her say a kind word to him in all the time I spent with them. Yet he was always kind and thoughtful to her, just like he was with everyone else he was around.

I had been spending my summers with them for as far back as I can remember. I especially recall that summer when I was between four and five. Grandma showed me how to make apple pie. She did have a lot of patience with me when she was teaching me something back then. When I was almost eleven, she felt I was finally big enough to start carrying my own weight.

Grandma was always up by six each morning, and if she was up she felt everyone else should be up too. She would say, "Tommie, go out and gather them new eggs so we can have fresh eggs for breakfast."

Then she would say, "Tommie, while I am fixing breakfast, you go and make sure the chickens and sheep and goats are fed. You feed the goats last so Grandpa can milk them while they are eating." Then she would add, "Remember when there is work to be done, there is no time for chasing butterflies."

Grandpa would get up early same as Grandma. He'd wash up, put on his work boots, grab his cap, and then head for the old barn to milk Old Betsy. When he was through he'd take her milk to the house, and then go back out to milk the three mama goats. He always counted on me to feed them through their stanchions so they would be still while he did their milking. The other three mama goats still nursed their young, so they were fed separate. Big Buck goat was fed last. He didn't like having to wait till last so he would always make enough noise to wake the dead.

The sheep grazed so all I had to do for them is make sure they had plenty of fresh water in their water tank. This last was Grandma's instruction for me to do a least every other day. But I decided to do it every day so I wouldn't forget which day was which.

After all our chores, Grandpa and I would be back in the house for a well-earned breakfast. Grandma always fixed a big plate full of scrambled eggs, along with bacon and a big stack of toast made from her home baked bread. She often said, "God gave us those chickens so we are going to be grateful for the eggs they lay for us." Then she would add, "We never turn down any of these benefits that God gives to us."

After breakfast Grandpa would end up in his garden. He told me, "If you talk to them plants you make them smile, and if they are happy they make the best produce."

He must be right, I thought, because we always got lots of tomatoes and squash. The cucumbers and melons were the biggest and best you could ever wish for. The potatoes, carrots, onions and beets always overfill Grandpa's root cellar. And what they didn't store there, Grandma filled their basement with jars and jars of can goods.

My work was not yet done, because after breakfast I helped Grandpa bring in ripe produce from the garden, and then I helped her with canning. We washed, cut, and placed most of the fruit and veggies in jars to boil and seal. Then we'd let them cool before taking them to the basement. We moved the last of the previous year's canning to the front so it would be used first.

The only time I would hear her sound happy was when she was doing her canning. She would sing to herself, and to all within her hearing. She only knew three songs, so she would sing one and then another and then the last, Then she would start all over again. I asked her one day if she wanted me to sing with her. She told me I first needed to learn how to carry a tune.

So, the summers always pass with a lot of work and very little play. But still I loved being there on God's Best Two Acres with my Grandparents. Mom and Dad would come for me a week before school started so Mom could take me to buy my school clothes. I did miss my parents during those summers, but they knew I was in good hands, and I would learn a lot about life when I could see it up close and personal. They also knew that my grandparents needed whatever help I could give them. They had chosen their way of life when they were much younger and stronger. Now that they were older, the work could almost be too much for them without my help.

The middle weekend in September was always a great time to go back to visit Grandpa and Grandma. This was the weekend at their county fair. They always had several entries at the fair. They always had one or more of their younger goats and sheep entered, along with many number of different fresh and canned fruits and vegetables. And, Grandma always entered one of each of her preserves, along with her special goat cheese.

This was always an especially fun time for me because there were lots of carnival rides. Grandpa always gave me some money at the end of the summer as payment for all my help. I took a part of that to go have a fun day at the fair. Mom, Dad and I spent that weekend at Grandpa and Grandma's to help them with the chores both at home and with their animal entries at the fair.

At the end of the weekend we always checked on all their entries to see how they placed at each exhibit. To my amazement they almost always got blue ribbons. The ones they didn't get first place always made Grandma mad. She felt the judges must have some bias against her. Grandpa always said, "You can't win first place all of the time, but next year we'll just try all the harder."

I liked Grandpa's way of looking at it. He knew they had done all they could to win first place, but he said, "Other people also worked hard, and this time they were also rewarded for their efforts."

Then Grandma answered, "Oh, you just keep your opinions to yourself old man."

He just smile and change the subject. He must have found it was easier to avoid an argument with her on this or any other topic. It was amazing to me how he always looked on the bright side of everything.

Grandpa took me aside on the fair weekend. He told me that he didn't think he could keep up with all the work around God's Best two Acres anymore. He was thinking of telling Grandma that it was time to sell out and move into one of those retirement villages. He didn't think Grandma would like that idea but he was going to bring up the subject after the weekend when the fair was over.

I hated to see them move away. I loved going out there every summer. He later told me that I had been a big part of the reason he had stayed out there this long. He had said, "I like having a place for you to come to spend your summers." He added, "Having you with us each summer has been the most enjoyable thing I can do with my time for these last few years."

I spent that last night out there thinking how I could convince Grandpa to try to make it one more year. I then started thinking of a plan B if Grandpa still was not convinced to stay.

Suddenly it hit me; we could move here and build another house right next door, so Grandpa and Grandma could stay on. We could all share the work on the daily chores. Dad worked at his editing job from our home now, why couldn't he do it from here just as well?

It meant I'd have to change schools and church, and I would have to find new friends. It would mean lots of changes and adjustments for Mom and Dad as well, but wouldn't it be worth it to have the whole family together all year around.

On the flip side, I'd get to spend all four seasons with both my parents and my grandparents. It would mean no more summers away from Mom and Dad, and no more winters away from Grandpa and Grandma. Since they all were such a big part of my life, it will be a win win situation for us all. I believe Grandma would be the real beneficiary. I really didn't think she would ever agree to leave their place, and try to get used to another place after all those years.

Now, all I had to do is to convince Mom and Dad of my idea. The timing will have to be just right, and I'll need to have to list all the pluses and minuses when I present this idea to them.

I decided to first tell Grandpa of my plan. When I approached him he said, "That is the best idea I've ever heard. If they agree it will be God's answer to my prayers."

He and I both knew Grandma would be elated with this idea. She would never like the idea of moving to a new place. She had said many times, "This is my home no matter what comes."

Then Grandpa asked, "Have you talked to your Mom and Dad about your great idea?

"No, I just came up with it during the night, but I wanted to tell you first."

His answer, "I'm glad you shared it with me first." Then he added, "What do you think they will think of your idea?"

"I can only hope they will like it, or that they will think it all through before they answer yes or no."

Then I added, "I plan to ask them on our drive back home, and I'll let you know as soon as possible what they say."

We left late in the afternoon that Sunday. We hadn't taken time to go to church, and Mom was wishing we could have all gone together with Grandpa and Grandma. But, it had been a busy weekend and even that morning had gone way to fast for everyone.

I remember Mom said, "I really liked Grandpa and Grandma's church. There are so many good people there and they are so friendly and welcoming."

I had thought, *'Wow, maybe this is the time!'*

"So I started to tell them "Mom and Dad, I have been thinking. How would it be if we were able to go the Grandpa and Grandma's church every week?"

Mom turned to look back at me, "Tommie, what are you saying?"

I told them all I had been thinking about like moving out to Grandpa and Grandma's place; to help them with their chores; go to church with them and live there year around. That I would have to change schools and make new friends, plus adjust to living on a farm, and all the work that goes on with living there. I mentioned that there is plenty of room to build a new house out there, or even add on to their house. Then I added, "Dad you can still do your editing work from home just like you do now."

Dad nodded his head before he said, "Son, you have really been thinking this through, haven't you?

I answered, "Yeah, Grandpa told me he was considering selling and moving to one of those retirement villages because he is having trouble keeping up with all the work around the place. He doesn't think Grandma would ever volunteer to leave the place on their own. She has said a thousand times or more, "When you stop doing, you die."

Mom said, "You know son, you have really come up with an idea this time. We will have to think this through just like you have, and we will need to pray about it as well."

I told them, "I really want to do this. Besides, it would be very hard on both Grandpa and Grandma to move away after all the years they have lived there. We could adjust so much easier to their way of life. I love their little farm, and all the animals, and even all the work to be done."

Then I went on, "I told Grandpa I'd call him when we get back home, I'll tell him you are thinking and praying about my idea, and I'll ask him to not do anything til we've made our decision."

Dad was nodding his head and Mom smiled and answered, "Fair enough."

We arrived home after dark that evening. After a quick dinner and bath I was off to bed as school was on my schedule for the next day. In the morning nothing was said about my idea, and although I would've liked to ask, I knew Mom and Dad would let me know as soon as they had time to think through all the pros and cons of my plan.

At school that day I looked at all the friends I had there. They would have to be left behind. Most of them were friends during the school year, but not in the summer because I was not around then. I also thought about friends at church. It was the same there. I saw them while I was home, but not during the summer. I would miss the children's church camp every year as well. But my summers were so full of everything I loved so I didn't feel I was missing anything.

When I got off the school bus that afternoon both Dad and Mom were standing out in front of our house. They had been waiting for me to get home. I knew something big was up, and I wondered what to expect.

Dad spoke first, "He said let's go in the house and talk. We have some interesting news to share with you." But first, "Would you like some milk and cookies?"

I said, "Yes, but first I would rather hear the news you wanted to share with me."

Dad turned towards mother and said, "Mother would you like to share the news?"

Mom shook her head, "No, they're your parents, I think you should be the one to share this news with Tommie."

I thought as I sat on the edge of my seat, "Well, at least I know the news involves Grandpa and Grandma."

Dad smiled, "Okay, Tommie it's like this, we have done some thinking and praying about what we talked about yesterday. The only thing we can tell you is this, we found out that I can move my office without any complications; also our house may be sold, or at least rented to some people from our church. They want to buy it, but won't be in a position to do that for about one year so they want to rent until then. We haven't talked to Grandpa and Grandma as yet. We wanted you to be in on that conversation. So, if they are in agreement with your idea, then I guess we are moving."

I said, "Wow, I've got to call Grandpa! He made me promise that I would call just as soon as I had your answer. And I know Grandpa and Grandma will both be in agreement with this plan."

We called Grandpa and Grandma that afternoon. They were both so happy to hear the news.

Grandpa added, "I just found out my next door neighbor is selling his two acres right between our two places. They asked if we knew anyone who might want to buy the land. I told them I just might know of someone, but I would have to get back with them in a few days." Then Grandpa said, "Does Tommie want to talk to Grandma?"

"Oh yes, I do want to talk with her."

Grandma came on the line, I could hear the change in her voice before we even said more than hello, she said, "Hello Tommie, I'm so glad to hear that you are coming for the whole year. Grandpa has told me more often than I can remember he just can't do all the work around here anymore, but now we will have you and your folks to help."

Then she added, "Maybe now I will find some time where you and I can go out to chase the butterflies together."

I laughed at that and asked her where she came up with the saying about chasing butterflies.

She told me the story about the very first summer I stayed with them. Her words were, "You was only four years old then."

She added, "Every time I turned around you wanted to go outside. I had asked you what you wanted to do outside. You told me you liked chasing butterflies. I've always wanted to have time to go chasing those butterflies with you. Now, maybe I should have more time to do that."

I Remember Dad

Life was good back then when we were all together. My dad, without a single doubt, was my biggest hero. He called himself just a regular cowboy, but I remember him as the best champion rodeo bronc rider. He had that cowboy look with his rugged suntanned complexion, his wavy light brown hair sticking out from beneath his well-worn cowboy hat. He had those bowed legs from all those years of riding. He was the best looking cowboy I ever saw. Of course, I was probably partial.

Dad always knew Mom didn't like him riding dangerous bucking horses in the professional rodeo circuit, but whenever we needed some extra money for whatever reason, he would enter in the closest rodeo. And he always won big in whatever contest he entered, and he has so many trophies and fancy belt buckles to prove it. He had long ago cut a deal with Mom that he would only compete maybe four or five times a year. And then only when the estimated taxes bill or doctor or dentist bills were mounting without enough funds to cover them. He would then go for enough money to cover the cost of these.

She always asked, "How do you know you will win enough to cover these bills?"

His response, "There is no one out there in the circuit who can ride as good as me, so it's a sure bet."

Then I heard her say more than once, "I hope you are right because if you don't win, we may not be able to pay them what we owe."

He would take her in his arms and whisper in her ear just loud enough for the rest of us to hear, "Sweet Precious Minute, you are not to worry one bit about that."

Mom is a little bitty thing. Dad called her his Precious Minute because he said she is no bigger than a minute. But, he knew she had her way of keeping him on the straight and narrow. He would say, "Britt, you may be the prettiest thing this side of the Mississippi, and you may be little, but you sure do carry a big stick."

She'd blush when he said anything like that. She almost always wore britches. She had many pretty dresses hanging in her closet, but they were rarely pulled off the hangers. Oh, there was their wedding picture where he wore his fancy cowboy dress jacket, white shirt, bow tie and new blue jeans over his new boots, and she wore the most beautiful white petticoat dress. It covered her from her neck down to her shoes in frills and lace. Or on Sundays when we all, even Dad, went to church to hear the Word of God preached, and where we gathered with some of our neighbors in fellowship.

Mom said one time, "Why would I ever wear anything fancy like that out in here in that red clay. It would permanently change the colors of my beautiful wedding dress, or all of my other dresses I keep for special occasions like to church."

Before Dad married Mom he followed the rodeo circuit full time. He had won enough prize money to stake the purchase of our ranch here in Southern Idaho. When he met Mom he decided traveling all around the country and sometimes even around the world was not the place for a married family man. When my twin sister, Tina, and I were born he promised Mom he wouldn't compete on a regular basis. Only often enough to keep his name on the rodeo circuit mailing lists, and only when we needed a quick fix in our cash flow.

We had cows, horses, and chicken, plus at times during any year, we had sheep and even a couple goats. The chickens kept us in fresh eggs, and butchering some young for meat, but when we all traveled for rodeos, Mom would chop the heads off of all the chickens and dress them for the freezer. She would say, "That way we will always have a steady supply of chicken dinners for quite a while after we came back home. That way we won't go hungry for some time if Dad doesn't win.

Mom chose to home school Tina and me. This way we could never get too far away from home without having to do school work. Even when we are away from home we had to keep up with our studies.

I didn't mind school all that much, but I would rather be out riding or helping Dad with his horse training. He trained horses for other people besides all the ranching and rodeo riding.

On one of his rodeo competitions he had earned enough winnings to cover the tax payment, as well as, buy a used ranch truck to replace our old one. The newly acquired truck is a king cab pickup truck beefy enough to pull one of our big stock trailers loaded with cattle, but still nice enough to use to take our family to church on Sundays. Dad called this new truck his Cowboy Cadillac.

On one of Mom's shopping trips into town shortly after we purchased that truck she found a bumper sticker with the words, "Cowboy Cadillac." This sticker quickly found a place on the back tail gate.

In the summer months we grazed our cattle on BLM land. This meant we branded them shortly after they were born, as they were to be out on the grazing land with cattle from other ranches. It also meant that in the fall we had to do our annual roundup. It would take all of us to separate ours from cattle that belonged to other ranches.

Tina and I had ridden going back for as long as I can remember. We both liked the fall roundup because we would get to camp out for several nights while we did our work. We also got to ride with other kids from other families. We would help one another with the herd separation. When we had most of our cattle separated we would drive them back into our fenced pastures. Then we went back out to see if we had any more strays. Dad would spend days out looking for any of our cattle that had strayed beyond the territory we had covered in our initial roundup.

He used to signal his location using the old Indian smoke signals when he found cows that belonged to one of our neighbors. They would also do the same for him. This method worked fairly well. Of course, that was long before the invention of cell phones.

I remember one of those fall roundups when Tina and I came across a brown bear and her cubs. She blocked our path thinking we were a threat to her little ones. Tina was just behind me, and was able to get her horse, Strawberry, turned back, but I was face to face with that she bear. I backed my horse, Boots, up one step at a time until there was some distance between me and that mama. She stood her ground until I was able to turn Boots completely around. She then turned and moved her cubs off in the other direction. When we got back to camp that evening and told Dad about our encounter he said, "I met her just yesterday myself. She is looking for a place to spend the winter, but I guess she will be out and about for some time yet because the weather is still too warm to go into hibernation. Be careful if you see her again. Keep your eyes open at all times. She's not to be trusted as long as she has her young with her. I'm proud of how you two handled that mamma bear situation."

After each fall roundup was a very busy time. We had to brand all the calves that were born out on the summer BLM graze. Then Dad separated out all the cattle which he planned to take to auction. This is always an important time for ranchers as this is often the biggest source of income for ranchers during the entire year. These cattle sales are needed to bring in enough money to cover most of the expenses for the rest of the winter months. If the market is down, the ranchers must find some other ways to produce income to make up the difference. Dad did better than most ranchers because of his horse training, boarding fees, along with his rodeo winnings. He had broken horses for several of our neighbors. He also boarded several horses all throughout the year for five families that live in town. They were, and still are, frequent visitors to our place when they wanted to ride, and we had lots of room for them to do that once they get through all the gates and past our fenced pastures.

After the fall roundup Tina and I were back to hitting the books, and Mom was always busy preparing for these teaching times. Along with catching up with all the things she didn't get done while we were all out rounding up our cattle. She rode with us every day out on the trail, and then also fixed our meals out in our makeshift camp wagon while we were out there. She always looked forward to getting back to her daily routine once we were back home.

She also did a lot of canning of fruits and vegetables from her summer garden. Most of this she did in the summer months. And it's something else both Tina and I helped her with. Mom would put up stewed tomatoes, squash, peas, carrots, green beans and pickles. She also raised several different herbs which she dried for spices. She dug up the onions and garlic too, but she waited until after our fall roundup to dig up the potatoes, turnips, and the rest of the carrots to fill our root cellar.

She said, "It's no use buying all these things when we can have them fresh from our very own garden. With our long growing season we can put up enough preserves to store in the root cellar the rest of the year."

Then she would add, "I've always found that the food always tastes better when you grow it yourself."

Dad would always say, "Amen to that my Sweet Sugar Pie."

Mom would blush when he called her that, and then she'd say, "You need to go back to work, as I have other things on my mind, and don't have time for all this name calling right now."

He'd smile and come back with, "Okay my Sweet Sugar Pie, but I'll be back when you are not so busy and have more time to pay attention to me."

It was right after Tina and I celebrated our eleventh birthdays when Dad announced that he had just signed up to ride in the late summer two day rodeo in Pocatello. He would compete and when we got back we would start the fall cattle roundup. He told Mom he felt that this would be his last rodeo as the competition was getting better all the time, and he felt that his chances of winning were diminishing. He was glad to get to compete in this rodeo as it was one of his favorites.

On the second day of the event he was in the running for top rider. He took us to Cowboy Church at nine that morning, and his competition was to start at eleven. He rode his first horse to the eight count. Only one other rider was able to do that. On Dad's last ride of the competition he again rode to the count, but in his dismount the horse turned and kicked him on the back of his head. He went down so quickly that some in the crowd didn't realize what had happened. Mom saw the whole thing and was over the fence and out to him almost before the rodeo people. She fell to her knees beside him and yelled for someone to get an ambulance in there pronto. Tina and I pushed so hard on that tall fence we were sure we would break it.

The ambulance was there in just seconds, and Dad was loaded up into the back as soon as they got his neck stabilized. Mom yelled to us that she was riding in the ambulance and for us to ask our friends for a ride to the hospital.

Then she said, "Dad is hurt bad and I need to be with him right now."

Georgia Steele gave Tina and me a ride to the local hospital, while her husband, Fred, drove our truck over there. She stayed with us until Mom came out to find us. I could tell Mom had been crying. She kneeled down in front of us and told us that we needed to be strong and to pray for Dad and for her right now.

She then added, "The doctors don't think Dad is going to pull through. They feel his injury is so bad that it may take him from us.

Even if he does survive, he will have some brain injuries which may cause him to be completely helpless."

She then held both of us for the longest time, and then she slipped back in where they were monitoring Dad.

Well, we lost Dad on his second day in that hospital. He lived like he wanted to live. He enjoyed life to the fullest and left us doing what he loved best.

My hero died young. He was my example of what a man should be. He was always here for us every day until that last day. He won the top rider spot that last day and Mom collected his winnings and his trophy. That trophy still sits in a prominent place in our main ranch house today as a reminder of who he was.

Tina and I both left for college eight years after Dad died.

Mom shared with us that day on the way to our first day of college, "I can't believe I have succeeded in raising my two kids up to adulthood this quickly and easily. I feel like my work should not be done yet, and here you two are all grown up and off to start the next part of your life. My advice to you is to go as your Dad would have done. Live your lives to the fullest just as he did."

Mom had hired a foreman, Frank is his name, to come in to help us with the roundup that fall, and he never left. He has been with us ever since and has become part of our family over the years. He does all the ranching and horse training that Dad had done while he was alive. Every year Frank says he is going to find a real job, but each time he brings it up to Mom, she tells him he can't go because he is needed here. She kept the ranch and added more boarding stalls. To this day she still keeps her garden and shares the bounty with Tina and her family, as well as, with me and my family and from the abundance from her canning.

Tina married right out of college and now has two children of her own. I married two years later and my wife and I have two sons and one daughter. We all work the annual cattle roundup each fall.

It's much easier now as we communicate with each other and with our neighbors with cell phones.

My wife and I built our house right here on the ranch property, and not far from Mom. Tina and her family also built here. We spend many wonderful hours with Mom. And her grandchildren are growing up to call her blessed.

Mom recently told me that Dad had taken out a life insurance policy for a million dollars just two years before he died. That money had been invested and over the years has since doubled. The return on investment had been more than enough for her to keep the ranch for all these years since. She had placed this asset along with the ranch in a revocable living trust. This will one day be passed along to Tina and me.

Mom recently shared that her and Frank have decided to marry after twenty three years. She asked if I would walk her down the aisle on her wedding day.

I told her, "I would be the proudest son on the planet to do this for her. Let's make this the biggest and best ceremony this county has ever seen."

Then I added. "Mom, next to Dad, Frank is the most honorable man I have ever known. He has been faithful to help you run this place for all these years. He has never complained about all the work it takes to keep this place going. I also know you have been in love with him for so many years, so why have you been so long in getting this done? Congratulations Mom, I can't wait to see you do this."

Her answer, "Thanks son, that's exactly how I feel about this. I remember how I felt when your dad and I were waiting to be married more than thirty years ago. He was my hero then and he still is after all these years. My love for him has never stopped, but now I have finally found room for my love for Frank to grow."

She continued, "Son, never forget your dad. He was the very best man in your life for your early years, and Frank has taken up where your dad left off. Now he will be your dad from now on."

"Mom, Frank has been like a Dad to me for twenty plus years, so my transition to accept him will be a very easy one. I love you Mom, and I am so very proud of you."

No Harmless Hattie

The bridge was just ahead. Melanie wasn't sure she could get home in time. She had left her friend, Lydia's place, at four that morning. Lydia had packed a snack for her to eat on the way. The trip was to take most of the day, but an accident delayed her. She saw the whole thing right in front of her. That person in the black SUV ran a little sports car off the road at a very bad spot. The little car with two occupants left the road on the cliff side.

The last thing Melanie saw was someone's arm waving, maybe throwing something out, from the passenger side, just before their car went through the guardrail and down out of sight. Melanie quickly pulled over, grabbed her cell phone, and then ran over to the edge of the road. She could see the sports car maybe thirty feet below sitting upside down at the bottom.

It was impossible to get down from where she was standing. Her long golden brown hair was whipping past her face in the wind as she dialed 911. The operator took all the information Melanie could give him, including about where it happened. She told him she would try to get down to the car and occupants. Then she ran back to her car, stashed her purse out of sight, and slipped her keys into her jeans pocket before locking her car. She ran back down the road to a spot she thought might be a way down.

The going was hard, but she needed to get to the car to help in any way she could. If she were in their situation she hoped someone would do the same for her. The gravel trail was treacherous and she nearly lost her footing more than once. Almost at the bottom she did fall, landing on her hands and knees. The gravel biting into her hands. She was thankful she was wearing her jeans or her knees would be looking like her hands. She stood up and continued on towards the car. This was no easier as the long grass and weeds at the bottom seemed to hold her back. She couldn't run, but she did push on as fast as she could. Almost there she could see the car.

Trying to see if there was any movement inside the car, she thought she saw a hand move. She called out but no one responded.

She thought, *'Why didn't I think to grab my first aid kit from the trunk of my car?'*

Melanie was almost to the car when she heard a car up on the road. It stopped and she heard its brakes squeal. Hopefully that would be help coming.

She called up, "Hey, they are down here. Please hurry."

"That's funny, no response from up there. Maybe they didn't hear me. Hey, please come down and help. There are people who need help."

There was still no response. Then she heard that same car speed off. She didn't take time to think about this as she needed to get to the people in the car, to find out if they were alive, and then tell them help is on the way.

The driver, a young man with long stringy dirty brown hair, was not conscious, but the passenger, a smaller man, a little older, and with a full beard and a receding hair line was moving, but was a little incoherent. She was able to ask him where he hurt. He moaned, "M—y head hurts and my—my shoulder is screaming at me. I think my leg is caught up under the dash."

Then he passed out. As Melanie was trying to get the door open on his side she heard a gunshot and instantly heard a bullet ricochet off the bottom of the car. She dropped down beside the car and said, "God please help us."

She wondered which direction this shot was coming from. A second gunshot broke the glass on the other side of the car. Next she heard the sound of sirens coming from the same direction she had come from. It was like sweet music to her ears.

There were no more gun shots, only the sound of a car racing away just before the sound of emergency units stopping up on the road.

She yelled up, "Hey, we are down here. Please hurry, there are two fellows badly hurt."

The trooper yelled back, "Are you hurt too?"

"No, but I am a witness to all that has happened and I need to tell you the whole story. There is a black SUV involved. Whoever was driving it purposely ran these two poor guys off the road, and then left. I think they came back and tried to kill us. They fired two shots at us just before we heard your sirens. Then they left heading towards the bridge to the south."

"Okay, I'll call that in and ask for backup. We will pursue the black SUV based upon what you just told us."

Melanie stayed with the car until the paramedics got there. Neither man regained consciousness while she was there and she was not able to get either of the doors open.

Finally she was able to tell the whole story to the officer. She also gave him her phone numbers and address so she could be contacted if needed. By the time all this was done both men had been pulled from the car. The younger one was pronounced dead at the scene either from his injuries from the accident, or the one gunshot wound, while the older one was brought up by sling to the road and taken off in an ambulance. She heard the officer tell his fellow officer they had found drugs in their car along with drug paraphernalia. She had apparently gotten caught up in the middle of a shootout between some drug runners.

They also hauled her up to the top with that same sling apparatus. She found her car had been broken into. Both her purse and her luggage were missing. She remembered locking her car. The bad guys had come back and taken her things. She reported the theft and gave the authorities a detailed report of what was missing.

Her clothes, makeup kit, and several papers inside her portable small metal chest containing all of her financial records, bills and invoices. Her check book and credit cards, driver's license were in her purse. Her car keys were still in her pocket, and she had her cell phone and thirty four dollars cash in her pocket. It would be enough to get home, but not enough if she stopped at motel before getting home.

Finally, after what seemed like hours of delay, she was back on the road. Home sounded so good about now. She couldn't wait to get there. She thought about all the things that had happened. She came so close. But is thankful to be alive. One of those bullets could have had her name on it.

And, now she might be a target for these bad guys. They know who she is and where she lives. They probably even had her vital numbers since they had all of her financial records. This meant she had to do whatever it takes to make sure the authorities catch them. She had no idea who they are except for that black SUV car, and they could likely get rid of it. It would stand out like a shining beacon for all to see.

On her drive she was amazed how many black SUVs are on the road. Every one put that much more a spark of fear in her. Any one of them could be that same car. They knew what she was driving and she had no way to change that.

Finally she decided she had to call her mom and dad. She wouldn't tell them all that had happened, not wanting them to worry, but she did ask if she could stay with them for a couple nights. When the bad guys are locked up she could finally go home and feel reasonably safe.

The bridge was just ahead. It would take her on into Wisconsin and on home.

It had been a long time since she last ate. Maybe she could spend some of her thirty four dollars on a good dinner before she traveled on. The remainder would have to go for gasoline. She might even get home with money to spare, "Wait a minute, her passport was in her purse! How was she to get across the border? Would she be able to go across on the sly? Would the Canadians believe her story? It sounded too far-fetched even to her, and she had lived it. Could the Canadian state police verify her story and allow her to go through? The Trooper gave me his card, I'll call him and explain my dilemma. He will surely be able to help me."

She spoke out loud, "Oh no, there, another black SUV. How many has that been now? Too many and each time I almost run off the road. It's very unnerving. Home sounds better and better, but so does food. There, a nice looking dinner house. I'll pull in and eat. Maybe when I have a full stomach things will look a whole lot better."

Melanie ordered the biggest steak on the menu. It came with all the fixings. That snack Lydia packed was long ago history.

The ladies room was a nice addition as she had not had a chance to clean up since early this morning. When she returned to her table her food was there for her. She couldn't remember the last time she enjoyed a meal more. She left the money for her meal along with a nice tip and headed for her car. She had just unlocked the door when someone with a raspy voice said, "Hold it you need to come with me. Don't try anything funny or you're a dead chick."

Melanie snapped her head around in the declining daylight to find that the bad guy was not a guy at all, but a woman close to her same age. She wore this leather collar with silver decorations all around, and she had a black leather vest buttoned up, but barely covering her womanly figure. She wore a pair of tight leather pants and boots that came up almost to her knees. Her long blonde hair was matted and pulled back into a single pony tail held by a leather looking band. Her big deep blue eyes looked hard and piercing, almost menacing, recessed in her round stark pale face. She had shaved her eye brows and painted lines in their place. Her hands shook and she was shivering like she was cold even though the evening was still warm with hardly any wind. She produced the biggest hand gun Melanie had ever seen. She must have had it hidden behind her when she approached.

She said, "Give me your keys to your car, get in, and shut the door. Melanie followed her instructions, while the gal ran around to the other side and got in the passenger seat. The gun was still in her right hand, so she handed Melanie the keys with her left hand, "Start the car and drive where I tell you. No funny stuff or you're a goner."

"Where is all my stuff you took out of my car back there?"

The gal laughed, "If you look over to the back of this parking lot you'll see the SUV. It's all still there. I borrowed a couple of your credit cards, but decided they may be more trouble to me than they are worth. So, I put them back, but you don't have to worry about that anymore. How are my two friends in the sports car?"

Melanie thought about telling her the truth; that one was dead, but thought better of that. If this gal knew she had cause his death maybe she would not hesitate to kill again so she said, "They're headed for the hospital, in fact, they are probably both there right now, since it's been a while since they went off the side of the road."

"Did you see what happened to them?'

"All I know is that they were in trouble. I stopped to help and call the troopers. They are getting the care they need now."

Melanie noticed that the gal didn't have her seat belt on. Melanie, out of habit, had put her seat belt on. Maybe this was the answer. It would take great chance and maybe it would back fire, but maybe it was her only chance. As they drove she watched for the right opportunity. The street was completely dark now except for the street lights. It would be easier to do this in the dark. She waited thinking something would come up that might help finish her plan. If she didn't do something rash she was probably going to be killed anyway. She was a witness to what this gal had done, and then to the shootings, "Were you the one shooting at us?"

"I suppose there's no need to lie to you. Yes, I shot at you first and then at the guys in the car. I can't leave any witnesses behind. You already know what I look like. The only thing you don't know is my name. It's Hattie. Some my friends call me Harmful Hattie, probably with good reason."

It was now clear that Hattie didn't intend for her to live. This knowledge just made her plan even more necessary, or this drive could be her last unless she found some way to disrupt Hattie's plan.

It was about that time Melanie saw it. A police car was parked at the side of the road with his lights flashing. The officer had pulled over another car and was out of his car talking to the other driver. She would have to be quick about what she was about to do. Just before they came up on the police car Melanie jerked the wheel to the right throwing Hattie of balance. Melanie used both hands to grab the gun from Hattie just as her car collided with the police sedan. Melanie now had the gun and Hattie was screaming in her ear, "Give my back that gun you bitch."

But Melanie had it pointed directly at Hattie's chest and she told her to put both of her hands out the other window. By that time the officer was at Melanie's door demanding the gun. He had his gun pulled and aimed directly at her.

When all was explained, and after the police had called the trooper, Melanie was released and Hattie was taken off to jail. The officer gladly gave Melanie a ride back to where the SUV was parked and she was able to retrieve her belongings. They took copies of her passport and credit cards, and then kept all of her other belongings as evidence.

The content of the SUV contained still more drugs and paraphernalia. She truly was No Harmless Hattie.

Melanie had to stay over that night. She called her mom and dad back and only told them she had been in an accident. She explained she was all right and she would rent a car in next morning to drive the rest of the way home. She decided it was best to wait until later to tell them the rest of her whole story when she was safely back across the border and home at last.

Melanie was called to testify when Hattie's trial came up. Hattie ended up with a long list of charges against her. The strongest ones were kidnapping and second degree murder, along with possession for sale of illegal drugs. She was convicted on all charges.

Melanie didn't stay for the sentencing but believed that Hattie will end up spending much of the rest of her adult life behind bars.

Melanie's insurance company rendered her car totaled from the collision with the police sedan, and only after they confirmed the reason for the accident did they agree to honor her claim. She ended up with a new car out of the deal, and, she eventually got all of her stuff back that No Harmless Hattie had stolen, but some of it was only after the Hattie's trial.

She says, "God was with her all through this really bad time, and He is so good!

All in a Day's Work

Barney owned a one ton vacuum truck which he used for cleaning the duck systems in homes and offices buildings, as well as, chimney sweeping. He worked by appointment. He rarely needed a helper to run this vacuum truck.

He is a big man with a great smile and a drawing personality. Most people remembered him for that, and for his extended waxed mustache. It had grown to several inches out beyond his cheeks.

One sunny cold day in late fall his second appointment was cleaning a chimney for a customer not far from his home. It was still early enough in the morning, where the frost had melted away, but there was still a chill in the air.

Barney quickly set up the big hoses and was getting ready to start the cleaning work when he discovered the hot ashes still in the fireplace. He couldn't suck these into his vacuum and cause a real fire hazard. He had to stop the big vacuum, hand removed the hot ashes before connecting the last big vacuum hose to the fireplace, and then start the big vacuum. This whole process normally takes about fifteen minutes, which includes setting up his ladders, then getting up on the roof to brush down the inside of the chimney.

When done, he shut down the vacuum system before starting his final take down. He always started the takedown inside the house to shorten the time the front door is kept open, and then continued removing the rest of the hoses until he reaches his truck.

That's when he heard the sound. It sounded like muffled kitten meowing. He first thought, *'Was it coming from under his truck.'*

However, with further investigation, he found the kitten was inside that last vacuum hose. He raced through this process. That poor kitten came waddling out so covered with soot it was almost impossible to recognize it was a kitten. Barney picked it up and was trying to wipe the soot away from its nose when his customer came out of her house.

He turned to look at her just she yelled, "Hey, where on earth has that kitten been?"

It had ashes from the tip of its nose to the end of its tail. Even his nose and eyes were so full of soot it couldn't see, and likely could hardly breathe.

Barney felt so bad for her kitten he didn't know what to say, except that he wouldn't charge her for his work.

She nodded her head, took the kitten from him, and then responded, "I'll give the kitten a bath, and see if it is ok..."

Each time that day, and every day following that incident, while Barney set up the vacuum truck he remembered the near disaster experience with the kitten. He couldn't help but wonder how many times he had unknowingly come close to a similar situation with someone's pet, or even with a small child.

Work place accidents are all too frequent as it is, and when they happen to you, it really makes you become very cautious at every step in your work.

A few days later Barney was close by her house and decided to stopped back to check with the lady about her kitten.

When he asked her how the little kitten was, she quickly exclaimed, "Oh, he died."

Barney's heart sank at hearing this news. He had never killed anything with his vacuum truck before, not even a wild animal on a road kill accident.

When she saw his reaction to her statement she laughed and added, "Oh don't worry Barney, the vacuum truck accident didn't kill my kitten, it was run over by a car out on the road."

Buttermilk and Cheese Crackers

I remember Grandma Polly probably differently than any of her other twelve spoiled grandchildren. She was that one person who personally influenced everything about who I am and how I feel about almost everything. Oh, she had her short comings just like anyone else. None of us are perfect, but for a long, long time I thought she was just about as close to being there as anyone could be.

You see, she took me in when I was a little four year old brat. I'm told my dad left before my first birthday, and then Grandma Polly took me in when mom was dying of cancer. That's a word that still strikes terror in the hearts of anyone who has it, or loves someone who does.

Grandma Polly was my dad's mom and I was kind of in the middle of her many grandkids, but the only one who didn't have a mom and dad around, so she brought me into her home, loved and nurtured me all through my remaining childhood.

I don't remember Grandma Polly with anything but long gray hair which was always wrapped up in a bun at the back of her head. She had lots of wrinkles and wore eye glasses, *'spectacles' as she called them.'* She wore them way out on the tip of her nose, and she always wore a faded, floral dress. She was barefoot most of the time, except in the snow. Her feet were so calloused that she could walk almost anywhere without complaining. And her hands felt like sandpaper, but they could be so comforting in times when nothing but being held by her comforted me more.

Granny, a name I always called her, helped me with my homework, even when I was in high school. She had dropped out of school in her freshman year, but she had the intellect of someone with a much higher education. She was especially good in math. She could read a math question once, and then know instantly in her head the right answer. I would sit there for what seemed like forever.

She would come over, look over my shoulder, and have the right answer before taking her second breath.

She would smile at me and say, "Jasper, you can do this. I know you can. All you have to do is work from the back end of the problem towards its nose. I never did figure out how she did it, but I did get pretty good at math over time. It was probably because of her faith in me. It sure wasn't because I understood and remembered all those dizzy formulas.

Granny was the only one that I let call me Jasper. It had been her nickname for me from the day I was born. She once told me I reminded her of a jasper stone, because my face was so red when I was born, and I kept that red shade even as I grew. I looked up jasper in the Webster and it said. "An opaque variety of quartz, reddish, yellow or brown in color." I guess I must be the reddish variety.

My given name is James, but everyone else, my cousins, my aunts and uncles all called me Jimmy until after I graduated from college. Some still do now, even after all these years.

From the time I first came to live with Granny, she would share her fresh buttermilk and cheese crackers with me for an afternoon snack. The milk came from our two cows. Granny would milk them twice a day, and then let the milk set over night in the refrigadaire, *'her name for it,'* until the cream floated to the top. She would skim the cream off so she could use it to churn butter. She then let some of the milk stay in the refrigadaire for many days, until it went sour. The left over milk we didn't use for cereal and other cooking she would use to make her secret buttermilk recipe. This was a secret formula which she wouldn't share with anyone, not even me. But, her buttermilk was always the best. Nothing you bought in any store could ever match it.

Granny sold her fresh butter and buttermilk, along with eggs to several of our neighbors. They always called to find out if she had any fresh supplies before they came over to buy. Between that and her government benefits, we always had enough money to get by. I found out years later, she got a social security benefit from her late husband, my Grandpa. His long time employment at the feed store, and then from survivor's benefits from his railroad retirement. I only later found out that Granny had socked away enough money to put me all the way through four years of college. That was just one more of the bigger thing I can be grateful for when I think of all the things that Granny did for me.

I remember that day I climbed up in our big oak tree in front of our house and couldn't get down. I must have been only five or six at the time. Granny went back and got the old leaning ladder Grandpa had stored in the old shed behind the house. It was so full of cobwebs but she didn't bother to remove them before she leaned that old ladder against the tree, and then climbed up to the top and pulled me out of that tree. She told me later that one of the few things she was deathly afraid of was heights. But, she didn't even think about her fear until she had us both back on the ground. She then leaned back against that old ladder and started to shake. She told me to run get her a cold, wet cloth to cover her face because she thought she was having a heart attack. Well, it turned out that she just had her heart racing out of fear. You know, I never climbed up in that old oak tree again, not even when I was older.

There was that other time when I was in first grade when I missed the school bus coming home. Granny always watched for me every day. That day the bus went right on by our house without stopping. Granny ran out to flag down the bus driver, Mr. Flanagan, but he didn't see her. She then jumped in our old Ford truck and chased down the bus. She was ready to have it out with Mr. Flanagan, only to find out that I wasn't on board.

She then drove over to the school to see if I was still there, but unbeknownst to them, and to her, I had started walking home. I knew a short cut through the Miller's corn field, so I wasn't on the main road. No one at the school knew anything, and she took them to task for not keeping better track of the children place in their care. Then she went to the sheriff's department to report me missing. By that time she was so rattled that she could barely talk. The sheriff radioed his patrol cars to keep a watch for me, and then told her to go home and wait for word. She reluctantly drove back home, thinking that there must be something else she could do to find me. When she drove in our drive, she spotted me sitting on the steps of the front porch. She slammed on the brakes to stop the truck, jumped out and ran the rest of the way to where I was now standing. My mouth was open, but I couldn't say anything. All I could do was point to the truck. She had failed to put it in park when she stopped. It rolled off the right side of the driveway, and broke through the wooden fence where we kept our cows. It came to a stop next to the barn when the front tires hit a railroad tie we used to separate our garden from the grass.

Let me tell you, I never missed the bus again, unless it was planned like it was done intentionally years later because of football or baseball practice.

Granny had me help her rebuild the fence that day so our cows couldn't get out. We missed our buttermilk and cheese cracker snack that day, and she didn't say anything about my bus problem until later that evening after supper and we had the dishes all washed. She finally then only asked what had happened. When I told her that I had a call of nature, *'those were her words,'* at the time the bus was due to come. She seemed to understand, but she said, "Make sure you get those duties over with long before it's time for the bus. Is that understood?"

The last thing she said before I went to bed that night, "Jasper, I thought I lost you today and it scared me more than I've ever been scared before. I guess I needed a reminder of how important you are to me. Well, today I got that reminder big time. It's something I will never forget. I love you son, and don't you ever forget it. I saw tears building up in her eyes. She just turned her head away, and I saw her take her apron and wipe them away before she turned off my light.

I lay there for a long time dwelling on her words. It was one of the few times she had called me "son" and I will never forget that night either. She was my Granny, but she was also the closest thing I would ever have to a Mom and Dad too. What a special moment that was. One that, like aging wine, just gets better with age.

Later, on my tenth birthday Granny gave me my camera. She put the following in my birthday card, "Jasper, memories are priceless treasures, but pictures are the road that drives you back to your treasured memories."

I took her saying literally because I started a memory book the next day. In it I saved that card along with hundreds of pictures, and hundreds of sayings Granny shared with me. That picture book still gives me so much pleasure. I have pictures of Granny milking the cows and gathering eggs; of her churning butter and making her special buttermilk. And of the two of us, I have pictures of us dressed in our Sunday best each year from that time on, along with pictures of our Christmas and birthday celebrations; of her driving her new Ford car the same year I turned old enough to go for my driver's license. There are also before and after pictures of our house the year we painted it along with the old shed behind the house; of the new fence we built around the house and along both sides of the driveway. My favorite one is of Granny working in her favorite spot, her garden.

She said, "Growing things reminds me of where we all come from. God put us here and He put all those plants here for us to work our talents. I plan to work my talents in His garden up there for as long as He wants me to."

When I turned fourteen I started milking the cows and doing most of the outside chores. Granny again shared her wisdom, "It's time you started doing manly things. Man's work is right outside our front door. That work is now all yours to enjoy, while my woman's work is right here inside our front door." Then she added, "But, I still want to be involved in our garden. Working in the soil is good both for the body and the soul. I can't allow you to have all the blessings from that very special place. You must agree to share that garden with me for as long as I am able."

When she said that I couldn't ever conceive of a time when she wouldn't be able to spend time in her garden. Of course, that day did come, but fortunately not for many years.

Granny gave me so many pearls of wisdom. Here is one of the ones that I didn't really understand and wrap my arms around until after she was gone, "Too many people look at work as drudgery, but I look at it as a gift from God, and a challenge to be completed. Only when it's finished can we have a sense of accomplishment. We all know what happens to idle hands. My desire is to never have such a pair."

Granny accomplished what she set out to do. She told me once, "I'm so glad God gave you to me. If you had not come along I would have gone away long ago. You kept me young and busy. Busy hands are also contented hands. You kept me busy and I was always content because of that."

My memories of my Granny will be with me forever. She was that one person who made my life so rich in so many ways. She is even more special to me today because I miss her so much. That old saying, "You don't appreciate what you have until you lose it." It's so true. I appreciate her more today than I ever did when she was still here. I truly hope she knew that. My one wish is that I could tell her that right here and right now.

Early Start

The sun was just peeking over the eastern horizon as I was driving on a certain country road that morning. The ever changing orange light reflecting off the clouds made me realize how temporary things of life are. First, it started from a slight darker glow highlighting a smaller part of the clouds. Then, it expanded to be wider and stronger, with more brilliant colors. Before long, a sliver of light crested the ridge, and grows still wider and higher into the eastern sky. These colors went from a deep orange to a yellow, and then to a blue as the sun fully lifts above the horizon.

At this same time the landscape gradually started from complete darkness, except for the headlights of my car, to full light during that whole process. That light spread over the land making visible the hills and trees, along with the buildings and roads that man has added to the landscape.

Another new day had sprung up; with it the prospects for the repeating of old experiences; while anticipating some new ones. Like meeting with old friends and hoping to make new ones.

Just like the sun rise, our experiences, and who we see are not always the same from one day to the next.

I'm thankful for the diversity of changes we see and encounter along the way that keep life interesting. Even though we sometimes resist changes, or even fight against them, we must come to realize they are much a part of our everyday trip down this path of life. If we resist them, we often times needlessly spend too much of our energy, as they are going to happen anyway. We should plan to add flexibility into our lives so we don't get thrown too far off our planned course. Whether any changes are major or minor, we must make room for them, and be willing to give up some things, or someone that is very dear to us. It could mean changing much of our daily routine.

The effects might involve our finance, our emotions, or even our relationships with family and friends.

It's so much easier to accept these changes that are positive, when they are for our good and to our liking. However, it's much harder when we need to brace ourselves for those negative changes that are sure to come.

We must choose to make the best of whatever comes, living our lives in such a way that we minimize the disruption both to our own lives, along with the people around us. We must plan to be prepared for the unexpected. This is not always easy to do, but we can make the effort to prepare nonetheless.

This first example is about a young married couple who planned to start their family at some future time, however, they unexpectedly found themselves expecting. They're going to be parents in just a few short months and had made no preparations. They need to move quickly to make ready their lives and their home for their new arrival.

The second example is another young couple who also planned to wait to start their family when they discovered their news. But, this couple had been planning ahead by starting a baby fund. They were two steps ahead of the first couple by being both financially and mentally prepared for this change.

So, go your way expecting changes to come, making provisions ahead of time, so they will not come as such a shocking surprise when they show up on your door step. You will then meet them with your best foot forward.

Grandpa Sage

"A person with great virtue is far better than one with great riches." This is just one of Grandpa's one liners that made me think. He had thousands of them that always made me search for there meaning.

Grandpa was one of those rare birds who always made you feel like he was glad to see you. That glint in his eyes said he was either poking fun at you, or pulling your leg about something or other. Or maybe, he was just telling you how glad he was to be with you. He didn't have the typical grandfather look. He wasn't bald, but had plenty of fine, thick dark brown hair with just a hint of salt sprinkled around the edges.

One of his good friends called Grandpa Sage the Silver Fox. I first thought it was because of his hair, but maybe it was because he was such a wise old fox. Either reason was good enough for me. He was not short and stout but rather tall and thin. He kept his hair rather long, but not long enough to wear a pony tail. He wore wire rim eye glasses, he called them his spectacles. He wore them out on the end of his nose. He loved to read. He was always reading something whenever he wasn't with me or one of his many friends.

I honestly don't know if he ever slept. I mean to lay down on his bed and sleep through the night. Grandpa always stayed up beyond the time I could, and he was always up and dressed each morning when I got up. He didn't like to watch TV either, except to catch the latest news and weather reports.

He had this same saying whenever I told him I was bored, "A bored mind lacks imagination." I didn't like to hear it back then. I thought he meant I was stupid or lazy. But one day he told me what he meant.

He explained, "If I needed something to do, all I needed to do was look around. Something will catch my eye to take my boredom away."

He then added, "Try that next time and see if you find something to occupy your time."

Another of his sayings that sticks in my mind, "There is a good reason we each have two ears but only one mouth."

I caught on to this one quickly. He wanted me to be a good listener. If we spend all of our time talking and little listening, we lose the benefit of the wisdom from others. I determined to apply this to my best advantage both in school and later at work. I felt it will give me the advantage by realizing what my teachers were trying to get into my head, and then later, what my boss is trying to convey to me.

Adding more advice, Grandpa said, "The dumbest question is usually the one you fail to ask. If you don't understand something, or directions, you need to ask again until you do understand."

One of many things that made me admire Grandpa was his way of including one of his sayings into any conversation. I remember he told me more than once, "Truth is always better regardless of the consequences."

He used this whenever he heard someone say something he suspected was untrue. Or was maybe not telling their whole story.

He was skeptical of most political leaders. He felt they were in their position for personal gain, and not for the benefit of the people who elected them. He qualified that saying, "They are not all bad, but too many have forgotten why they are where they are."

Another of his sayings, "Feelings can be misleading, but truth is sure. Wisdom comes hard, but foolishness comes easy."

Grandpa believed we should all live honest lives, avoid foolishness, but seek wisdom even before wealth or happiness.

Grandpa had many friendships that lasted for three or four decades. Some would come spend many hours visiting him. Most knew each other so well that they could almost predict what the other was about to say. Grandpa told me, "Son, make a friend and gain an ally." He also told me, "Most friendships are costly, but worth the price."

He explained that the cost of most friendships are in emotions and patience rather than in money."

Then he added, "I wouldn't trade any of my good friends for all the wealth of the world."

I remember another of his favorite sayings, "A book's cover is only a glimpse of what is inside. They hold a whole world of discoveries far beyond our ability to go see, but are all available to us in print and pictures format. If you can't travel to Japan, or anywhere else in the world, all we have to do is read up on these places from books found at your library. With your vivid imagination you can picture and experience all these amazing places."

Grandpa Sage told me that he and Grandma had the very best marriage. He said, "Young man, if you marry, look for a virtuous wife to spend your life with, and be willing to take counsel from her."

He continued, "A good marriage, for the most part, depends upon how much work and effort both partners are willing to put into their relationship."

Then he added, "Love is one of the most powerful words. Unless both partners in a marriage are willing to give each other their all, the marriage will be only mediocre at best. When your Grandma died I almost lost my will to live. She was the reason I came home from work every evening; the reason I kept my life in good order for all of those years we were together. She was the one who encouraged me when I was discouraged; who cheered me up when I was sad; who loved me when I was not worthy of being loved, and who made our house a special home in every way."

Before Grandpa Sage left this world he made this writing for me, "My hope and my prayer for you, my grandson, is that you spend your life making life better for all those you come in contact with; that you look for the best in everyone; that you speak the truth in all matters; that you build bridges rather than walls; that you keep a good attitude for the purpose of making someone's day better each day; that you value each friendship as pure gold, and that whatever you do, you do it with all of your might. When your life is near over my hope is that your friends and family will gather around you as a confirmation that they hold great value in your presence."

When he left us, those who came spoke volumes to me and to the rest of our family. The gathering was very large and the day serene. Many came from great distances to pay their last respects. Not one person I talked with at his memorial had anything bad to say about him. They each came and spoke of their memories of how Grandpa Sage had affected them in some good and meaningful way.

Grandpa Sage lived in such a way that he will not soon be forgotten. He left his mark on many lives. He will never be forgotten by me. He left me with examples of actions that I can only hope to follow. My prayer is that I will use all that Grandpa modeled to me for good and not for evil, and that I will continue to be a blessing to all others from this time on.

Amen!

Ducks for Dr. Dewey

It all started back in '81 when my son, Kirk received one little duckling as an Easter present from his mom. I think she didn't consider what this one surprise gift Easter gift might cause for all of us she left behind when she moved on away from her own family. Well, maybe she did!

Our house sat on three bare acres lacking any trees. Oh, we have lots of olive trees just across the road. There was plenty of room for Kirk's one little duckling, probably more than enough for a cow, or a horse or even a few sheep. But she chose this one little duckling.

Two days after the duckling arrived Kirk, a smarter than average thirteen year old, was concerned that his pet might get lonely without another webbed foot friend around. He wanted to take some of his hard earned chores money to buy a second duck. He was always tight with his funds and rarely spent his money foolishly. I had even kidded him about still having the first dollar he had earned.

Since we had already made a pen out of some scrape lumber and wire we had on hand for the duckling, and since Kirk had agreed to keep up with any work with his ducks, I couldn't say no. So, off we went to the local feed store looking for another little fine feathered friend. We could have bought a whole flock, and Kirk had a problem deciding which one to pick. When he finally made his choice, he paid the man and we took this new critter home in a little box to introduce him or her to the other duck.

The first couple weeks went fine on our little duck farm. The two settled in and started to grow. Oh, on occasion we found that they had escaped and stopped for too long in the shade on our front porch, no harm done that a little water from our garden hose couldn't solve.

But then, Kirk received an invitation from his grandparents to travel some distance to stay with them for the whole month of June while he was out of school for the summer. His grandparents were planning an extended trip, and it was the best chance for Kirk to spend quality time with them. I'd miss him being gone that long, and then it hit me, who would take care of his ducks? He couldn't take them with him.

I really wanted Kirk to spend this time with his grandparents. I must decide what to do about those ducks. And now I'd also have to take over his mowing and other chores as well. But, it would still be worth him traveling and spending this time away.

Finally I agreed to take over his work for at least the four weeks he'd be gone. As a single parent, it meant feeding those hungry ducks three times a day until they grew past their duckling stage. So, I'd go home on my lunch to feed them the special mash. I had no other choice short of hiring someone to do this. That was too expensive, and certainly not in my budget.

Kirk left the weekend after school was out. He told me he really appreciated my offering to cover for him.

What could I say but, "Son, you're worth it."

It wasn't too long before those two critters were no longer little ducklings. They seemed to grow over night, and as they grew they started consuming more food. Also, they started venturing out further and further beyond our yard. They soon discovered the flooded olive orchard across the road as great fun. The farmer had one low spot in the middle of that orchard which had water in it most of the time. The ducks would spend most of their day swimming, but, they were always make it back before dark to be herded through the garage and out into their pen behind the garage.

One night, about three months after Easter, I woke to some strange sounds. First, I heard a dog barking, then ducks quacking, and then a chase was on through my back yard. It was over so fast I was not able to come to the aid of the ducks. I couldn't even locate them nor could I find that strange dog that had started the chase.

The next morning when I went out to check on the ducks. One was gone and the other looked kind of ruffled up. It didn't appear to seriously wounded. It was Saturday so I didn't plan to go in to work. With Kirk gone Saturday was usually my catch up day with all the mowing along with household work was on my to-do list. These would take up most of my morning, but that particular Saturday turned out to be a whole lot different.

One quick phone call from Mrs. Foremost next door changed my whole schedule. Her first question, "Are you missing a duck?"

My answer, "Yes."

"Do you know your duck is in my swimming pool?"

"Oh no, I'll be right over!"

The next hour and a half seemed like two days. We coaxed, bribed, shewed and herded that duck from one side of that pool to the other. It was not coming out of that pool until it was good and ready. Finally, I managed to coax it out of the pool and herded it back home. I told Mrs. Foremost I would come right back and vacuum out her swimming pool, but she declined my offer. She was probably glad to be rid of me and my little, fine, feathered friend.

Something had to be done about these ducks. So I called my son. Kirk agreed we should find a good home for them. I also reworked on their pen so hopefully they couldn't escape again, and still be safe from that middle of the night doggy visitor.

I've always had a good relationship with all of my neighbors, but if these ducks put an end to that. That pool chaos, if news of it spreads could be in deep water in the whole neighborhood.

I checked with several neighbors, friends, bank customers and anyone else who could be interested in taking the two ducks off my hands. I even considered making baked duck out of them, but I wouldn't be able to face Kirk afterward.

By the end of June Kirk returned home only to find that we still had his ducks.

Then on the last day of June my boss's friend, Dr. Dewy, approached me about the ducks. He explained he really liked bar-b-que duck and wanted duck for his birthday on the 4th of July. He agreed take those ducks off our hands and even offered to invite Kirk and I to his celebration. He offered to come over the next day to pick up the ducks, giving himself plenty of time to prepare them for his birthday duck feed.

When the 4th of July came and went with no invitation, I knew he had pulled my leg about our invitation. He had either forgotten about his offer, or he was just trying to appease me.

The next few months passed quickly, and I forgot about the ducks. I didn't see the good doctor come into the bank to make his deposits so that was a reminder either.

It was maybe a month or so after the 4th of July that I met and started courting June. How we met for our first date is another a whole interesting story which we can share some another time.

On the Saturday before Easter in '82 I had to work to finish at the bank for most of the day. June agreed to come over to the house to spend with Kirk when I was working. When I drove in my driveway about four that afternoon, Kirk ran out to meet me. He was all excited. He told me about these two mysterious men that had been casing our place earlier that day.

He described one of them, "He looks just like Rolley Fingers, you know Dad, the waxed mustache relief pitcher for the Oakland A's baseball team."

Kirk continued, "The two men had left a box on our front porch addressed to you. They didn't ring the doorbell or knock. They just sneaked up to the front door, left this box, and then hurried away."

I didn't have to look in the box to know what was there. From Kirk's description of the men, especially the guy with the waved mustache, I knew who had been there, and why. All I needed to know was how many they had left.

When I opened the box, sure enough, there were four little baby ducklings along with a small container of feed. It was starting all over again!

I thought back to all the problems the first pair had given us. I had to come home every day on my lunch time for a couple weeks to feed those critters. Also those two had left messes on my front porch more times than I could count. And, oh there was the swimming pool experience at my neighbors that also came to mind. There were only two ducks back then, but now there were four.

My next thought was to drive over to Dr. Dewey's house and deposit those ducks on his doorstep, but Kirk and June talked me out of that.

Then it hit me, Kirk and I would keep these ducks. We would not say anything to anyone about them. We would enlist the help of my friend and co-worker, Herb, to keep Dr. Dewey and my boss worried about the well-being of those ducks.

Two weeks went by without a word to or from Dr. Dewey or my boss about the ducks, then a full month.

The ducks started eating a lot of feed. Something had to be done. This joke was starting to cost too much money.

I stopped by to see my friend, Harry, at the feed store. I paid him $2.50 for some feed and asked him for one of his store blank invoices and one of their envelop. I decided to make up a billing to Dr. Dewey Silvan and mail it in the mail box right in front of his office. Let's see what kind of reaction we get from this.

Within a week Harry from the feed store called me to tell me my credit was good at the feed store. Dr. Dewey and his accomplice, my boss, had left $10.00 towards future duck feed purchases.

Now it turned out that Dr. Dewey was a bank customer. He must have his help bring in his deposits, but now he started bringing them in himself. I made sure he didn't see me watching him, but couple times I caught him peeking at me around the column next to the counter. Still he didn't approach me and I sure wasn't going to approach him.

I felt it was time to start adding a little more spice to our little joke. So, I enlisted Herb's help again. His desk was not far from mine, so it was easy to plan out the next move. Herb agreed to pass along my tales about the ducks to my boss, who in turn would certainly keep Dr. Dewey posted.

Each week we came up with a new story about some terrible problem with the ducks. The first one was that a dog attack had resulted with one of the ducks dead and two more injured. Our stories became taller each week, until just two weeks before the 4th of July. During that week I told Herb that during that terrible storm a lightning bolt struck and killed all of the remaining ducks.

News travels fast because shortly after I arrived home from work that same day my neighbor, Mrs. Foremost, came over to tell me about the two prowlers at my place that afternoon. She almost called the sheriff department, but these guys didn't seem to take anything. They just walked around the back of my house, spent several minutes just standing behind the garage, and then they were laughing when they left. I asked her what they looked like, and when she answered that one of them had a waxed handle bar mustache I knew exactly who had been there and why.

That strange visit to my place that afternoon must not go on without some form of response. The next morning Herb agreed to pass along the news that some prowlers had been at my place yesterday. I had booby trapped my place and who ever got caught would not be able to be around people for a while after dealing with my pet skunk. "That little guy is fine around family, but we could not be responsible for what he would do around strangers. Any uninvited visitors would be in for an unpleasant surprise.

The following Saturday morning while I was doing my Saturday morning routine of housework and general cleaning, I heard a car pull into my driveway. It was my boss's car. Instead of going to the front door, he walked around to the back of my house, and I invited him in through the patio door.

The first thing he said, "I see you have some more ducks."

I said, "Yes." Then I quickly changed the subject.

During his hour stay he brought up the duck subject twice more, and each time I changed the subject again.

At last he flat asked me, "What are you going to do with those ducks?"

I could close my eyes and almost see Dr. Dewey licking his chops, or maybe I only imagined that part in my dreams.

Now it dawned on me that the 4th of July was only a couple weeks away, no need to give up on this joke just yet, so I told my boss that the grasshoppers have been thick this year, and the ducks have done such a good job of keeping them out of the yard and my garden, I've decided to keep the ducks until fall or maybe even longer.

With that answer my boss stood up to leave. He certainly had some things to pass on to Dr. Dewey.

Nine day later, just three days before the Fourth of July, I was at my desk. It was almost my lunch time. Suddenly, my boss bursts out of his office and walks straight over to me, at the same time Dr. Dewey came in the door, and he too came over to stand next to my boss in front of my desk. After a quick greeting I almost laughed before I decided wait to see how this was going to go down.

I thought, *'last a direct confrontation.'*

But all they wanted to do was make some small talk. They talked about the Lyons and Rotary Clubs baseball game last night. Dr. Dewey told that he was up to bat and he had to DUCK to avoid a wild pitch. Then, my boss told about a house he once visited where you had to DUCK to walk through the front door. Next, Dr. Dewey told his story of crossing the street, just this morning, and he had to DUCK out of the path of a speeding car.

Now I sadly realized just what an indirect approach really means.

Finally after still more small talk I looked at the clock and told them I needed to get to lunch as I had an early afternoon customer appointment. I also stole a glance over at Herb and knew that he had been listening in all that was being said at my desk.

My lunch statement must have been their que, for finally a direct approach. Dr. Dewey asked, "What are you going to do with those four ducks?"

I said, "I'm undecided whether to keep them myself, or to give them to June because she and her family really like roast ....." Dr. Dewey interrupted me, "I'll tell you what, you give me the ducks, and I'll invite you, June and your son over for a duck and chicken bar-b-que."

I considered carrying this out a little further, I could have said something about Dr. Dewey's promised an invitation last year.

But I decided to accept this year's invitation, "I'll have to see if June and Kirk are both available come, but I for sure plan to be there."

We set this Saturday as the time for Dr. Dewey and my boss to come for the ducks. They said they would come over early as they needed to have time to prepare the ducks for the bar-b-que.

Well that Saturday just happened to be the day the farmer across the road decided to irrigate his orchard. When Dr. Dewey and my boss showed up, the ducks were off for their swim.

I wish I had my movie camera out there to record the action. The next couple hours would have been good materials for a Disney movie called, "The Doctor and the Ducks."

They coaxed, shewed, quacked and bribed those ducks, but they were not going to leave that pond until they were good and ready. Dr. Dewey and my boss were about to take off their shoes and roll up their pants legs and wade out into the pond in their effort to drive the ducks out of the water, when the four ducks finally waddled out of the flooded orchard and we herded them back across the road and into my yard.

Then, one by one Dr. Dewey chased them down on the dead run. We would see him running one step behind a duck as they disappeared around the corner of my house. A few seconds later, he would reappear with the duck tucked under his arm.

One duck ended up under his car, and would not come out. That too was eventually caught, and with all four boxed up and placed in the back of Dr. Dewey's car, they were ready to leave.

We set a time for his birthday party on the 4th of July, and they drove off with the all four ducks.

The birthday dinner was a great time. June and Kirk were with me and Herb and his wife were also there. We spent most of our time recalling the various things that transpired during the past few months. We were finally were able to compare reactions, and feelings from both sides of our stories. They told of their reaction when they received the billing from the feed store, and I told them about my neighbor's report of prowlers at my home, and how she almost called the sheriff to report the incident.

At the end of the evening as Kirk, June, and I were about to leave, Dr. Dewey stood up to give a toast. He thanked us all for coming out to help him celebrate his birthday.

Then he added, "This duck situation had turned into the most fun I have ever had in my whole life."

Dr. Dewey's last words as we were walking out his front door, "I am really looking forward to next year!"

One Day in the Life of Fritz Sorenson

Fritz rubbed his sleepy blue eyes and ran his hands through his unruly sandy brown hair as he headed out. He pulled on his gray sweat shirt and matching sweat pants, slipped into his running shoes before tying them, took a big gulp of water, and then he was ready. His plan was to go out for his normal early morning walk.

He had just turned onto the main road when he heard the roar coming from behind him. It sounded like a car coming very fast; too fast for this old country road and its conditions. As a precaution he moved off the road and stood back waiting to see who was coming. It was just a couple seconds later he saw the cloud of dust, and then not one but two sheriff cars with lights flashing heading his way. They both pulled up and stopped right next to him. With guns drawn both deputies stepped out of their cars.

The first yelled, "Mr. stand where you are!"

They then both came around one on each side of Fritz. They told him to raise his hands up around the back of his neck, and then one deputy took one hand at a time and brought it down to cuff him. When he started to ask what this was all about he was told to be quiet and hold his questions.

"B....But I'm just out for my morning walk. I live right over there in that grey house with a blue roof. What on earth do you want with me?"

"You're a suspect in the armed robbery that just took place at the Mini Mart at the west end of town. You and two others left the store manager lying in his own pool of blood when you left heading in this direction. He told us you are wearing these same gray sweats. We need to see you're ID. So where is it, and what happened to your two pals who were in with you on that job?"

"I....It's in my wallet back at my house. And, I don't have any two pals that would do such a thing. I never carry my driver's license when I go out for a walk. You fellows have the wrong guy. I do shop at that Mini Mart at times, but I have not been there for a couple days, and the last time I stopped was for fuel for my old car."

"Okay, where is your car, and is it the same one you guys used to do your dirty work. How about the guns you used? Are they in the car?"

"No, no, you have this all wrong. I have never been involved in anything like this before. I am just a law abiding citizen. I don't have any buddies who would be doing this kind of stuff either."

The second officer finally spoke up, "Hey Frank lets read him his rights and let's take him in for questioning. Old Sarge Ferguson can make him talk much better than you and I."

Fritz shook his head, "This seems like some kind of joke, but it's really not funny. I live right over there and I work construction building roads and bridges. I don't rob or shoot people. Now tell me who put you up to this?"

"Hey Frank we have a real prize here. He thinks we are just poking fun. He thinks we are doing this so someone can take pictures and make some home movie or something. I think that's funny."

"Yeah Sam. He thinks we are clowns or imposters. Maybe if we take him in he will see that we are not joking. Come on. Let's get him in your car. We can come back and deal with his car and those guns later."

Fritz sank down in the back seat when Sam drove him past his neighbor's houses. He had seen some of them standing out watching the whole thing.

When they arrived at the county jail he shook his head in total disbelief, *'This is really happening. I'm being jailed for something I had no part in. I wondered who I can call. I have no alibi for this morning. No one who could verify where I was from midnight until now.'*

Fritz had gone out with a friend last night, and had dropped her off at her place about midnight. *'This is turning into a real nightmare, but it's happening in broad day light.'*

Fritz was booked into the jail where they took down his name and address and employment information. They even took his picture. And then, he was taken to a room similar to what he had seen on TV as an interrogation room. He sat there alone for several minutes; it seemed like hours before Sarge Ferguson came in. At first Sarge just looked at him for the longest time. When he finally he spoke, "Okay, you've had a chance to think about what's going on and what you did. Do you want to start talking? Can you tell me who else was in on the heist? Can you tell me where the car and guns are? Can you make this easy on yourself, or do you want to do this thing the hard way?"

"Sarge, I'll tell you the same thing I told the two deputies. I was out for my morning walk. I live just down the road from where they found me. I didn't rob or hurt anyone. I am a law abiding citizen who pays his taxes, votes in every election and have never stolen anything from anyone. You have the wrong guy. You got to believe me. I need to get someone's help as I don't think you and your people understand how wrong you are. Where do I go from here?"

"Okay, you want to do this the hard way. You can fess up now or you can later, but I believe you will find it better to do it sooner rather than later."

"What, are you threatening me with bodily harm unless I lie and tell you something that I never did?"

"Tell me again what happened. Start from the first and give me every detail. We are recording each of your statements, so if you change anything, I will know that you are pulling my leg. Go ahead, tell me your story."

"On TV the suspect gets to ask for legal representative. Maybe that's what I should do. Maybe I should not say anything further unless I have a lawyer."

"Is that what you want to do? Do you have money for an attorney or do we call in someone?"

"This is the strangest thing I have ever been involved with. I woke up early this morning and decided to go for a walk. I was only a little ways down the road from my house when I heard your deputies coming. I moved off the road expecting them to go on by me, but the rest is history. Now, I am expected to spend my own money to have legal representatives solve this problem. How can this be? How can I, an honest citizen, be caught up in something like this? Why don't you spend your time going out to look for who really did what you're suspecting me of doing?"

"I guess you need more time to think about telling the truth. I will have the Lieutenant come in. He is better at getting to the truth than I am. He can persuade you to give us the information we need. You just sit tight and he will be in shortly. I encourage you to be straight with him. He is your last resort before we take you back and assign a cot and jail garb."

Fritz just shook his head in total exasperation when the Sarge walked out. "Will nobody believe him? What must I do to convince them? Would the Lieutenant be more understanding and figure out that I'm innocent? Or, will I end up spending the night in this place?"

Fritz sat there for another long spell. It was obvious what their tactics were. They made you sit there and stew on your dilemma. If the time felt long to someone who was innocent, Fritz imagined how it would feel to someone who was guilty. He decided to make it look like he was taking a nap. Maybe this would bring someone in faster, and let him tell his story again. Maybe he could convince the

Lieutenant that he was innocent. Or, maybe if he told the story over and over exactly the same each time they would finally believe him.

He put his head down and wrapped his arms around his head, and then did a count to thirty before the Lieutenant came in.

"We can't have you sleeping in here. We need this room for other reasons. Now, let's go over your statement again. I need to hear every little detail. Don't leave anything out."

Fritz looked at the Lieutenant. His stern gray eyes seemed to look straight through him. The Lieutenant ran his fingers through his salt and pepper short cropped hair. He then looked at the file in front of him, "This is not the first time you have done something like this, is it? You have a book here telling us of all your priors. It is a long list. But, it's the first time for you to pull a trick like you did today. Did your buddies con you into this job?"

Fritz just shook his head, "Okay, you win. I'll tell you my story just as it happened. I woke up early this morning. Made my daily trip to the bathroom, and then washed my face and put on sun screen before putting on my sweats. I went to the kitchen for a drink of water, and then I headed out the door for my daily walk. I did some stretching before I walked down my driveway. I turned left on the old road and was about two football field lengths away from my driveway before I heard your two deputies coming. I heard them before I saw them. I saw the dust trailing behind them first and decided to move off the road to let them go by. Only they didn't go by and you know the rest of the story from there. I've never robbed anyone or shot anyone. I've been a tax paying citizen for all of my adult life. Truth be known, some of my tax dollars likely go towards paying your salary. This so called book you have on me is a fake. I have never even been stopped for a traffic violation, much less for any criminal activity. Now, if you don't believe me then lock me up, and then go after the real culprits. Just get out of my face before I say something that will do more harm than good."

Suddenly it dawned on Fritz that he was hungry. He had skipped breakfast, planning to eat after his walk. It was two thirty in the afternoon when the Lieutenant started his interrogation. Probably more like three or three thirty by the end of that conversation, and still no food or water had been mentioned. "When do I get to go home, and if you will not turn me loose, when do I get to eat? I haven't eaten since dinner last night and all I have had is one glass of water at home this morning. I am parched and starved. That is inhumane treatment to even the worst criminal, not to mention someone like me who is totally innocent of any crime."

Just then the phone on the wall rang. The lieutenant stood up and grabbed it. He was quiet for a time, listening to whatever was being passed on to him. He then hung up the phone and sat down.

He looked at Fritz for the first time with compassion before he said, "Well we have the culprits. They tried to rob another mini mart in Emeryville. Two of them are in the hospital there with gunshot wounds and one is in the Clark County jail. They were wearing sweats just like yours. The day manager at the mini mart is being called the hero in the case. He shot two and held the third until the police came in. They have confessed to also robbing the mini mart here. It looks like we can send you home."

Fritz finally had the controls, "Oh no you don't! You are going to buy me the biggest steak dinner in town, and then you are going to drive me home. If that doesn't take place, I plan to sue the county for false arrest and undue harassment. Do we have a deal?"

"Okay, okay, we have a deal, along with our sincere apologies. Now let's get you out of this place."

Mystery Uncovered

Shelly froze in place with her brilliant emerald green eyes in a full dark stare at him after Cyrus had shook his head and looked down without any further comment. She then turned on her heel, and with her long auburn hair following in the whirl she stomped off in a huff. He didn't have a chance to even call her back as she was out the door and gone before he could take two breaths. He ran both hands through his wavy brown hair and leaned back in his favorite chair to contemplate what he should do next.

Shelly had been his best friend for longer than he could remember. They'd had some differences before, just like anyone else does, but never had their views been so far apart as now on this subject. He closed his eyes and took time to consider it all. Maybe he was wrong, or maybe some middle ground could be reached between them. But, no, he was right and no amount of rationalizing could make him bend. He felt that they were at a stalemate. He would not compromise and he also knew Shelly well enough to know that she wouldn't either. Her stubborn streak wouldn't let her move his way no matter what. So, where can they go from here? Could this difference be enough to end their great, longtime friendship? One that had survived for the better part of two decades? Would they, or could they, ever be close again?

Finally Cyrus decided he needed some guidance from someone he held a great respect for. He'd go see his longtime friend, the English professor, to seek his advice about how to approach Shelly.

His call to Professor Marlin's office went to voicemail, so he left a message. He hoped the professor would get right back to him so he could get with Shelly as soon as possible.

The next morning Professor Marlin called and agreed for him to come right down before the Professor's next class an hour from now. Cyrus raced out the door and sped off in his old Plymouth.

While he drove he planned out his questions for the professor. Due to the time restraints he needed to summarize his questions making the most of the time. His first question for professor was his opinion who was right and who was wrong. This would help to overcome the gulf between the two of them.

If professor wasn't able to referee, could he and Shelly just agree to disagree without losing everything? Maybe they could move on without losing their friendship. Maybe in time she could see his POV. People do change their minds on important issues from time to time. Surely she would see the error of her ways on this one important issue? Surely she would eventually conclude that he was right and she would then concede?

Professor opened the door at his knock. Cyrus thanked him for his time, before he quickly shared their dilemma. He didn't go long into the subject, but only asked how to approach Shelly and, if nothing else, how to persuade her to agree to disagree.

Professor's quick solution, "Okay Cyrus, Call her and offer to take her out for a nice dinner. Then, in your time together, let Shelly know you want to give her the right to her own opinion on every subject, and that you hoped she will give you the same. Tell her you want to peacefully agree to disagree without losing your long, precious friendship. Then make no speculation on whether either of you will ever share the same opinion on this particular subject."

Cyrus nodded his head. He liked Professor Marlin's advice. Time normally is the best healer. These are the words Cyrus knew his friend, Professor Marlin, would gladly share. He would say, "It is the way of making biggest mountains erode into little mole hills."

Cyrus never got around to explaining to Professor the troubling subject. He was so anxious to call Shelly that he only excused himself and thanked Professor again, and shook his hand before heading out the door.

His call went to Shelly's voicemail. Still another wait for her to call him back. He could only hope it wouldn't take her long to respond. But then, he knew how stubborn she can be. She may keep him waiting and guessing for a while. Sure enough, it was the next morning just as Cyrus was going out the door when his cell phone went off. He answered it as he was unlocking his car. He got in, closed the door before he took a deep breath, and asked if she would go out to dinner. He knew they needed to talk, to share their feelings for one another. He wanted nothing more than move to restore their relationship. He waited for her to respond. It felt like a super long pause before she finally agreed to meet him that evening at the restaurant they often liked to go to together.

But she firmly added "But you're buying, right?"

He smiled, "Well, I invited you so, yes, this is my treat. So does seven tonight work for you?"

"Seven will be fine. I'll see you at Charles Place then?"

"Well no, I thought we would go somewhere really nice. Why don't I meet you at The Steak House? It's time we did something really special."

Again a pause before she said, "Oh, okay Cy. That sounds really nice. Seven it is. But, do I need to dress up for the occasion?"

"You decide on that subject. I plan to wear slakes and a nice shirt with a collar, just not blue jeans and a tee shirt. I'll see you there at seven then."

Cyrus knew she would have liked to have more conversation then just his invite. She seemed reluctant to end their conversation, but he cut it short so he could leave her hanging for the rest of the day about what he was up to. The time between would make her think, and it would give him time to plan his approach to the subject that had cause this big riff.

Finally seven o'clock was almost here. Cyrus arrived about five minutes to seven. Shelly was not there yet. He asked for a table off in a corner with more privacy. Just as he sat down he spotted her coming in. He waved her over. She approached and smiled at him as she took her seat. He said, "Let's order drinks first and then our dinner later if that's all right with you."

She looked at him strangely, but said, "Oh okay. Is that because you think I won't stay long enough for dinner?"

He shook his head and smiled, "No, It's just that I would like us to talk a while before we start our meal. I've missed you a lot the last couple days. I hope that you missed me as well. I want to catch up on what's happening and I want to tell you some conclusions I have come to, some conclusions since we last talked on Monday."

She looked at him with her brilliant sleigh look, "Oh, so you have decided that I was right after all and you want this dinner to be your way of offering an apology?"

"Well Shelly, I think we still need to talk. I haven't changed my mind on that subject, but I have come to the conclusion that you have every right to have your own opinions on any subject. I also hope you will give me the right to hold my own opinions. I don't want to lose what we've had since we were both kids over a difference of opinion on one subject. I want you in my life. I want your friendship and your support in every other area in my life. To lose you now just because we agree to disagree on one issue would be a terrible loss to me. I hope you feel the same way. The decision is up to you."

"Wow Cy, you've said a lot. But, I totally agree. I don't want to lose what we've had for so long. I agree with you on so many other things. You're right. To lose our relationship over this one difference would be a tragedy. Can we agree to peacefully disagree on this or any other issue? Can we continue to hold discussions on our views on any other subject without making each other angry?"

Then she went on, "I just believe there should be more to what we already have. I've been too patient with what we've had until now.

Isn't there something you want more than just our long time good friendship?"

She looked him straight in the eyes and added, "There I've spoken my mind. You think about what I just told you! Now, can we order now because I'm starved?"

"Yes Shelly. I think it is time to order. But before we do, "Have I ever told you that I'm in love with you? I have really missed you these last two days. It's made me realize that I want to spend the rest of our lives trying to convince you to change your opinion on our big disagreement."

"Oh Cy, that sounds like a marriage proposal. Did you just propose to me? If you did, the answer is Yes, Yes! I will marry you just as soon as we can get everything arranged. I can't wait to tell my folks and yours. I think they have all been expecting this to happen for a very, long, long time."

Cyrus stood up and came around to her. He got down on one knee and took both her hands in his and kissed her for the very first time.

When they parted she looked at him with tears in her eyes, "Cy, you don't know how long I have waited for you to do that, and now we've had our first kiss and I have your marriage proposal all in the same day. How awesome it that?"

"Oh, for the Record, Cy, I went to see our mutual friend, Professor Marlin, for advice. He told me to purposely take a totally extreme opposite position from you on whatever subject we came up with to shake up our relationship and make you realize that you and I have been stuck in neutral for a very long time. I was in total agreement with you on that certain subject, but Professor's advice to me was that I needed to create a smoke screen to make you realize your feelings for me. I have known for a long time how you feel, but you seemed to be stuck and needed a push. I was taking a chance, but

I felt you would come around in time. It didn't take very long and I am so very glad of that."

That's Life

Each of us arrives here naked, helpless, seemingly speechless, and mindless. We are also toothless and penniless because we don't own a thing. We spend a few years finding out who we are, and the rest of our lifetime finding out just why we are here.

For the first few weeks we have only three natural abilities; the ability to cry, to soil our pants, and to learn to eat. And we have a lot more to learn in our future. Learning to suck is a very important lesson for our survival. The next few weeks we learn to smile, and later to laugh when some giant sticks their funny face in ours and says "goo, or tickle our ribs. At about that same time our eyes begin to show us more than just brief glimpse of movement around us. We follow them and get to know these strange, noisy creatures.

We also start reacting to various sounds. And, we discover the hand to mouth trip, which later is refined to the thumb to mouth trick.

It's not long before we discover another interesting trick, wow, every time we cry some giant comes running our way. They pick us up, check our pants and run for the kitchen making ready that bottle contraption for our mouth. And, the louder we get, the faster this all happens.

We soon find that even a whimper brings someone to take up our time. If we get real vocal we get their fast attention, so we continue to train them to come as often as is possible, after all, we have all this time on our hands, why not let them entertain us? Before long our learning is coming by leaps and bounds. We have taught all those giants to meet our every need and desire. Then, unbeknown to us, still more of these giants come from miles away just to see us. They all stand in line to hold us and play with us. Wow, we must be someone very special!

Our first tooth shows up. It is a real pain, but it also gains us lots of attention. We may as well ride these occasions for all they are worth.

Next a cold shows up. It is not as painful as the tooth, but it too gets us loads of attention. Hey, here is still another way to get all these giants to help take up our time.

Somewhere along the way we discover we have a name. This same sound keeps recurring, and each time it seems to involve us. Maybe, just maybe these giants are referring to us. So each time we hear this same sound we respond, and guess what?

Hey, it works!

We now fast forward through many teaching sessions. Like the giants reaction the first time we rolled over, then the first time we scooted across the room, the first time they found us standing in the crib. And wow, the really big one is first time we take a couple steps!

But the real excitement comes when the first "Mama" came out of our mouth. This created such a stir of dancing, laughing, and phone calls. So we started putting this to work whenever we are hungry, or wet, or just want some attention. This works really good for a while, but the uniqueness does wears off. We must continue creating and developing more teaching lessons for all these giants around us.

That's life!

Memories

What we remember and what others remember about any one event can vary. We remember that the car ran off the road, while someone else may remember that the cow in the middle of the road was the reason for the car going off the road. We couldn't see the cow from our vantage point. Watching the car go off the road distracted our attention away from the cow still standing in the road.

The same can be said for any story. We remember that Johnnie drove to the store for groceries, while someone else remembers that he was just out for a ride. They may not have been privy to Johnnie's plans to go to the store.

Most stories can really be embellished when they are passed along from one person to another, and then to others several times over. For an example, Pete caught a fish that weighed five pounds, but after the story had been passed along to several people the fish had grown to twenty five pounds and took him two hours to land it. This makes it becomes much more news worthy, even though it might be embellished. We have all heard personal stories, or even news reports, which have been stretched, possibly to make them more interesting. We may unknowingly passed these along to someone else. Even if we shared the story just as we heard it, we cannot be certain the next person may or may not add even more color.

What we heard, or the parts of what we heard, may stay in our recall while other parts might be forgotten. So, when we retell the story, we may accidentally leave off a critical part of the original story. When several people do this, the story can have a very different version from when it was first told.

So, to summarize, we must never take a story as all complete and factual when it has been passed along to a long story line of people. If we have a need to know the original version we must go to the original teller and hope they will share the truth, and/or will recall all the original details.

Also, remember open communication is always very necessary. When we share our experiences and allow others to share their own, we open the possibilities of creating friendships, and we expand our relationships with those around us.

Best of all, we make others feel valued when we seek mutual sharing of their interests.

So, go out and make someone feel valuable today.

God Bless.

Picture This - The Unknowns

You were riding down the road on your bicycle on that clear, cool morning. The birds were singing their brilliant chorus. The breeze felt like a soft whisper about your face and arms. You had a great night's rest and a delicious farmer style breakfast before venturing out for your bike ride. You had time to ride because the demands of work, family and chores were not on your early morning schedule. Oh, they are all important, but they will wait until after your most enjoyable outing. You like to use these times to pray and meditate. Then beyond that, to plan how to deal with the many things that will take up the rest of your day. These quiet times are such a blessing. You wish you had the time to schedule more of them.

You just started around the sharp curve when you hear a car coming up behind you. You move over to the right as far as possible to allow the speeding vehicle plenty of room to pass you on your left. You looked down over the side of the road for only a second. It's a long ways down to the bottom. You then looked back to see if the driver approaching the curve will be able to see you. It sounded like the car is coming way too fast. That driver is taking a great chance because this curve does not allow for such great speed. So you quickly stepped off your bike and moved even further towards the railing and the steep bank. There's no further time to do anything else before the car reaches your spot.

You saw the car first before you see the driver's face. The young man had a look for terror. He knew he was in trouble. He swerved his car to avoid hitting you, but over corrected making the car to spin out of control. The very last second before the car flew past you see the second person in the passenger seat and realize he's your teenage son. That's the last glimpse before they were spinning towards the railing and the edge. Your heart nearly stopped in your chest at that very moment.

Then you hear the sound of their car crashing through the guard rail, and descend through the thick brush on the bank. That audio and visual picture will stay with you in your mind for the rest of your life.

Your first thoughts, *'Dear God, how can I help them? Will they survive that terrible crash?'*

That steep cliff is impossible for you to climb down, so you start running back up the road to find a place where you can climb down. Then you remember your bike. You can ride back faster. You dared to look over the edge and see their car below setting up side down on a narrow ledge. Beyond that is another drop all the way to the bottom.

You remember your cell phone in your backpack and hope it's a good signal area from this spot. You called 911, and then quickly called home to alert the rest of your family before riding back in search of a place to get down to those two boys. Just as you think you've found what appears to be the right spot, Deputy Sheriff Martin pulls up alongside. He has you leave your bike, and you both head for a good spot to climb down.

He has a first aid kit already in his hand, and shared important information with you, "A medical team is on their way."

As you climb down you give him some quick details of what happened, and also who is in that car. That fresh realization causes a chill to run down your back.

He told of a similar experience he had with one of his kids. It had occurred one night while he was on duty.

He said, "I know just how you must feel right now. Listen, I'll tell you the whole story when we have more time."

Finally we found a likely spot to move toward the car. We were both wading through stickers and tall grass. Deputy Martin is clearing a path. We trudged a good half mile before we finally saw their car. It's really scary seeing it hanging out over that ledge. It wouldn't take much for it to drop the rest of the way down to the bottom.

Then we both saw the movement inside of the car. It was just an arm moving, but any movement could be both good and bad. Good if the two boys were okay, but bad if they moved wrong and caused the car to fall further. I was having all kinds of strange apprehensions as we drew closer. But we had to hurry.

To our relief, they both were not seriously hurt. They had bumps and bruises, and a couple cuts from broken glass. The hardest thing was getting them out of that car without having it fall further. We talked to them, asking them to stay very still until the car could be tied off so it wouldn't move in the wrong direction.

While we waited for help, Randy told me, "Boy Mom that was a real scary ride. I'm so glad Scott and I had our seat belts on. It could have been a lot worse."

After we had them out of the car and attended to, I finally looked over that ledge. It was still maybe another three hundred feet down. "Yeah, it could have been a whole lot worse. Thank God, He was looking out for us."

My day had started off so quiet and peaceful, but it didn't stay that way very long. It just goes to show that none of us knows what the future holds for us. Only God knows all that was and is now and what is to come.

We all need to be both physically and spiritually ready for whatever comes our way.

Picture This = Memory Loss

When you woke up very early this morning you had that strange feeling that you had forgotten to do something very important yesterday. You are convinced it wasn't anything to do with your work, even though you are seldom caught up there. It must be something from home or maybe at church.

You wanted to go back to sleep, but with this puzzled feeling, sleep was not going to happen. As you lay there starting to retrace your steps from yesterday you think maybe this process will help jog your memory. Maybe recalling these activities will help to shake out all those cobwebs that were clouding your brain.

Since this brain freeze might cause you to look bad, you choose not to enlist the help of anyone around you. So, you choose to bare your burden alone.

You also decide to get out of bed in hopes that something you see around the house will give you some clue. You see nothing in the living room, the family room, or kitchen that rings a bell, or turns on that illusive light.

Now you must take drastic measures. You decide to pray for God's help. After all, you cannot swallow your pride by going to family and friends for help. That would confirm yet another one of your faults. They already know too many of those now, "Father God, I don't come to you very often, but today I really need Your help. Please bring my memory back. What did I forget to do yesterday? Amen."

Maybe if you find something to occupy your attention your mind can relax enough to sort out the matter. You decide to fix breakfast for yourself, and why not go ahead and make it for the rest of the family. This will give your dear sweet wife a break and you know all the many benefits this will bring. Maybe you will even fix the children's lunches as well. This will make her day even better, and with all these mental distractions maybe, just maybe, this will help you figure out what you lost.

You decide on scrambled eggs, turkey bacon, toast with blackberry jam and that home pressed apple cider you've had in the freezer for months, and only two days ago you had decided to defrost and use.

Your timing should work out just right to get all the breakfast and lunches ready when the radio wakes up your wife. You could even be able to wake the children so they can get ready for their day.

You have the toast ready to pop down in the toaster. The bacon is baking in the toaster oven, and the eggs are started on the stove. The table is set, and the kid's sandwiches are almost ready. You decide to send an apple and a healthy snack bar along with their sandwiches. Their mom would be happy with this decision. She is always trying to get the kids to eat healthy.

Just as you push the toast down you hear the radio come on in your bedroom. She will wake up and be in the kitchen shortly.

In a few minutes your wife appears in the kitchen looking for you. She said, "I woke to the smell of bacon cooking."

Then she looked around to find all the work she normally does each morning was already done.

She walks over to me and gives you a big hug and kiss before she offers "How wonderful to have all this done for me, and especially today, on *my birthday*."

"YEAH, OH, HAPPY BIRTHDAY SWEETHEART!"

Pea Soup and Other Delights

"Why are you getting on my case again? Don't you think I have enough brain power to make up my own mind which way to go?"

Trig was so upset when Thad, his older brother, had put his two cents in for the umpteenth time. Thad is only thirteen months older, but he had always been that big brother know-it-all for as long as Trig could remember.

Thad always would screw up his round face like he was in pain, and then come up with his corny opinion on any subject. The truth he is a real pain according to Trig.

Because Thad rarely combed his buff brown hair it usually stuck up at several points on his head. He would cross his gray blue eyes before he threw out his lame suggestion. Most of the time his ideas kind of made sense, but on more than one occasion, what he added had no merit and fit like a round peg in a square hole. This was one of those times.

Trig was working on his latest model airplane. The expensive kit showed how to do all the basics to assemble the plane, but it also gave you several options for how the finished plane should look. The decals and strips could be altered, along with the paint color to make it look different from the picture on the outside of the box.

Thad suggested that Trig change the basic assembly. Also, he suggested altering the motor and propeller to the back end of the plane. He threw out, "There are any number of ways this can be done."

He then pushed Trig out of the chair and started working on his assembly idea.

When Trig tried to stop Thad from doing this but tail assembly broke in their pushing match. This would need to be glued back together, but it might never be right. The plane might never fly right after that.

Normally Trig, at sixteen years old, was old enough to not have Mom and Dad intervene. He didn't want to sound like an overgrown cry baby. But this time, because he had spent most of his hard earned savings on this special kit, he needed to get them involved. He hoped they would come to his rescue and make Thad come up with the funds to buy a replacement kit.

Trig had learned years ago that timing was everything with his folks. He just didn't pop downstairs and hit them with his problem. They liked their peaceful evenings. At breakfast in the morning might be the best time to bring this problem up, and then only if Dad seemed like he was in a good mood. If Dad is cheerful then Mom will be too.

The next morning didn't start off like Trig had hoped. It was a Monday. He and Thad had forgotten to set their alarm so they were late waking up and were rushed to get ready for school. Trig was a sophomore and Thad was a senior at Lincoln High. Thad had yelled at Trig that morning about forgetting to setting the alarm and Trig had responded with, "I'm not the only idiot who knows how to do that. Next they battled over time in the bathroom, and by the time they arrived downstairs Mom was unhappy with their attitude, and if Mom is unhappy then Dad will be also. It was not the best morning to bring up the problem with Trig's model plane.

On their way to school Trig always followed Thad and his buddies. This was another source of contention between them. Thad would tell him to get lost and Trig would say, "I'm going to the same place you are, so how am I going to get there, by flying in my own plane?"

"Yeah right, go jump out when you get over the school for all I care."

The verbal fight was on, and from that time on no one was going to stop the flow of remarks. But when one of Thad's friends joined in Thad was suddenly in Trig's corner. This was the way it always went.

A spat between brothers was acceptable, don't let anyone else come into their battle.

The end result of the plane mishap was settled that very evening. Mom found the broken plane when she was putting clean laundry away in their bedroom. She asked Trig about the plane, and it was then that he told her what had happened.

She and Dad concluded that both boys were responsible. Thus Thad would need to pay for one half of the replacement and Trig would pay for the rest. And then Trig would be the only one working on the replacement, as well as, decide how to finish it. Thad had to agree to stay out of the picture, or he would be paying for the full price for the kit.

That was not the end of the brother's disagreements. Over the next couple years they had more than their share, but never again did they battle over one of Trig's model projects. In fact, it was Thad who convinced Trig to enter his first remote model plane contest. That was the beginning of a long run of contests. Most of which Trig came in either first or very close to the top in each event. In his senior year he had been so successful that he won the Oregon state championship with a cash prize sufficient to pay for the whole family to travel to Denver for the National event. He came in second at Nationals. The awards for that included a cash prize and an opportunity to visit Washington DC, as well as, a visit with the President in the Oval office for himself, and for the person who won first place.

To Trig's surprise that person was a young lady his same age. Samantha Donnelly, a petite little package with fiery red hair and emerald green eyes that sparkled with what looked like specks of gold. Her award winning smile and her pure beauty took his breath away. They met with the President and later went out to eat with both families. Samantha and her family were also from Oregon, just one hundred ten miles to the south. Trig and Samantha competed against each other in several more contests. She always came in first and he was right behind her. Their families always dined together on these trips and became fast friends.

But the real story came later after both Trig and Samantha graduated from high school. They both were big Beaver football fans, and decided to apply at the Oregon State University in Corvallis. They both received their acceptance notice the same week, Trig called her and arranged a celebration dinner for both families. The whole idea that both families had become such good friends because of Trig and Samantha's interest in remote model plane flying contests was unique, but it did happen and it brought great joy to everyone.

Over the next four years Trig and Samantha's relationship grew, all the while the bond for their two families became closer.

Their graduation celebration included both families, and Thad who was home on a 30 days leave from his military duties with the U.S. Navy. He had joined right out of high school. He reenlisted after his first four years and plans to make a career out of it. His new assignment was the USS Ronald Regan, an aircraft carrier. He was to report for duty after his leave time was over.

He still picked on Trig from time to time, but their relationship had never been closer, even though they are hundreds, and sometimes thousands of miles apart. Trig couldn't have been more proud of his brother and his service to our country.

It was mid-summer after graduation; Trig was serving as a short term intern with the Spiral Engineering Company with the promise of full time employment after the ninety day intern training was finished, and Samantha was waiting for word from two possible placements in her field when Trig's parents were notified of the accident on board Ship. Thad had been in the middle of the action when an explosion occurred. He and two other sailors were killed and five others had received serious injuries. Later, one of the other five also succumb to his injuries.

The Navy was involved in the planning of the memorial for Thad. He was honored for his bravery, in that he had saved the lives of many more by putting himself in the path of the explosion. They estimated that eight or more could have been lost but for his actions to protect his comrades. They gave him the greatest honor given to any non-war time casualty. He was buried at the Veteran's Cemetery closest to where Trig's parents lived.

Samantha was there during the family visit after the memorial. She witnessed the various comments by family members in remembrance of Thad. How Trig brought up the broken tail assembly of that very first plane he was building; how the parents had made Thad pay for half of the cost of a new kit.

Trig also shared a time when Thad and some of his friends became stranded overnight on the island in the middle of the lake because their boat floated away. Somebody forgot to tie it off properly, but no one had ever owned up to that. Then how the boys had piled up pine straw to sleep under to keep warm.

How Trig had bugged his big brother almost every day in some way or other, but Thad had grudgingly put up with most all of Trig's antics.

How Mom had recalled Thad's all-time favorite lunch. Pea soup and BLT sandwiches were his specialty. When she would ask him what he wanted, his answer was always, "Pea soup and other delights."

On Labor Day weekend of that year Trig sprung a surprise on Samantha. He had asked her to go with him for a picnic at the lake. Yes, the same lake where Thad and his friends had spent their night roughing it. Trig had planned a lunch for two of them, and then both of their families were to come out for a bar-b-queue that evening. Samantha didn't know what his plans were. He had just gotten confirmation that he was hired with full salary at Spiral Engineering. His first day on the job was next Tuesday. She still hadn't heard from either of the two promising companies where she had applied.

Right after they ate lunch Trig told her he had something he wanted to give her. He said, "That is if you will accept it."

She look at him in her own special way, "Okay Trig, but what is it?"

He pulled out the little box he had stashed in the bottom of the cooler. When he opened it she could see that it was a ring, an engagement ring.

She looked at it and then said, "If you're going to ask me to marry you the answer is "Yes," but, we first need to talk about something."

"Well, yes I'm going to ask, well it looks like you already knew what I had planned for today, but what else do we need to talk about?"

"Well, I know how much you miss Thad. He was a great brother to you and he was taken away way too young. So, I have been thinking if you and I ever get married and have a son, we should name him after his late Uncle Thad."

"Oh Sammy, what a great idea! I couldn't be more pleased with your answer, and with your plan for our future. Now can I slip this ring on your finger? And I want to tell you I'd like to have a very short engagement," as he reach over and grabbed her into a big hug. "I can't wait to tell our folks about our plans."

What We Throw Away

Most of us throw away items that may have some value to others, and a few of us often toss these out in a most careless way. Drive down most any highway you see evidence of these discards. Walking down these same roads gives you a closer look. Among some of the items you will find are cans, bottles, cardboard, plastic jugs, tools, old tires, clothing, toys, newspapers, disposable diapers, books, old furniture and so much more. Some of these will eventually breakdown into the soil, but others like plastics, old tires, aluminum cans and disposable diaper could take years, or may never go away, unless someone comes along to properly dispose of them.

Now, most people don't want used disposable diapers, but the aluminum, plastics, tires, newspapers, books and old furniture, to name a few, might have a recycle value.

Maybe we should have a swap day once a month in each city, town and village so people can give away all of their unwanted items. With the right price, which is most likely FREE, we shouldn't have to bring too many unwanted items back home.

In contrast some things are meant to be tossed, but for some reason we hold onto them. I am reminded of an old pair of tennis shoes I have. They should have been tossed in the garbage long ago, but every time I think about doing so, mowing, painting, or some other project calls for shoes which won't change much in appearance with a few more grass stains or with extra drops of paint. In fact, these usually temporarily improve the appearance of those old shoes.

I don't store those old shoes in my closet anymore because of the odor, so they are kept in the garage for those frequent, but necessary occasions.

One day I will part with those old tennis shoes. And I may miss them only when the next project comes along when they could be useful.

It never ceases to amaze me What We Do Throw Away.

Borrowed Trouble

Francine thought back to where she was just ten days ago. Much had happened and changed in that short time. She'd lost her job on day one. Her sister, Marta came to stay with her on day two. The biggest change was when Marta introduced Francine to Josh, Marta's ex-boyfriend on day three. Marta had just broken up with him and she apparently believed he would ask Francine out. She had even told Josh she was okay with him asking Francine out, since she had told him their relationship has no future.

Josh did ask her out. He proved to be not that soft spoken, polite reserved personality that Francine might have envisioned for her future, but she found she still enjoyed spending time him. He's a handsome hunk, with a little too long hair, more like Marta would like. His gorgeous big brown eyes and ready smile seemed to be glued on his handsome face.

Francine knew he had an ego problem, that he thought he was something special. He had this way of presenting himself in that way from the first time they had spent time together, and now, ten days later, she was totally entranced with his presence. She had been able to avoid his advances to sleep with him up until now, but her will power was running a little thin. If she didn't put a little distance between them she would do something that was totally against all that she believed in. But, what should she do to slow down the process? How could she control his advances, as well as, get control of her wilting will power, especially now that she wasn't working every day?

A thought came to her that she had not considered before. She wondered if Marta had had the same problem with him, and how she had handled it. She needed to talk with Marta before Josh showed up again, and before she gave in to his next romantic advances.

Marta was due home from work about three thirty, while Josh worked until six, and he wouldn't be over until about eight. That would give her and Marta plenty of time to have this little discussion. It would also give Francine time to shore up her waning determination to keep her resolve to live as she had always planned. Her plan to remain pure until she had a wedding ring on her finger.

Marta came home early. Francine approached her with her question. Marta had a beautiful complexion, but that changed when Francine opened this delicate subject. Marta immediately turned as red as a ripe tomato. She almost left the room, but when Francine grabbed her arm and brought her into a hug, she melted and began to cry. She then turned angry, not at Francine, but at Josh. He had taken advantage of her.

She had let her guard down just once in a moment of weakness, and that is all it took. When he wanted her to do it a second time a couple days later she refused and he became angry. He didn't stay around that day. He left in a huff.

Marta's mood changed after that. She then quickly apologized to Francine.

She said, "I should have never introduced him to you. He is out for whatever he can get, and when he doesn't win he moves on. I'm sorry I didn't tell you sooner, but I was so embarrassed with what I did. I moved in with you so that I wouldn't live alone and be open to giving in again. Can you ever forgive me?"

"Marta, let me ask you the next question. Did you use protection?"

"No, it was just that one time and I was not ready to think things through. I am hopeful that my moment of weakness was not at my most dangerous time. I should know in a few days."

"Marta, whatever comes, I want you to know I am here for you. I too am very angry with Josh. I would like you to be here when he shows up tonight. I want you to witness what I am going to say to him.

Josh showed up right on schedule, but he had no idea about what was about to come down. When Francine opened the door, he strutted in just as he had done each time before. He tried to kiss her and when she drew back, he had his first inkling of what was about to come.

He looked puzzled, "What's the matter Sugar?"

She looked up at him and smiled, "We need to talk. You go sit on the couch and I'll be right with you."

Then she knocked on Marta's door, "Marta, Josh is here and we need to have our little talk."

Then she turned back to look at Josh. He looked like a trapped animal. He didn't have anything he could say to defend himself. He didn't stay very long that evening after their little talk. He quickly found a way to make a quick exit. His last words before going out the door, "I'll see ya whenever I see ya."

Francine and Marta watched him from the kitchen window as he raced to his car. That was the last time either of them ever saw Josh. Fortunately for Marta, she never had a reason to go looking for him ever again.

The Heart of Our Nation

What is the heart of our nation?

After much thought, I feel we must first consider what it IS NOT. These areas will open our eyes to the most important areas we must each, both individually and corporately, can concentrate our own positive efforts.

The first "NOT" is government. It is not the heart; even though it might be a major player. It should be of and for the people; in that it should be about doing the will of the people.

Our government was first created not to rule over, but to do the will of the people. If government rules over the people it becomes a dictatorship where just one, or only a very few, make(s) the majority bow to their wishes.

By contrast, a government of and by the people is one who sees that the will of the people will be carried out. It is a representative of the people where the people must have the final say on all things pertaining to equal rights. It is where the majority rules; where our people rule with their votes; with an elected representative leads on behalf of the people.

The second "NOT" is our schools, both public and private. They too play a major role in educating and training our young. The people's concern must continually remain on what and how they accomplish this teaching process. Are all the subjects being taught there with truth and accuracy, and not just conjectures or theories? Are these schools keeping with the basics of reading, writing, science, and arithmetic? Are they teaching only studies that are pertinent and age appropriate? Or, do they mix small portions of theory within their remaining factual ideas to be studied and to be taught? Are these theories limited to teaching only one side of any topic while refusing to teach any other points of view? Do they encourage our young students to keep an open mind on some of the subjects, while closing the possibility of consideration for any others?

The next "NOT" is the news media. Their role should be to keep the general population well informed of all of the daily news events both locally, nationally, and worldwide. We must consider the possibility that the media may report only the news that sells newspapers; or that they report only areas which will agree with their own agenda; while avoiding stories that may contradict their own standing? Do they practice selective reporting; telling us only the news that they want us to know?

Years ago the media simply reported each and all news worthy events. But today they also do analysis of what their interpretation of the news may mean both for the present and often even the future. We must demand that both their news reports and analysis be unbiased and impartial. However, we have to wonder if this is the way it comes across slanted in only one direction or another; either accidentally or on purpose. Both of these are wrong, and it leads the listeners to a different belief in what truly took place.

I believe we would be foolish to take all that we hear reported today to be completely accurate and unbiased. I believe it is safe to say that how they report stories does have an effect upon decisions people make about any given subject. This may be especially true when we show up at the voting booth.

It is easy to determine that the news media falls far short of being the heart of the nation. I am so glad to not be an active member of their occupation. I do not believe it is possible to write and/or broadcast these stories without injecting a little of my own personal opinions within the context of any given story. It is human nature to try to persuade others to think and to believe as we do.

The media, along with the government and schools are all major players in our daily lives. They influence how we make decisions at every level including when we decide who we want in a political office.

How powerful are these news reports and their analysis?

It will depend upon how much we each individually believe these reports, and how often we each accept them as accurate and true.

The next "NOT" is money and power. It is not what we own or how much influence we carry. Money is simply a means of barter. It allows us to acquire the things we need, then beyond that, some of the things we may want. Great wealth and power often can shrink the heart. This can cause us to hoard instead of share from our abundance. It can cause us to elevate our own sense of self-importance, and then look down on those that have less. Fortunately, not all people with great wealth are like this.

We can change our attitude towards others by changing our mindset on how we value others. We should look for ways to share our blessings, especially, if our sharing is done anonymously, without expectations of recognition for our good deeds.

The needs out there are many and are seemingly endless. There are so many people in need. This is not a new thing as there have always been people lacking even the bare necessities of life.

The real heart of our nation engulfs many areas. All of these are included in how we individually and corporately interact with our neighbors; how we treat people who are in need; how we look out for one another; and how we choose to be willing to serve when we see the needs all around us.

It's when we open up our doors, open up our wallets, and give of our time to help our neighbors, and even people half way around the world who may lack the things to feed or house themselves.

Our country and our people have long been known for our generosity. We have always been willing to come along side of those who have a need.

My hope and prayer is that we will continue to be there, ready and able to help out when any real occasion arises.

I just read a heartwarming story of a nineteen year old young man who has used up all of his $1,000,000.00 maximum medical insurance coverage, but he still needs a bone marrow transplant. A plea has gone out on his behalf. His neighbors and friends, as well as, total strangers have contributed over $400,000.00 towards this life saving procedure. This is just one of many cases where people have come along side of someone who they will likely never get to meet but are willing to help unconditionally. This is truly an action taken by a Good Samaritan as exampled by the story in the Bible of unconditional love shown to a stranger. He came to the aid of a man wounded and left by thieves alongside the road. This wounded man was passed by two others before the Good Samaritan came to his rescue. He dressed the man's wounds and took him to an Inn. He paid for his stay and even agreed to come back later to pay any amount over and above the first cost of the wounded man's stay.

Sometimes, coming to someone's aid does not always involve money, but can be an expenditure of our time and our efforts. Whatever the cost, the action taken is always worth the energy spent. Someone receives the benefits from whatever good deed done, both in getting their needs covered, as well as, getting confirmation that there still are people willing to show compassion.

We too can benefit from our actions to provide the help to others when we know that we have come along side of one of our neighbors in their time of need.

May this desire to help others continue to be the way we; each and everyone one of us live. I believe this is truly the real heart of our Nation.

Old Blue

It was a really rough time in my life. I was a single dad with two little ones to raise, and not much money or time to try to get ahead. Also, my only means of travel was an older car with a blown engine. I had been accustom to driving a nice car and living in a very comfortable home with nice furniture and clothes. Most all of my needs and almost all of my wants were being met.

"It's called the good life."

What came next was a drastic drop in my income after an employment change. This resulted in financial problems when my income remained very low for an extended period of time. That's when the nice car, the comfortable home and much of our furniture had to go away to help cover my family's living costs. The house was sold on a quick sale leaving very little equity money after all the selling costs were paid.

It may have appeared that we were in good financial shape, but in reality, we were living from one pay check to another with no savings plan in place. We simply spent every penny we brought in from pay check to pay check. We were living just one paycheck away from total poverty.

Since I lacked sound transportation and being without much money to buy another car, my ten speed bike was my only way to and from work for the next couple of months.

Finally, a small tax refund and some desperate saving methods enabled me to put together a total of seven hundred dollars towards a replacement car. I knew this amount was not going to buy much. My income still was not sufficient to take on a monthly car payment.

My neighbor told me about an auction where they sold former police, telephone company and power company cars, along with various other items from many other sources being sold to the highest bidder. This auction was located about 15 miles away.

I remember it was Valentine's Day, February 14,1982. I'd arranged to catch a ride to within a mile of the auction with another neighbor and his wife. They were planning to spend the day in the big city. They got me to within a mile of the auction. A quick walk from where they left me off brought me to the entrance of the auction.

I was overwhelmed by the number of cars and light trucks, jeeps and motorcycles, along with travel trailers, tow trailers of every kind to be sold. It had to be the biggest auction lot I had ever seen in my life.

They had everything from pitiful wrecks that looked like an accordion, to many late model cars and trucks that would likely sell for way more the amount that I had with me.

My plan was to list all the cars and light trucks that would run and might sell somewhere within my price range. It was about a half hour before the auction was scheduled to start. The first 100 or so vehicles were motorcycles and big trucks, so I had ample time to look over the remaining 200, or so, without missing my chance to bid on any that might be closer to my price range.

I spent the next couple hours walking up and down rows of cars and trucks. I started each one that would start, and made a list of each one I might bid on. I remember thinking as I finished my list, I hope to buy one before they get to that last row. Most of these had more than their share of dents and rust.

Finally the auction reached the cars and light trucks section. That was the biggest part of the auction for the day, and the part I had come for.

The first car on my list was an old Plymouth Valiant. It sold for sixteen hundred dollars; the next was a Ford Maverick for fourteen hundred. Even a disabled power company pickup sold for nine hundred fifty dollars.

For the next three hours and three auctioneers later, I still didn't have the right price. I was beginning to think I shouldn't have come.

About 3:30 in the afternoon they had gone through all the rows except that last one. Yes, we had reached the dents and rusted section. I almost headed for the main gate; but sheer stubbornness, and the fact that I had no ride home kept me right there.

The most of the bidders were gone by this time. Many had either bought their prize auto or they had no interest in these on this last row.

The first two trucks sold for eight hundred twenty and the other for one thousand dollars. I had four more trucks on my list out of twenty some still there. I had started all four of these trucks.

Just as before during the bidding that day, I would join in on the bidding, and would lose out when the price went over my seven hundred dollar limit. It was looking less and less likely that I would come up with the top bid.

Finally with five trucks left in the row and only two left on my list the bidding seemed to stop at my bid of six hundred dollars. The man in the straw hat had bid five hundred seventy five. Now he seemed to hesitate after I bid. The auctioneer turned to him and told him, "The ball is in your court."

He took off his straw hat and rubbed the top of his bald head, and then bid six hundred twenty five.

Now the ball was in my court. I knew I had a chance as my competitor had waited so long before he returned his bid. I held up for only a second before putting my bid out for six hundred thirty dollars.

Now the wait as the auctioneer turned back to the man. He had put his straw hat back on so I couldn't see his eyes from where I stood. The auctioneer turned back to him again for his response. For a moment I thought he would counter my bid; but when the auctioneer said, "Going once, going twice, and sold for six hundred thirty dollars."

I knew I had a potential ride home.

The next few moments were filled with a mixture of emotions. I was so glad this long day at the auction was all but over. But what had I done?

To the eye, this old, faded, blue truck with so many dents and rust spots looked like a bad mistake. But to the ear it ran like it was brand new. It simply ran like a top.

Now to the nose it smelled of dirt and oil and stale cigarettes. Even some empty beer cans had been left behind by the previous owner.

This was going to be a humbling experience. Even after the two months with nothing but my ten speed bike. Driving this old blue truck around town would be hard on my pride.

The last few months had been like a, "Riches to Rags" story, and this old blue truck would show even the people I didn't know just what my plight was.

"Ole Blue," as that old truck was later affectionately named got me back home that day without any problems. In fact I drove "Ole Blue" for four more years. At some time along the way "It" became "Him." He was faithful until the end. In his last few days he started to burn almost as much oil and he did gasoline. But, I can truthfully tell you he never failed me one time. He always started when needed him. I was never left stranded due to a breakdown.

One time I was invited to a big wedding for the daughter of a friend of mine. When I arrived the only parking spot still available was right between a late model Cadillac and a Lincoln Continental. I did not hesitate to park there knowing that those expensive cars can get just as dusty and dirty as "Ole Blue."

When the sad day came to part with "Ole Blue" I was still able to drive him to the Junk yard where I got three hundred dollars for him. The employee there said his boss plans to make a junk yard part runner out of "Ole Blue."

In retrospect, I can truthfully say that six hundred thirty dollars was the best six hundred thirty dollars I have ever spent. Old Blue had been faithful to the very end, and driving him for the four years removed all that pride in my life and replaced it with a heart of thankfulness for all of my other blessings. It showed me that I needed to learn this lesson, and to look at my life and the way I set my priorities in a very different way.

A Fourth of July to Forget

The road didn't show up on any map, but it was one I needed to travel that certain busy, exhausting holiday. The whole family, along with several friends of various members of our family, were gathered at Lake Francis. We had been doing this every Fourth of July for as long as I can remember.

The day was beautiful and sunny with very little wind. The crystal blue sky had just the right amount of those white puffy clouds to make for a great day for photos. We had the best picnic location, thanks to Cousin Pete. He showed up at nine that morning to claim our area. Past years we often settled for second or third choice, but not this year.

We had fifty plus come out for our annual gathering. Pete's wife, Melinda, a sinisterly looking gal who owns maybe two dresses to her name, both mid-calf length, one blue and one gray with high collars and roses embroidered on each lapel. That day she wore her blue one. For many years she had been in charge of taking a head count and getting updates from each family. Then she notified every one of the time and place for each year's event. She had this system down to a science, and our mailings always came in plenty of time to plan and prepare our food and stuff to bring to this fun outing.

Cousin Pete fit the picture of an appropriate better half for Melinda. He had that walking banana look with his curved spine, his usual yellow stripped shirt, and yellow colored pants held up by yellow suspenders. His pants stopped about three inches above his shoes. He always wore yellow soaks. He must have many pairs to choose from. His little crop of dark brown hair stood up much like the stem of a banana. He had very little neck, and his flat face looked like it had been painted on the concave side of his banana look. His extra-long body and very short legs made it look like he had a hard time walking, but he always got around to say hello to everyone during one of our gatherings.

He and Melinda had no kids, but they sort of adopted all of their nieces and nephews. They always remembered our kid's birthdays and were especially generous to our kids at Christmas time. Melinda always hugged each of the kids. I remember when she grabbed Clinton, our ten year old son, around his neck and kissed him on both cheeks. He looked like he wanted to be anywhere else but in her grasp. He later told me he might skip next year's picnic so he wouldn't have to be embarrassed again by his Great Aunt Melinda.

The lunch selection of food was unreal. We had everything one could possibly ever wish for. My biggest challenge was not taking more than I could ever eat in one sitting. Then Cousin Pete pulled out his battery powered freezer on wheels and started dishing out four different favors of ice cream.

After our meal, we set up badminton nets and several stakes to play horse shoes.

It was in our rules for no one to go swimming for at least a full hour after eating. Unbeknownst to us, a couple young fellows sneaked around and jumped into the water right after eating. It only took a few minutes before one of them was shouting for help. Little eight year old Johnny was cramping up so much that he almost couldn't keep his head above water.

Three of us dropped our shoes and dove in. I was the first to reach Johnny so I simply lifted him up over my shoulder and brought him back to shore. It took some time for his cramps to go away, but it took much longer for the three of us who jumped in to dry off and keep the sand out of our shoes.

It was during our rescue effort Cousin Pete stepped on something sharp. This sharp object had been buried in the sand. He yelled and dropped like someone had shot him. When we investigated a bailing hook had gone right through his shoe and into his foot.

I agreed to take him and Melinda to the hospital, and while they were being attended to at the emergency location I went home to change into some dry clothes before heading back to the hospital.

After a tetanus shot and some wound care and bandages they released him. He chose to go straight home. I took him there, and agreed to take Melinda back to the lake get Pete's truck, along with his battery powered freezer, their picnic supplies, and Melinda's lap top computer.

It was on our way that my car was rear ended while we were stopped at a red light on Main Street. The other driver left the scene without stopping. I could see when he backed away from my car there was considerable damage to the front of his car. I get his plate number and I called 911.

Another car stopped right behind us and the driver put on his emergency flashers. I was about to get out to check on the damage to my car when I looked over at Melinda. She was passed out with her head leaning against the side widow. I again called 911 and asked for an ambulance to come as soon as possible. They asked if I had injuries, and then about her injuries, but all I could tell them was she said she was fine two minutes ago, but was now passed out. It looked like she was breathing, so I passed that information along to them.

The police arrived first just ahead of the ambulance. Melinda was taken back to the same hospital. An accident report was taken, along with the information about the other car including the license plate numbers.

I determined my car was drivable, but I needed to use hand signals because my brake and back signal lights were broken. I called Cousin Pete and told him I would come right back to get him, so we went back to that same hospital.

Melinda had fainted due to a heart condition, possibly a mild heart attack brought on by our accident. They kept her overnight to keep an eye on her. I offered to get all of Pete's things and his truck back to his house, and then come back to get him if he wanted. He looked at me with a puzzled look and said, "I'm not sure what to do, but if you will at least bring my truck back here, then I can decide to either stay here over tonight or go back home."

Back at the lake again I had some of the others help me load the freezer and other things that belonged to Pete and Melinda. We delivered these items to Pete's house. We moved the left over ice cream into their main freezer, and then took his truck to the hospital.

I brought Pete his keys, let him know where we had parked his truck, and asked how Melinda was doing.

He smiled and said, "She is a doing, but Doc told me she is determined enough to live and continue to harass everyone."

We then drove back to the lake just in time to see my son, Clinton, fall out of a tree and injure his arm. I suspected it was broken, so Mary and I loaded him in the back of our car before heading back to that same hospital.

The doctor set Clinton's arm, gave us some pain pills in case he had some pain during the night, and we drove back to the lake with our broken car, my wounded son, and my exhausted body.

When we got there we found all of our family had left, and so were our chairs and all of our picnic supplies. I called my brother, Gary, but he didn't know what happened to our stuff. He suggested we call Cousin Pete, but I reminded him that Pete had been at the hospital for most of the afternoon.

When I got off the call to Gary my phone rang. The police had caught the driver of the other car. He was an unlicensed driver with no insurance and no means to pay for the repairs on my car. They asked me to be available if needed to testify when the driver went to court.

The last thing that happened on that Fourth of July was when we got home we found someone had run over our mail box and our precious old dog had died. He was in our back yard lying right next to our patio door.

I told Mary and Clinton we needed to look on the bright side. We are all still alive, with limited injuries. We still have our health, our life, and our jobs, along with our family and many friends. Everything that happened that day would eventually heal, could be replaced or repaired, except for Buddy, our dog. He was a one of a kind. There was no replacing the likes of him, even if we did decided to get another dog.

Oh, our picnic supplies were stacked right in front of our garage door. Everything was accounted for, including a left over rhubarb pie that we didn't bring to the gathering. We never did find out who gave us that great pie, but its one of my favorite pies.

God is so good!

Rainy Day Monday

Buzz woke up early, somewhat confused that certain morning. His dark brown eyes didn't focus for a moment or two. He rubbed them, and then looked at the alarm clock a second time. He thought, *'It can't be time to get up yet. It's still dark outside. Maybe someone messed with the alarm.'*

He looked over at his sleeping wife. She hadn't moved when the alarm when off. She must be still deep in sleep. He lay back for another minute before getting up. How tempting it would be to just cuddle up to Diane and go back to sleep. What did he have going today? His list of customers to call on was long just like almost every Monday. He could shorten his list by spreading the calls through the rest of the week. He had done that before, but every time he did, things always seem to get all mixed up.

As he laid there he thought he heard it raining.

Diane turned, lay back and stretched before she looked over at him in the dim light, "Good morning sweetheart. Why are you awake? Is it time to get up?"

He turned towards her with a puzzled look, "Good morning, did someone fool with our alarm? It's still dark outside and the clock says it's time to get up. It's also raining out I think."

His next thought was to lay back over, go back to sleep, and then get up later, "I could spread my calls just like I've done before. Calling on customers in the rain is not always the most pleasant way anyway."

She smiled and spoke, "You're the boss. You can do whatever you choose. The customers will always be there, but they may have made their purchases from some other source by the time you get there. Remember the last time you shortened your day. Some of your people had already gone elsewhere for their goods."

She reached for the remote and switched on the TV. The news reporter immediately said, "It's a rainy day Monday here in the city.

The time is now fifteen minutes past seven. Time to rise and shine. Now we'll give you one of my favorite song artists, Dolly with her best-selling song, "Rainy Day Mondays Always Make Me Cry."

Buzz leaned over and kissed Diane, then jumped out of bed, headed for the shower, and said, "I guess that's my que Sweetheart, I'll be ready for my breakfast in twenty minutes."

He could only hope the rest of the day went better than it started. He needed a good day after his strange start. Rain or no rain, he would make the most of it. Salesmanship was his trade and he needed to have his mind and his body going in the same positive direction, and at the same time.

Jumping forward to the end of Buzz's work day....

He ended up selling more goods than any other day prior to that time. He couldn't wait to get home and share this with Diane and the kids. His last thought when driving onto his driveway, "I could use a whole lot more Rainy Day Mondays just like today in the future, just like that song he'd heard while he was shaving this morning."

My Space

Sherman (Woody) climbed up in the old oak tree near the back fence to see what was causing all the ruckus over at his neighbors. He couldn't see anything from the ground, or not even at five feet off the ground so he climbed higher.

That branch just above his head looked strong enough to hold his two hundred ten pounds, so up he went. He then climbed out away from the trunk of the tree to get a better look.

He saw Sam, his neighbor, running a power washer. The sound seemed different than what he had heard just minutes before.

He was about to climb down when he heard the first crack. Before he could move the branch gave away. He bounced off a lower branch before he had a chance to grab hold of it. He doesn't remember feeling anything at that sudden stop when he hit the wet ground.

His first thought, *'I'll just lay here a minute to see if I hurt anything.'*

When he tried to get up he couldn't move. His cell phone in his back pocket felt strange. He was able pulled it out, but it came out in pieces.

That sound from Sam's place was still going on, so he knew he wouldn't know what had happened to him, and his own house was far enough away that Marta wouldn't hear him yelling for her help. Besides, she's probably gone grocery shopping, *"I may as well lay here until Sam shuts off that power washer."*

A good half hour passed, but it seemed much longer, like a whole day. He was wet and began shivering. He discovered he could roll onto his side, but wasn't able to get up on all fours. The cold breeze felt worse on his wet back so he rolled back, only to find he had rewarm the ground where he had been laying.

He spoke out loud to distract himself, "Think... of something... other than you...your...prob..problem, maybe...think of what you we...weres...sup...supposed to be...do...doing instead of...climb..ing trees. Think about...how I wou...would do it once you got...start...ed, while still...list...listening for Sam. Once he...st...stops that..da...darn... mach...machine you..c...can get...his atten...attention. You...can think...ab...about what my..grand...kids would want to...do for the...the...their Grand...grandma's...birth...day. They al...always want to...to do...something really...sp.. special."

After an hour Sherman (Woody) was getting desperate, *Sam must be washing his whole house. Seems like he could take a break before long. Maybe he will soon, I can only hope.*

There, the noise stopped. Sherman yelled as loud as he could, "Sam, hey...S.. Sam, I need...help."

"Is that you Sherman, a...a Woody? What do you need? I was just going in to take a little rest before I finish the rest of the house."

"I'm over...here under this...tree, and I need...help!"

Sam yelled back, "Let me come round to see where you are."

Sam came around the house, "Well Woody, what on earth are you doing lying under that tree?"

Then he saw the broken limb and smiled, "Oh' I see you were climbing up to snoop on your neighbors when that branch broke. Can you get up, or do I have to call someone to come help."

Sherman's face change from a cold pale to red cold red, "Yes, I was...sn...snooping when that...branch gave away. I can't get up. I don't think anything is.... broke...broken other than that darn...branch. But, I may need a ...stret...stretcher. Can you call...call for the EMT...wagon?"

Sam took off his coat and laid it over Sherman before he turned to hurry back to his place to call. "Don't go away. I'll be right back."

He heard Sherman say, "Don't wo...worry I...I promise I'll be...right here."

The EMTs showed up in about twenty minutes. They lifted Sherman off the ground. They took him to the hospital, and then to Dr. Barton, his chiropractor. Woody's back was out which effected his legs. Once his back was in place he able to function normally. It was three days later when he developed a deep cough that Marta became concerned. She took him in to the doctor, who in turn sent him on to the hospital with pneumonia. Three days under their nurses care was all that he could handle.

Marta begged him to stay put until the illness was gone, but he said, "I need my space, and I need it like yesterday. Hospitals are for really sick people. I'm just a little under the weather."

He moped around the house for days. Marta told him every chance she got, "If only you would have stayed in the hospital two extra days you would have been well enough to avoid this condition you're in now.

He would give her an answer like "Your right again." He knew she was right, but he wanted to be home is where his heart is. It was three full weeks before he really felt like himself.

With his bout of pneumonia history and he could now could get back to his normal things. The lesson learned was to stay out of the trees and keep his feet planted firmly on the solid ground.

Oh, Sam and Woody had had several times while Woody was recuperating when Sam kidded him about trying to be a big kid again, "Climbing trees and breaking things are really for true kids, next you will start drawing up plans to build a tree house or tree fort or something. When you do, please do not include me in your project."

Woody would say, "Sam, if you didn't come here to cheer me up, well then maybe you should just go back home."

"Okay Woody, I'll try to behave myself, but tell Marta if she needs anything, I mean anything at all, she can just give me a call."

"Okay, now you've gone too far and said too much, Marta, show this so called friend of mine the door."

"Now Woody, I was only jesting. I do miss not seeing you out rambling around, trying to get something done. I do wish you would pay me for all the mowing I've done around here. Payment can come in good home cooked meals. In fact, I would prefer that over money. Marta is the best cook this side of the Rockies, and you have been the beneficiary of that for several decades, and to be totally honest, it shows. I lost my partner almost five years ago, and I still haven't come close to perfecting my mastery in the kitchen. Frankly, I don't want to because it's my weakness in that area that makes me continue getting out there to find my second soul mate. Why, just last week I lunched at the senior center and had two proposals, at least I think they were only marriage proposals. Now, that's a record for me. Unfortunately, neither of the two admitted to liking to cook. One even told me that she goes out to eat three times a day, and frankly that showed as well."

"But, enough about my love life, or lack thereof, how are you doing? Are you ready to come out and race me with your riding mower anytime soon? I need the practice for the big lawn mower race is coming up in a couple months. I plan to take first place in it. That will make me a big cheese with the ladies around town. I know this fellow who lives on the other side of the tracks, if you know what I mean, who has tampered with his mower, maybe jury-rigged his mower is a better description. I'm told that guy can do twenty five MPH on his machine."

"Sam, it's never a dull moment having you as my neighbor. You have more crazy schemes going than anyone I have ever met."

Woody felt the challenge. He thought he might try racing against Sam one day soon once his health was better. He could beef up his belt driven mower by mounting a larger pulley on the drive shaft. He was not sure how fast it would go, but he was convinced it would give Sam a run for his money. They could set up the run on Sam's driveway.

They made a deal that they would shut down the race about fifty yards before the main road. This way it would not allow either of them to reach the road. Sam's driveway Teed at the main road and the ditch on the other side was pretty deep. Their race would go about two hundred yards at tops. Woody had asked Marta to officiate, but she declined. She thought the whole idea was foolish, if not also way too dangerous. Sam wanted to wager on the race, but Woody was not a gambling man, so all that would happen was all the gloating and ribbing the winner would be able to give the loser.

So Sam and Woody made it official by shaking hands on this deal.

The first of the very next week they were out marking off the starting line and finish line before they lined up to start the race.

Sam looked at Woody, "We need someone to officiate our race? Who can we find to get us started?"

Woody offered, "How about we throw a rock in the air, when it hits the ground we start the race."

Sam agreed, "Maybe if it hits metal that will work. Now who gets to throw the rock? How about we flip a coin to see who gets that honor. The winner throws the rock. Will that work for you?"

"Okay Sam. Do you have a coin?"

"Just so happens I do. You call it in the air."

Woody spoke, "I call heads."

"Heads it is. Woody, you get to toss the rock. But, how about we get the metal garbage can cover? We can set it just ahead and between our race paths, and then we can finally get started."

Woody said, "I'll go get the cover and find a rock, then I can finally get the chance to beat you."

"Ha, wishful thinking, but I'm as ready as you are, probably more so."

Woody set the cover just three feet ahead of the two mowers and right between their two paths. He got on his mower before he said, "Gentlemen, start your engines."

When both were ready Woody tossed the rock up a good ten feet in the air, but Sam started ahead of the rock coming down. When the rock landed it failed to hit the cover.

Woody yelled, "False start. Come on back Sam."

This time Woody set the cover three feet behind their mowers. He told Sam it was the sound of the rock hitting the cover as their signal, not when the rock was in the air. They lined up again. This time Woody tossed the rock up and when they heard the clank they both started off at the same time.

Woody heard the belt on his mower squealing. It was obviously slipping. Sam pulled ahead from the start by a few feet, but when the squealing stopped Woody was gaining on Sam just inches at a time. Both mowers were now going at full speed. When they approached half way mark Sam was still a foot ahead of Woody. At three quarters the distance was down to six inches. And at the designed finish line they were neck and neck, but neither man was willing to let off the gas. The end of the road was coming up too fast. And then the steep ditch was just beyond that. Could they stop in time before......?

Woody was now in the lead. He looked both ways and saw a car coming from the right. He choose to make a sharp turn to the left, out of Sam's path. In doing so his mower tipped over to his right just before it reached the main road. He landed on his right shoulder and felt something give there. He swung his legs away from his mower and turned to look in time to see Sam fly off the far side of the road before he disappear into the ditch.

The driver of the car had seen what was coming and was able to stop his car to avoid hitting either mower or rider. He jumped out of his car and ran to where Sam was in the bottom of the ditch. The mower was on top of him and he was yelling that his pants were on fire. That third party jumped down and pulled the mower off Sam just as Woody arrived. Then he squatted down next to Sam to find out what else was wrong. Sam's pants were not on fire, but he had been burned by the hot exhaust pipe. He was definitely in pain. Both of his legs were hurt, and he had a big lump on his head. Woody told him not to move. He heard that third party calling for an ambulance.

The same ambulance people who had come to help Woody a few weeks ago showed up to help Sam. Woody heard the one who made this comment, "Hey George, we are getting to know this road all too well. It's just the other fellow who getting a ride from us today."

Woody had heard his comment, but chose to not take offense, or say anything because they might decide to leave without helping either Sam or himself.

Woody ended up with a broken right collar bone and Sam ended up with a concussion and both kneecaps badly bruised, along with burns on one leg. But, both of them had more permanent damage to their male egos after Marta got through with them, and after the local newspapers finished their articles about their practice mower race.

Part Two Short Stories – With a Christian Theme

Homeward Bound

Melvin left his doctor's office that day with his body and mind in a near panic mode. The information he had been given left him numbed. The future prospects that lay ahead were unsettling. That substance he had accidentally ingested the day before was lethal and had no antidote. He had waited too long to have his stomach pumped so the toxins are likely having an effect. Doctor gave him the saddest, most compassionate look before he spoke, "Melvin, it looks like at best you have seventy two hours."

He had forgotten to breath, and when he did he almost choked on his saliva, "Wait, wait, you-haa.. you mean I have seventy two hours to.....to live?"

Doc looked at the floor for a moment with his shoulders slumped, "Yes, that is my prognosis. You should feel okay today and even part of tomorrow, but on day three you'll start feeling the changes that will come quickly. By then, life won't be pleasant for you. My recommendation is you make the most of today and tomorrow. I'm so sorry to have to tell you this."

He walked out of the doctor's office with a thick, black cloud hanging over his head. He forced each step heading back to his car. Should he go back in and plead with doctor for a different diagnosis, or to ask him, "Doctor, isn't there something that can be done?"

When he crawled in he leaned over the steering wheel with his head in his hands. He prayed, "God send someone to help me figure out what to do with this shocking revelation. I need someone to help me make some sense out of this, someone to tell me what to do with my last three days.

He was lost in time, until he finally forced his mind to work. He needed to plan his next 48 hours. No one had showed up after his prayer. He needed to make a mental list of priorities, to set

them in order. He'd go home to Susan. He'd always liked driving his car. Doing all the other things he liked came to mind. As he walked up the steps he thought about their home. *'I really liked it, but it's not paid for. I need to find Susan.'* She has always been my mainstay from the first day I met her over thirty five years ago. *'She'll know what we are to do.'*

He found her in the kitchen cutting up vegetables for his all-time favorite stew. She looked up when he came in and knew instantly something was wrong. He stepped over and pulled her into his arms and just held her. She knew about the doctor's appointment. She had insisted that he go. She had almost gone with him, but he had convinced her that it was not necessary.

She knew he had bad news. She leaned back and looked up into his eyes, "Melvin, Honey, please tell me what's happening!"

He gently held her face in his hands, looking through his tears he shared what the doctor said. They cried together for a long time, before he told her of his mental list. She quickly agreed to follow his plan. They'd call the children first. Then start on his list. See as many people he wanted to see one more time, and then do as many things he still wanted to do in the short time he had left.

Before he got very far on his list, he started thinking of all the things that had suddenly become so very important, some silly things like being thankful he had just mowed the lawn and washed both cars. Susan wouldn't have to worry about these for a while. Then, how, thankful he is for Susan's prodding last year about all those legal matters. His will and living trust are now stored away in our safe. His organ donor records are in order, and his plan for cremation is also a matter of written record.

Susan could continue on with the business activities in his absence. Her income wouldn't change all that much. He was thankful he had listened to her about these. He had been guilty of putting off, procrastination is a more appropriate word, about all things that sound too morbid for far too long.

Then he thought about his Susan and the times they've had together. She's always been able to lift his spirits with her special little ways. He's been able to depend on her sweet, adorable presence from the start of the day and all through to the end of each day. She is his gift that keeps on giving even when he's not deserving of such a wonderful gift from above.

Next, Melvin thought of their grown children. They are kids that any dad can be proud of. Sherry, our oldest, newly married, is starting on her life after college. She and her husband, Tim, are getting their lives anchored, and in a good direction. Then there's our single care free young man, Brad, who is just now getting his feet solidly on the ground. He has the right ambitions and morale character to work with. And then there's Amber, our college whiz kid, who calls home every other evening to update us on the things going on in her life. She keeps her grades up better than anyone else in the family has ever done. She plans to get as much out of her schooling as she possibly can. But how will they each take this terrible news?

He then thought how important it is to share with them how important his faith is to him. How Jesus gives him the hope that his eternity is sure. He can encourage them all to go on with their pursuit to walk with God. He's glad to be given this time and this warning which still allows him time to pray for and with each of them.

Melvin then thought about all the things he will miss. He'll miss getting to know future spouses for both Brad and Amber. He would miss not being there for Amber's wedding day. He won't get to play with his future grandkids. He'll miss the future time not growing old with his Susan. She could spend the rest of her days either single, or she could remarry. How would that be for her after our thirty five years together?

He and Susan were going to ask their family to come home for an important family gathering. They choose to have them to come here to the house, rather than to share his fateful news over the phone.

He and Susan were about to start making these calls to their children when Susan answered the call coming in. It was from Doctor William's office. Judy there asked Melvin and Susan to hold the line for Doctor Williams.

Melvin had just come from there two hours ago. What could this call be about? They waited for maybe only a minute, but it felt longer. When Doctor came on he thanked Melvin for holding, then he said, "Melvin, have Susan listen in on speaker? I have some really good news for you. Your test results from the lab were mixed up with another man whose first name is also Melvin. For privacy reasons I can't tell you his full name. But, the real news is YOU ARE GOING to be OKAY! You are going to live for hopefully for a whole lot longer.

The bad news is for this other Melvin. He now has less than three days to get his affairs in order. He's not my patient, so it's not up to me to tell him of his situation. Melvin, you are going to be alright. I am so sorry for what this shocking news has put you through for the last two or three hours. I hope you are alright. Your test came back all clear. And no further treatments are needed."

Doctor went on, "I know you and Susan believe in the power of prayer, so please pray for the other Melvin and his family."

"Please tell your Susan and your children I'm so sorry to put you all through this strange shocker. Please tell them all I send my regards."

Above the Clouds

Have you ever wondered what is up there? Or, how the sun, the moon, those planets, and all those millions of stars can remain in place year after year, decade after decade, and century after century? Or, how the sun that gives us our daylight and warms us can keep on burning without burning out?

We continue to discover more and more of what's out there ever since mankind's curiosity and the pursuits of searching for all the vast unknowns out there beyond our earth's atmosphere. Each new and bigger telescope we build allows us to look even further out into space. We find an ever increasing number of stars, more than we've ever seen before. Each new search makes us want to look even further beyond, and then to wonder if there just might be other life forms in existence somewhere in the vastness of space. We further desire to determine if man, and all of the earth's inhabitants are not the only living creatures in existence.

It is this natural built-in curiosity in each of us to seek for all the unknowns around us, both near and far away. We all seem to like to search out these unknown mysteries. I guess that's why mystery books and space movies are so popular. It's that natural desire to find, "The rest of the story," as the well-known public radio personality, Paul Harvey, used this as his trademark during his many years of broadcasting. He'd tell us his lead subject, and then share the rest of the story. That's just like we humans (mankind) continue our search for the rest of the stars and galaxies to be found out in that vast unknown.

We can travel by airplane around this planet in less than a day. We seem to think time and distance are slight measurements until we consider how long it could take for anyone to travel to the farthest point we can see today through our latest telescopes. That distance even at the great speeds we can travel today, would consume a big part of an average lifetime or possibly more. It may not allow one man enough time for a return trip. Even if we were to try, such an effort would be beyond our human ability to withstand that amount of time in a state of weightlessness, away from earth's gravitational pull. Not to mention the need for ample supplies of food, water and oxygen. This adventure would probably require more than one person. Maybe we would have to make up a small community with occupations including all the needed services needed for medical, entertainment, recreational needs, along with replacement of needs as they are used up or wear out.

We are complex creatures. Ones that would not allow for solitary travel for such great distances over extended amounts of time. One person traveling alone would most likely lose his or her ability to maintain sanity. To use a modern day terminology, "It would eventually blow our mind."

One has to wonder is there any end to the space out there? It seems to go on forever. Surely it must end somewhere? Also, one has to question how long life, as we know it, can be sustained on our own planet. How long will the sun continue to burn, to light and warm our earth, without burning out? How long we can continue to use up the fossil fuels and other natural resources available before these supplies are exhausted? How can we continue to provide enough food and other needs as the populations of each country around the world continues to grow?

There is no reason to panic at this time, however, we must convince our neighbors that we must be good stewards of all the things we have today. We all must make use of all sources of energy so our children and grandchildren, and all future generations to follow will have enough to meet their needs as well. This means we must put the power of the sun, the seas and all other natural sources to work for us now. If we invest in all the available sources which will help us, as well as, the people who come behind us, we will be better off and so will they.

Another benefit from harnessing all natural sources is expanding their availability over time. Solar, hydro, atomic, and sea tide sources create little, if any, pollution problems. Also, these have investment costs that are mostly up front, with smaller maintenance costs to receive the long-term benefits.

Production of fossil fuel sources may create more pollution, but their continued use will insure daily availability and sustainability of the current power needed for now and for many years to come. Several of the experts in that field feel these are sufficient to supply us for maybe a couple hundred years at our current rate of usage.

Still another way is being good stewards is the methods and materials used when we build our new homes and offices. We are doing better in our selection of methods; however, we can do a lot more. When we demolish existing structures we should be able to recycle much of those materials rather than just burying them in some landfill. Much of the wood, as well as the metal items could be reused to make other new products. This may create some additional upfront costs. But in the long run would eliminate the need to find new sources of raw materials for milling and manufacturing many of our new products.

We can also design prototypes for homes, schools and office buildings using materials which will prove to be energy efficient, biodegradable and/or recyclable. These will need to meet all the requirements for keeping the use of new raw materials to a minimum, while making them more energy efficient, thus requiring less costs to heat and/or cooling these living and working spaces.

We can find so many how-to-books in print, along with on-line instructions, which will help us to understand not only the importance of being good stewards, but also give us instructions on what to do to be successful in our efforts to be good stewards. There are so many new and existing ideas from exterior wall construction, and how to produce our own electricity and hot water, along with long standing ideas on crop rotations, and with food and water storage. The most unique of these long standing ideas which may be becoming more widely used is the growing of our own vegetable gardens. These can be individual or community efforts from either small or huge areas designated for this purpose. They can be gardening in containers to big plots of land with greenhouse covers in community efforts. Either way, these methods can be most rewarding, not only in the gain of fresh from the vine produce but also as a means of getting people to share in the experience of accomplishment and working towards either complete or partial self-sufficiency.

The Bible, God's Word, is a great source of information to encourage us on the importance of being good stewards of all that God has placed in our hands. He gives us both strength and abilities, along with knowledge, to make the most of all that is available to each of us. All we have to do is put this information to good use. Then to help and encourage others to see how valuable this same information to make the most of each situation.

In the book of Psalms, chapter eight, verses three and four, "When I consider Your Heavens, the work of Your fingers, the moon and the stars, which You have ordained, what is man that You are mindful of Him, and the Son of man that You visit Him?"

In the book of Job, He speaks of God in Chapter twenty six, verses seven through fourteen, "He stretches out the north over empty space; He hangs the earth on nothing. He stores up the water in His thick cloud, yet the clouds are not broken under it. He covers the face of His throne, and spread His cloud over it. He drew a circular horizon on the face of the waters, at the boundary of light and darkness. The pillars of Heaven tremble, and are astonished at His rebuke. He stirs up the sea with His power, and by His understanding He breaks up the storm. By His spirit He adorned the Heavens; His hand pierced the fleeing serpent. Indeed these are the mere edges of His ways, and how small a whisper we hear of Him! But, who can understand the power of His thunder?"

When we read and understand in part how powerful is His Word, only then, can we partially understand who it is that hung the sun, moon and stars in their place, and who keeps the tiny atom from imploding upon itself? And, who keeps the planets continuing in their rotating upon their axis and their orbiting around the sun, as well as, who keeps the sun from burning out.

God's Word tells us He gave man dominion over all the creatures on the earth. It is our responsibility to take care of this planet, to be good stewards of all. This means we must be careful not to abuse or take for granted these things in our care. I liken it to being a parent where we are constantly watchful of those little ones in our care. We want the best for them and try to keep them from harm. Much as our children need to be taught to become good stewards and to carry on after we are gone, we must look at the earth with this same plan, to make it the best possible environment for all future generations who will come after us.

You are encouraged to use all the vast amount of valuable information available to you to do your part and to be an example of your good stewardship to your love ones, neighbors and friends.

May God bless your efforts.

I Spy

This is the story of the late Nancy Joanne Bristol during her final days. This story is told by her pastor.

"Why did I agree to do this? This could be dangerous," were Nancy's thoughts following her conversation with Monty Splean.

Monty, a skinny little man with a sharp pointed chin, receding hair line and eye glasses, which Nancy thought were way too big for his face, told her of his suspicions. He wasn't planning to do the investigative work himself. Instead, he told her that since she was a natural investigator because of her inquisitive mind, she should take it just one step further and just act on her suspicions.

She came back with, "You mean your suspicions don't you?"

Monty had spotted the weapon by accident that morning when he was in with Mr. Baron in his library. Mr. Baron was looking for his favorite pen when he opened his middle desk drawer a little too far. The gun was there, big and bold as life. Mr. Baron had quickly closed the drawer, more like slammed the drawer closed.

Monty told Nancy that day, "If I go back there tonight Mr. Baron is bound to question it. Besides, you're the one with the invitation to his big shindig. All you have to do is slip up there while you are at the party, pretending to be looking for the lady's room. Nobody will be the wiser."

When she objected, Monty added, "Nan, you owe me. All the things I have done for you and Josh, and now I plan to collect. This is your way to repay me. You just sneak into his library and bring back that gun so it can be tested. You know it meets the description Lt. Herald gave me. Mr. Baron has motive for the crime. This needs to be checked out and the sooner the better."

Monty had been a long time partner to Nan's late husband, Josh. In fact, Monty had brought Josh into his business and taught him all that he knew. He had treated Josh like his own son and made him a full partner just a couple years before Josh was tragically killed in that car accident two years ago.

Finally, after much arm twisting by Monty, Nan agreed to his plan. She was to be all dressed in her finest when she arrived with her party invitation in hand. She'd chosen to wear her new purple evening dress. She had her silky golden brown hair done up in a bun with curls extending down both sides of her face.

The hostess opened the door and welcomed her in. She announced Nancy's arrival to Mr. Baron and the rest of his guests. Nancy was not even half way into the reception room when a waiter offered her a glass of champagne. Being a nondrinker, but not wanting to stand out in this crowd she took the glass. She carried it around with her as she blended in with the other guests. She almost wished she had brought a date after the second single man approached her with plans to see her home after the party. But, she had come unescorted on purpose so she would have the freedom to do her investigative work.

After mingling for over an hour, she asked one of the servers if there was a powder room close by. He directed her to a room just down the hallway, or if it was occupied, another one was upstairs just beyond the library.

'*Perfect,*' she had thought. So she set the glass down on a table, chose the one upstairs. and headed in that direction.

She followed the directions Monty had given her and found the double door entrance he had told her to look for. The hallway was semi dark. She could see a light on in the room so she opened the door only a little and very slowly to see if anyone was there. The room appeared empty. Taking off her heels, she tiptoed in. The room was big with rich, smooth oak wood planking and wood panels on every wall except where the bookcases were. She moved around the desk and set her high heels on the floor. She told herself, '*Go, don't spend any more time here than necessary.*'

Monty had told her the gun should still be in the desk. When she tried to open the middle drawer she discovered it was locked. She reached for a knife looking letter opener setting right next to the phone. To her surprise she was able to open the lock on her first effort, and, ditto, the gun was still there. She'd purposely brought her larger hand bag as the gun wouldn't fit in her smaller one. She grabbed a tissue from the box behind her and lifted the gun out, wrapped it in a second tissue, and then tucked it into her handbag. She closed the drawer, put the letter opener back in its place before heading for the door. As she was about to open it she remembered her shoes still on the floor under the desk. She turned back to get them when she heard a noise just outside the door. She ducked in under the big desk just as Mr. Baron came in with another man. Mr. Baron came around to the back side of the desk and reached for his cigarette case and offered one to his guest. At first Nan couldn't recognize the guest's voice, but she sure was interested in what he had to say. He told Mr. Baron about his plan to plant the evidence in Mrs. Summer's home to make it appear that she was the guilty party to the murder.

'Murder, oh good Lord help me. Monty, what have you gotten me into? How am I going to get out of this place? I could reach out to touch Mr. Barton's foot because he is standing so close to me.'

'Wait Nan, get your head on straight. You will need to see if they were going to stay. I pray Mr. Baron doesn't decide to sit down at his desk. If he does, I'm toast!'

The two men had finished their conversation and Mr. Baron said he needed to get back to his other guests. They headed for the door. Nan watched the feet of both men as they started out the door. She saw their shoes and for some reason thought she recognized the shoes of Mr. Baron's guest, but from where? Just then the lights went out. Now in total darkness, she slid out from under the desk. She brushed off her skirt and reached for her shoes. Then felt her way around the desk and headed for the door. Her eyes adjusted slowly as she found the door knob and opened the door so very slowly. She would find the powder room first before heading back down stairs.

She felt she needed to spend a little more time at the party so her early departure wouldn't look too suspicious. So for about another half hour Nan mingled among the other guests, before looking for her host to thank him for inviting her, and to let him know how much she appreciated him thinking of her.

She explained, "I'm sorry to leave so early but I have a little guy at home that likes for me to tuck him in every night."

Mr. Baron was most gracious when she approached him. "Well Nancy, I'm so glad you finally came to one of my functions, maybe, now you won't be such a stranger. I hope to see you again very soon."

Nan thanked him again, made her early departure after she said good night.

She heard him say, "Come back again when you can stay longer."

She just nodded her head and started towards the front door with more than she had come in with. Mr. Baron's gun weighed heavy in her handbag. As she reached the bottom step she resisted the urge to pull off her heels and run for her car.

She thought, *'Mr. Baron was nice, but did he suspect her of doing something? Could he know that she was not there just as a guest, but was there for some other reason?'*

She reached her car, unlocked the door and climbed in, hitting the lock behind her before she said out loud, "Monty, you just wait till I get my hand on your neck. When I'm through with you, you won't live long enough to send me out on another one of your schemes. Okay, I guess I won't murder you, but I'll sure be more careful what you talk me into after this."

Nan drove straight to Monty's place to drop off Mr. Baron's gun. Monty planned to take it right over to Lt. Herald so he can have it checked. She was now aware that it might be the murder weapon the police were looking for. They will then know for sure that Mr. Baron was involved in some way in their murder case.

Nan took him to task, "Monty, I can't believe you would send me into real harm's way when you asked me to go after that gun. I got caught in his library when Mr. Baron came in with someone. They had a conversation right there with me hiding under his desk. They plan to plant some phony evidence in Mrs. Summer's home to make it look like she is the guilty party. I heard them say that. I didn't recognize the other man's voice until I was out of the house and heading for my car. I believe it was my boss's boss, Mr. Maynard, the retired senior partner in the CPA firm where I work. I recognized his shoes first, then I remembered the many audio training CDs he made which we still use at the firm. I am certain it's his voice. When I saw those old style expensive Wingtip dress shoes just like my dad used to wear when he was still working. Dad still has a pair in his closet. Mom can't get him to give them away even though he never wears them anymore. I'll never forget what you had me do tonight."

Then she added, "I'm going to pick up my little boy and go home. I plan to lock us in for the night. Tomorrow I'm going in to see my boss and ask for some time off. I have vacation time coming and since it's the slow time of the year, my colleague, Joel can take over my clients for a couple weeks. Clay and I are going out of town for a while. I need to clear my head of all that has happened in the last few hours."

Nan picked up Clay from her twin sister, Lori's place, and drove home. She parked her car in the garage, picked up Clay, who had fallen asleep in the back seat, and carried him into the house. She and Clay hid out until morning.

She didn't sleep much, only off and on, for probably only a couple hours between bad dreams and her restless mind.

After fixing some breakfast for Clay and herself she took him back to Lori's. Her mom and dad were there visiting Lori. They had plans to take Lori and Clay out to lunch while Lori's husband, Tim, was at work.

After Nan's experience the previous night, she decided it was time to fill them in on some things she had been thinking about while she should have been sleeping. She told them she has all of her legal papers in her safety deposit box at Mid State Bank. She had designated Lori and Tim as care givers for Clay should something happen to her. Lori was good with that because she and Tim loved Clay almost as much as Nan.

Nan then added. "Lori spends more time with Clay than I do, especially during the heavy tax season."

She then told them all about her million dollar life insurance policy, and the fact that her house was paid for from Josh's life insurance when he died two years ago. With Josh gone, Nan hoped Lori and Tim could adopt Clay.

She went on, "Lori, the life insurance money will go towards the purchase of an annuity with enough return so you would have enough income to raise Clay, and then send him to the very best college."

Nan's mom gave her a strange look before asking, "Wait a minute, why are you going over all this now? Is there something that you're not telling us?"

Nan's quick response, "Mom, when would I do so, if not right now, with you and Dad as my witnesses?"

Her mom gave her another strange look, but didn't say anything further. Then Nan asked if anyone had any questions. When they shook their heads, she told them of her plans to ask her boss about taking some vacation time, and then about plans to go home and pack for their trip out of town. Adding, "We, Clay and I, are going to the cabin on the coast for a ten day break, and a little R and R."

"Lori, I'll be back later today to pick up Clay. See you then."

Nan hugged each of them, told them she loved them, just as she had always done, and then headed for the office.

Her boss told her to go, "Take a couple weeks to relax as you've certainly earned this time off."

He added, "We will cover for you, so don't worry about anything while you're gone. Just go and have a great vacation get-a-way."

She thought, '*You have no idea what I have to worry about now.*'

But she didn't say anything to him about what had happened last night. Or, that Mr. Maynard, his former boss may be involved in some way to the murder.

Nan grabbed a couple things from her office, told Nicki, her assistant, about her plans, and to give Joel anything that needed to be completed before she got back from vacation. Then she left.

She felt the need to go by her church to pray before going home. When she got there Pastor Mike was sitting in the lobby reading. He greeted her, and then asked if she needed him for anything. She told him she would like to share what had happened to her in the last 15 hours. She shared with him every last detail of the gun situation; how she had stayed up most of the night thinking about everything, even about her bad dreams. She also told him all the things she had shared with Lori and her parents. She spent a good two hours going over every detail.

Pastor then suggested they should spend some time in prayer.

They spent another hour praying. Pastor asked his wife, Millie, to come in to join them in prayer. Then Nan thanked them for their continued prayers and headed for home to pack.

Pastor Mike stood before the people gathered at the memorial for Nancy Joanne Bristol. Her little son, Clay, sat in the front row between his Aunt Lori and his Uncle Tim. Nancy and Lori's mom and dad were beside Tim. The church was filled to capacity with friends, family and many of Nancy's co-workers. The mourners were all subdued and intent on listening to what Pastor Mike had to say.

He began, "Nancy came to me last Wednesday morning with her heart heavy. She had been through a frightening experience the night before. She told me she had something she needed to get off her chest, and she chose me. Somehow she knew things were about to change for her. She told me every detail of her experience from the previous night; then about her hurried conversations with Monty about the gun, how she had lifted it from Mr. Baron's desk, and that she hadn't slept much during that night. She said she had several bad dreams that woke her. She spent the rest of the night planning what she needed to do. She told me of all the arrangements she had made with Lori and their mom and dad for Clay's care; for her work at the CPA firm and for Clay's future. We, Nancy, my wife, Millie, and I prayed for a long time, and somehow I also, not just felt, but knew that things would be changing for her. I didn't know what was to come, but I knew that something was about to happen. When she left my heart was heavy. I now wish I had told her not to even go home."

"Millie and I continued to pray for Nancy and her son, Clay. Not realizing how or what to pray about at the time. Just prayed for their safety and her concerns."

"It was not until the next morning's newspaper came that I found out what had happened. I read that article with such a heavy heart. Just as I was finishing with it, Lori called me in tears with the same terrible news."

Those headlines said, "EXPLOSION ROCKS NEIGHBORHOOD." It was reported as a rare accidental natural gas explosion. It happened at 2 PM yesterday. There was one fatality. One of our own, Mrs. Nancy Joanne Bristol died in the *accident*. The interior of her house is a total loss. But because of the high block walls around the back and two sides of her house, only the two story house next door on the west side sustained some minor damaged to the upper story. The blast shattered windows and blistered paint on the east side of that neighbor's house."

Pastor went on, "Just below that article was a second one. "LOCAL LEADER FACES MURDER CHARGES," Samuel Baron, a long time, local business man was arrested at his home that same evening on first degree murder charges. The police are looking for his alleged accomplice. They are withholding any further information until both suspects are in custody."

The following day Nancy's obituary appeared in the newspaper. It read, "Nancy Joanne Bristol, of Fort Wayne went home to be with her Lord on Wednesday afternoon. She was affectionately known as Nan. She was twenty eight years old. She was preceded in death by her husband, Joshua K. Bristol, who passed away just two years and two months ago, and by her baby sister, Victoria Meyers who died twenty years ago. Nancy is survived by her minor son, Clay M. Bristol; by her parents, John and Betty Meyers and by her twin sister, Lori Meyers Franklin and Lori's husband, Timothy Franklin all of Fort Wayne.

Pastor Mike went on to say, "Nancy will be sorely missed by all who knew her and loved her. Our loss is Heaven's gain. None of us knows when our time here on earth is finished. We do know that we have a choice where we spend our eternity. If any of you wants to know more about what you can do about your own eternity, I urge you to come see me after this service. Nancy's last prayer is that anyone who needs to come should realize that today is the day. Tomorrow, well we just don't know what tomorrow will bring. I was probably the last person to see Nancy alive. I know without any doubt that she is with the Lord Jesus Christ."

"Now, for an announcement: "The family welcomes you to gather after this service in our family center for food and refreshments. A memorial has been established in Nancy JoAnne Meyers Bristol's name with proceeds to be used in assisting families in need during the holidays, and at any other time of the year. Contributions can be made here at the church with a designation for this fund or at the Mid State Bank under Nancy's name. Her heart was to help take care of those who are hungry. This is a permanent memorial with tax exempt 501c3 status."

"This concludes our service in memory of Nancy Joanne Meyers Bristol."

Footnote: One year later Pastor Mike had the honor of officiating at a private family ceremony. A remembrance of Nancy Joanne Meyer Bristol, and the adoption party for Clay M. Bristol Franklin who now has both a mother and father. Tim and Lori Franklin adopted him, but allowed him to keep his birth name, along with adding their Franklin name. His permanent records are now changed to: Clay M. Bristol Franklin.

Margins

We all have our priorities, the things we put ahead of most other things. Yours might differ from everyone else. Much like our fingerprints, no two are exactly the same. What I like and what I hold important may be very similar to someone else, but some of my areas will differ from other people. Or, they may dramatically differ as if they lived on some different planet than me. They might seem to operate under different standards or walk to a different beat and believe in many things we can't, or couldn't even understand.

We each have friends who are thoughtful and considerate in every way, except for one difference. They could easily be our best friends except for this one area which drives us over the edge. It may be that they are late for every get together. If we invite them to dinner at our house for six, it may be six thirty or later before they show up. If we plan some outing, and plan to pick them up at their place, they are rarely ready on time. Then they might make no apologies for their lateness. I have even heard one or two of them say, "It is very "IN" to always be LATE."

Unfortunately, I feel it is very "OUT" to always be late, as well as, it is rude, inconsiderate, and lacking concern for our time.

Others who don't match up with what we want in a friendship might be what they believe in. Or, maybe it's their politics, their Christian belief, or unbelief. Others might have what we might call an attitude problem, or a negative response to any given subject. Whatever the differences, they make these a non-candidate for wanting to spend quality time with them.

Now, most things that people do shouldn't bother the rest of us that much. It's just their way of being individuals. It's their personality and we need to give them the right to be whoever they are. It is when they continue to often affect us that we finally need to take exception. And how we react to these differences may make or break any chance of a friendship or even a distant relationship.

Some might say that opposites attract, but I say people who hang together need to be on the same page most of the time. If they cannot agree on most issues, this can or may cause a great deal of strain on any relationship. They each must be able to come to an agreement on any vital areas of interests, time and work schedules, along with, eating habits and whatever areas where they spend greater amounts of time together. They each must be able to adapt to any differences, without over stepping on each other's comfort zone. If one will bend, but the other will not, this too will eventually cause a riff.

Good relationships take hard work from all parties. Each person must be willing to put their full effort into the maintenance of their relationship. They must be able to talk out and work out their differences. They must learn how to relate to one another in order to keep their bond intact. If only one of them is willing to make an effort to do this, eventually the relationship will come apart, or at least it will fall short of their expectations.

Many of us are involved in so many different types of relationships. These can be husband and wife, parent and child, brother and sister, brother and brother, sister and sister, employer and employee, neighbors, co-workers, cousins, friends, just to name a few. In each, how we treat one another, how we agree to spend our time together, our likes and dislikes, and our opinions on almost every subject can make a difference on how we get along. And, get along we must, if we wish to keep the relationship from being shipwrecked.

We are talking about margins. These must be part of every aspect of life.

Margins in finance means we must save back funds after all of our required bills are covered. This gives us the means to pay for any unexpected expenses to avoid the crunch which can and will come.

It also gives us room to avoid the possible eviction or repossession, or any other money problems which could occur. Margins in our time are another area which we must include in our plans. To do this means we must allow extra time in all of our daily activities. When we plan to meet others we need to allow (margins) for any unexpected delays. At work when working on a project we need to do the same. Our relationships with others should also require margins building in some wholesome, quality time. These times must be agreeable to all to make it work. If one tends to monopolize the other's time while the other wants some alone time, there is bound to be problems.

Margins can prove to be a very good thing especially when they are planned with all parties in agreement. They can prove to be useful in providing a solid basis in both work and in play.

The best starting place is in the planning. First, all parties must come together with their ideas of what they want included in the mix. Then, some mutual ground must be established for the future. Here much adaptation will be required. The more people are involved, the harder it will be to finalize a workable plan. It will require some give and take from all interested parties.

The old saying, "You can please some of the people all the time, but you cannot please all of the people all the time."

All of the people should get some of the things they want, and then be willing to allow others to get the same. With the final goal that everyone will get some benefit from the plan, and everyone can be better off with the final result.

So go out there and set up your margins with your money, your time and your relationships.

"No success can come from a lack of trying."

"Where there is no vision the people parish." Proverbs 29:18

Behold the Trees

Why, what are trees are so important to all of us?

In school I memorized that old poem, "Only God Can Make a Tree." It didn't mean much to me back then, just words that rhymed. Trees are so numerous it's easy to take them, as well as, those words in that poem for granted.

Years ago we had lots of trees on our family farm. My parents planted hundreds of them in five rows that ran for a half mile in a shelter belt along the Northern boundary of our farm. Our lack of appreciation for them came from the work that was involved when I, along with my brothers and sisters, pulled weeds and grass out from around those small, starter trees several times during those first two summers.

I also remember many grass clod fights happened each time we were out there working. This job seemed to go on and on, so throwing grass clods at each other was our way to break up the monotony.

Also, the word "work" was associated with our trees. It was too silly to place our blame on innocent objects, those trees.

After those first two years the trees continued to increase in size, along with their value to us. They grew to become a landmark in our community. Their value wasn't measured in dollars, but in how they slowed those cold northerlies in eastern North Dakota, plus in holding back the snow pack needed for spring water for the surrounding land. They also provided beauty in every season, along with their fruits and nuts in the harvest season. They gave bountiful treasures for several of our neighbors during these years. They also slowed the soil erosion caused by the winds and rains. They also provide a natural roosting place and hide-a-way homes for countless wildlife. These reasons go well beyond the benefits with visual value to our eyes.

The paper products we use, parts of our furniture, the floors we walk on, under the roof that protects us, and many other materials come from trees. Looking around we can see countless other items made from wood. Even some foods, like real maple syrup, walnut extract, and many by-products come from trees, shoe dyes and even parts of the brooms, shovels and rakes are a product that comes from them as well..

Trees come in all different sizes, shapes and colors. The red, yellow, white, silver, grey, brown and hundreds of shades of green add much to the magnificence of our landscapes. A tiny dwarf fruit trees are in contrast with the giant redwoods, both fall under the general title of a tree.

We can swing under them, get shade from some, climb up in some and rest against others. They help moderate the climate, and provide erosion control. We break their branches, prune them, beat on them, poison them with chemicals and petroleum, saw on them, chop them down and generally abuse them. Yet, many have strength to survive much of these abuses.

I had a tiny volunteer valley oak tree start up several years ago next to my garage. I almost dug it up to transplant it to a better location back then, but today it provides both shade and beauty to a big part of the yard. I wouldn't want to lose the value it adds.

Trees withstand severe heat and cold, drought and floods, insects and animals' abuses, but we humans are their biggest threat.

Trees provide so many necessary things. The bounty they supply is perhaps second in importance to one other element. That is the precious, life supporting oxygen the trees expel into our earth's atmosphere. This alone is just one more immeasurable by-product which comes from our trees.

Have you ever thought what our world would look like without them? Their beauty is still another benefit that cannot be measured in dollars. I believe without them our planet would dry up and blow away. I believe without them our survival here would be in peril.

We've come to realize all trees were placed here for our survival. They are our helpers, our friends and allies. We plant them, water them and cultivate around them, but to borrow a phrase from that old poem, "Only God can make them grow." They are a gift from above. They are an inanimate gift that keeps on giving expecting so little in return.

Thank God for these special gifts.

God's Greatest Gifts

We all experience some mixed emotional times. Perhaps one of these which can have the greatest impact is when a new baby arrives at your house. When it happens it will require more schedule changes, disrupt more peace, require less rest, and yet, create more joy and excitement, along with more innovation in your life, and in your schedule than almost any other one single memorable event.

The time leading to the first entrance of this new member into your household is what can be described as a time of waiting and a time of preparations. It's also a time for both changes and experiences. It causes you to really get to know your partner through mentally and physically challenging times; and then to get your minds prepared for what will be required of you by bringing this precious new little creature home, along with coming to the realization that you are responsible for raising up this child to adulthood.

The Bible describes the family in such a beautiful way. God said, "It is not good for man to be alone, I will make him a help mate."

Then God told us, that we should go forth and multiply.

We have certainly followed His instructions on this one point, if on no other!

Whether or not you believe in the Bible as God's word, you must admit the plan of marriage between a man and woman is certainly a beautiful plan.

I get tickled every time I see a young couple walking hand in hand, and if it is obvious the woman is carrying an unborn baby. This even adds to the sense of joy I feel. They are sharing something together beyond themselves. They are sharing the wonder and anticipation of the expected arrive of a new life. The apprehensions of the responsibilities that this change will demand of them, as well as, the joy and excitement of this new beginning can be also ever present.

Pregnancy is a condition not to be compared to any other. When is happens between a man and his wife, it starts them to working together setting goals and plans for their new birth. In most cases, it also gives them something very special to share that no one else can share with them so completely. It creates memories of this time of preparation that they will always be able to share, along with the joy and pride of being a part of the forming of this new miracle of life which is to be entrusted into their care.

By contrast, an unplanned pregnancy which occurs outside of the marriage union causes many different emotions. Some might be embarrassment, guilt, a loss of self-esteem, or it may even cause one or both parties to look for drastic alternatives to solve this possible unwanted problem. In essence, the unplanned pregnancy becomes an inconvenience instead of a source of joy and excitement. From day one, any expected new life will start off with so many unknown questions.

Who will be the primary parent, along with who will be there to support this little one both physically, financially, spiritually, and emotionally? Who will take him or her to all those fun activities that all kids hope one day to be involved?

Conception of life under the divine plan outlined in the Bible is a miraculous event. The joining of a few cells together transforming into a brand new life, the promise of a walking, talking, active human being; one who is full of emotions; one with a unique personality all of its own, and yet a person who may still have many of the characteristics of both parents. This can only be called one of God's amazing miracles.

Yes, man's place was created different from all the animals around him. He was to have dominion over all the animals, the birds of the air, and the living beings in the seas. And man was to have one mate for life, not many mates as do so many of the animal kingdom. He is to remain involved in the lives of both his mate and his children. He is to remain the protector and provider for his wife and to their children. And, he is to be an active partner with his wife in the ongoing care and rearing of their children remaining in their lives even beyond their rearing process.

Many animal species do not have these long term relationships. In fact, the female turtle lays her eggs in the sand, and then goes away leaving them to hatch and then fend for themselves from day one. This is just one of many types of animals with little or even no parental presence after the birth of their offspring.

What a privilege it is for us to become a parent!

We get to share in the joy and blessing, along with the challenges which surround raising a family. We get to have the pleasure of seeing our own children grow physically, mentally, intelligently and spiritually. We get to help direct their lives for a much larger ways and longer time than any other living being.

When our life is over we have a hope that those who we raise will carry on in our name as a big part of our lasting legacy and heritage.

With lots of prayer, love and care maybe we each will have an outstanding legacy carried on by those in the following generations God has given to us.

Amen!

A Bridge Uncrossed

More times than I want to admit, looking back to the many times when I had good intentions, I failed to follow through. I could have blessed someone who really was hurting by bringing a cup of cold water, and/or a word of encouragement and prayer. But now, I have to live with and ask for forgiveness of my past failures.

We all have known others who were or are now facing serious troubles. People hurting have an illness, or just need a friend willing to go out of our way by giving of our time, and of ourselves.

I've had times when someone came to help me, to show their love and encouragement. My Mother was that kind of person. She's been gone now for many years, but, she did model love to many others during her lifetime. She seemed to know other's needs, even before they recognized them themselves.

I remember my time in the Navy how many times my favorite oatmeal/raisin cookies arrived by mail, often without any special occasions other than a pure act of Motherly love. Then that special handmade quilt she made years ago for me and for my siblings. I still have mine to use on a cold winter nights. These are just two of many highlights, acts of love, she showed to me.

Another person that comes to mind is my Pastors and their inspiration to me over many years. They display so many Christ like attributes, their continued studies, prayer life, and their love for each of their parishioners. Their knowledge of God's word, and then the gifts of preaching and teaching God gave to each of them and called them each to share it. In this they showed true servant leadership in all that they did and do.

Next, there is this couple, very good friends of our family, who are people I should strive to emulate. They always remember birthdays, anniversaries, and other special occasions with special greeting cards. They've been known to host large or small gathering with such beautiful details. Oh, to have the talents, abilities, grace, as well as, their follow through they so often displayed.

Maybe we need a "How-To-Class" to teach us to rearrange our priorities and schedules in such a way...........No, I believe we need to learn to schedule our time better. We need to set our priorities on things that are important, to eliminate other activities where we spend our time spinning our wheels. Then we should place others ahead of ourselves both in our prayers and our actions. We need to prioritize our time so we can cross over these bridges to make others feel loved. And then, we should follow through on all these efforts.

Next we need to learn to say "No" to each area which carries a low priority where the result has little or no benefit, first to others, and then to ourselves. We need to make a "To-Do-List" writing in the high priority items. And then, we need to keep an assortment of greeting cards on hand, then to plan our schedule with a balance, allowing for adequate rest, family time, work time and leisure time into each day to do our To-Do-List.

As parents, with children still at home, we should schedule your own and your children's time setting limits on the number of activities everyone is involved with to avoid over scheduling.

Last, but certainly not least, we should pray. It changes all these things today, tomorrow and beyond. It will allow us to cross that bridge of love for others and for our own sake as well.

Please Direct My Path

Life has so many learning curves. We need to establish our plans to make life all it can possibly be. We start when we are very young just going from day to day activities. These were having fun and games and attention getting events, or we might get bored as our attention span likely was very short back then. We required lots of action, possibly lots of noise, along with a lack of imagination. "Oh yes," we liked colors, lots of bright colors. With these all available we could be entertained for fifteen or maybe even up to thirty minutes before we started losing interest. After that amount of time spent something different was needed to keep our attention.

As we grow older most of us come to realized our attention span expanded somewhat, requiring less noise and bright colors to keep us attentive. We also have more life experiences at our disposal than before. This normally helped us to be more inventive. We can pursue the things that are of interest to us. This usually allows us to make the most of many of those activities.

We also may gain additional abilities to display our individual characteristics. Most of us actually start to accomplish and finish more things.

We all are given so much potential to learn. We each have individual interests which, if pursued, could even take us to the moon and back. Or at least make the most of those things we are trying to accomplish.

The experts tell us we all use only a very small portion, like 20%, of our built in capability. So most of us have no excuse for what we lack or want to pursue.

Along the way we also discover we have available a lot of choices we can make. We were taught so many things during our formative earlier years. Hopefully we were taught the differences between right and wrong and to respect others, both their person and their property. These, coupled with our upbringing helped us to choose the directions we will select for our own lives.

Most of us will become productive citizens, while a few others may choose to be destructive and hurtful. These usually are our very own choices. We must each determine how we will use the time we are given. Most of us will choose a good path. One that is productive and helps ourselves and others around to us.

A few others may go off on a road that is neither helpful nor good choices for themselves or others. Most of these are rooted as a selfish life where everything is designed to be for self-gain, or self-recognition, or a power position. Where everyone around are subject to this power for bad and not for good. This is usually a self-appointed position which is often sought out by people who have self-doubts or an inferiority complex. They often work harder to do bad or hurtful deeds which most often lead to serious problems for themselves and others. For some others it may when a person is following others who may not be going in a good direction. That may not be a self-designed choice or goal, however it might appear to benefit them in the short run, but very likely will not work to the benefit of all when things go bad for whatever reason.

Most of us will choose the, "put others first position." These are people who have a built in concern for the welfare of others. Who are generally compassionate, loving, and caring people who have realized the value of their neighbors, friends, and loved ones. They have found the secret in the old saying, "It is better to give than receive." Their rewards come not always in personal self-gain, but in their sense of worth from coming alongside in helping others.

We have many examples of people who seemingly have everything that this world has to offer in personal possessions and wealth, but continue searching for what is missing, because all that they have never seems to be enough. If they ever discover the value of helping others, only then does life come to have full meaning. Only then can they stop their search and carry on with those things that really give them satisfaction.

I just read about an outstanding professional athlete who is now retired. He just started a summer camp for needy handicapped children. He says this is the best thing he has ever done. He claims it even tops all of his sports accomplishments and all the accolades that go with his stardom in sports. He has been introduced to a concept that opens doors for him and opened his eyes to what really counts. At the same time it makes life a little better for so many others who have great needs and great limitations. Should he continue to carry on with this project for the long run he will get more benefit from this activity than all his sports exposure ever gave him. Plus, this project has allowed so many others to come alongside him to help with his worthy cause.

The principals in the Bible give us a guideline for living which, if followed, will direct us in the way we each should live our lives. These principals of giving God authority over our lives; by putting others first ahead of ourselves; by loving our neighbors; seeking the things above rather than the things of earth; storing up treasures in Heaven not on earth are just a few of the attributes which will promote Biblical living.

When we choose to allow God to direct our path in every part of our life, then we will see the fruit of our labors. We will see what God has in mind for us, and we will learn to trust Him completely.

Please Lord Direct My Path. Amen

Earth Our Wondrous Home

Sitting at my dining room table, the large window gave me a tremendous view of the western mountain range with the peaks first catching the first brilliant colors of the early morning sun. It caused me to think of all the varieties of wild life sheltered in those cliffs and on the peaks out there. The bears, mountain lions, and other games of prey stalking these ranges looking for their next meal to pacify their own hunger and for their young for yet another day.

The grass and wild flowers compete for precious water and nutrients to sustain their mid-summer growth. These require an adequate supply of water to grow a beautiful blanket of colors upon the meadows and hillsides during the spring, summer and into the early fall. Only to not be seen again until the following spring when snow cover melts away and the days get longer and warmer.

The ground squirrels and chipmunks rely on their great instincts to hide from predators while gathering food not only for today, and also for their storehouse for the coming long, cold winter.

Then beyond those western peaks I think of the huge Pacific Ocean with its enumerable types of sustained wild life. These vary from the smallest organisms and marine life, to the huge graceful wale family who migrate north or south depending upon the changing seasons. They all depend upon the depths to sustain life. The oceans seems like an uninhabitable place to us, yet it's home to so many types of life. The size and depth allows for the development of threatening storms and waves, along with many dangerous living species. But its lack of oxygen makes it an inadequate home for us, as we can survive for a very short time in water. Especially in the vast oceans and seas which lacks many of our vital necessities.

Beyond the great oceans we think of our planet where the greatest surface is of water. The larger bodies, the oceans and seas, along with the many major lakes, rivers, and streams comprise the biggest surface areas. The land masses come in second to these waters, but which provide homes to all humans and the land animals.

Except for a very few of us who choose to live on houseboats or in ships, land is the natural place for us to sustain life which provides all of our basic needs for fresh water and much of our food sources. The land also protects us from the harsh environments found at sea.

Today we've advanced far beyond just survival. Our ingenuity, along with all the available raw materials, allows many of us to progress from a hand-to- mouth survival long ago to an amazing life with so many luxuries for people groups today. We have developed more ways to avoid manual labor than at any time in the history of man. We live, sleep, work, and play with more toys, gadgets, and appliances. We have found more ways to recreate and entertain ourselves, and yet we claim to have less time than all the generations who came before us. We have at our disposal so many inventions to make our lives easier. This technology of the recent past years is continuing in its expansion.

In considering all of the above, I'm reminded of the profound balances. Everything we need, and so many of our wants, are presently available to us. Further, everything for each living being, humans and animals, as well as, plants have the same separate balances needed to sustain existence. So, just where do these necessary balances come from?

Some will tell us that all this came about by chance. Some will call it an accident. That all the things we need, or will ever need, just happened. But, the real question is how can this be?

Logic tells us the odds of this being an accident, or happening by chance are just too great. To have all the elements for our survival arrive at the very exact place and time when we needed them would be next to impossible.

Further, plants and most animals require different needs than we humans. To have each element show up at just the appropriate time and place is beyond a stretch. Further, where did these all come from? What is their origin?

There must be someone with great wisdom and with the means to make this all possible. Someone who has the ability to plan and create this world with all the balances of the right life sustaining ingredients. Someone who took great care to first give us our life. Then someone who provides us with all that's needed to support our lives.

After considering all this, which can only be seen within our limitations, I now find it possible to believe that the only explanation is provided in God's word, the Holy Bible.

Geneses 1: 1 "In the beginning God created the heavens and earth."

I believe God also created all life and the necessary things required to support all life. He planned each of us to be different from all other life. Even our fingerprints are a testimony of our individual differences. We each think and act differently than any other living beings. After this revelation, it has become impossible for me to believe any other answer. When someone should ask this question," Where did we come from?"

The only possible answer that holds any credibility is God's answer.

The Bible tells us God knows the number of our days. He loves us as a father loves His children. In the Book of Jeremiah, God tells us He has a plan for each of us, and it is for good and not for evil.

Let's take Him at His word and acknowledge Him and His Son, Christ Jesus, as the only possible reason we, you and I, exist.

I believe God planned His creation with such intricate details. These are all part of such a mysterious and fine design by His power which is far above our abilities to understand. To believe, as so many do, that everything came about by accident or by chance takes a faith beyond human understanding. You contemplate all these various details about this subject, and then you should be willing to share your findings with the rest of us, with your full understanding of all things we can see and touch around us.

Do you agree or disagree with my findings and my summation? God Bless.

Who Can Tell?

Think of the honey bees, those hard workers who move from flower to flower picking up nectar, the raw materials needed to produce that sweet, wonderful, natural substance called honey. In their travels these hundreds and thousands of bees also transfer some the precious pollen from one plant to another, adding to the benefit of the plants. This is one more wonderful way all living things are tied together.

How many bees does it take to make just one cup of that pure sweet honey?

Who can tell?

The next subject is the tornado. This is one of the most powerful combined natural forces on earth. When one touches down on the surface, not much that man builds can withstand the direct force of its power. Yet some most unusual things can happen within the movement of one of these forces. Things which are impossible to explain. In Texas a path was left in an orchard one half mile wide and more than one mile long; where every tree was twisted off just a few inches above the ground. In a subdivision in Florida, every house in a two block area was flattened, except for this one certain house and one tree right in the middle of the damaged area. These were left standing, and neither the house nor the tree had more than minimal damage.

Why were these saved?

Who can tell?

Some autistic children seem to be living in some other reality, or fantasy. Sometimes he or she seems to be out of control, and at other times, very withdrawn or passive. But, one common trait for the ones with this condition is that most have a highly elevated talent in one of the arts. Some have unexplained, amazing abilities in playing musical instrument. Others excel in painting, or sculpture; while others may have unbelievable memory recall abilities.

How can this be explained?

But who can tell?

I believe everything natural around us was planned in such fine detail. I've written short stories about trees, the miracle of childbirth, the changes in a sunrise against the mountains, and so many other subjects. These are all part of some magnificent design by a power far above our abilities to comprehend. To believe that all that we have around us happened simply by chance takes far more faith than I have.

But, who can tell? You think about that.

Removing an overgrown ivy plant can prove to be an enormous challenge for the average homeowner. Just cutting them back only encourages more new growth. Digging up the roots helps, but too often some roots are left behind or are too deep in the ground and soon produce new growth. It may take years and sheer persistence to rid yourself of any trace of these determined plants.

Will the ivy show up again?

Who can tell?

These examples are just a part of our everyday life. We see these along with so many other examples. The trees around us provide cooling shade and life giving oxygen. The ground water from lakes, rivers and oceans evaporate, and form clouds, which are carried by wind currents to the far corners of the earth. There they drop as rain or snow, to replenish places in need of moisture.

Our food supply sources are from natural plant and animal growth found here for our needs. We have these at our disposal. Because they are readily available to us, we can survive and have our livelihood.

All those people around us, our family, friends and neighbors are here to provide company, companionship, and a helping hand. We all seem to need one another. Without these people around us our lives would be so very dull and very lonely.

Did all of the above originate either by some freak accident or by some big bang or explosion? Or were they amazingly and intricately planned?

Who can tell?

I believe everything that exists was planned in such fine detail. It is all part of a magnificent design by a power far above our abilities to comprehend. To believe that all that we have around us happened simply by chance takes far more faith then I have.

But, who can tell? You think about that.

Who is Confused?

In the Bible, the Holy Scriptures, John 1:1 reads, "In the beginning was the Word, and the Word was with God, and the Word was God." Then John 1:14 tells us, "And the Word became flesh and dwelt among us, and we have seen His glory as of the only Son from the Father, full of grace and truth."

Thousands of years before John 1:1 was written, Genesis was written. In the beginning there was only God in the form of three persons, the Father, Son and Holy Spirit. In Genesis chapter one God tells us of His creation of the Heavens and the earth; then of all of the rest of His creation, including day six, the creation of man, made in God's own image. Then He created woman as man's help meet. He tells us that we are fearfully and wonderfully made.

We know from our study that we need a very complex balance system for our being to survive. God did all of creation by speaking, "Let there be light, (or fill in the rest of the other words), and each appeared. If you read these scriptures found in Genesis chapter one, they tell us the sequence of when and where everything came into existence.

Who's confused? We can reveal the stories of some men's incomplete versions of where and how things happened. Some of these men and women say the Bible is a hoax and is full of myths. They claim these stories and explanations in the context of the Bible are fabricated. These same people go on to tell us that they are in complete control of their own lives, and that we all are in total control. They try to convince everyone that God does not exist. They even call God a crutch. Something to give us a false hope of some future beyond this life. They say that life is just that, when it is over, it's over. They say we will be buried in the ground and that is our final end. They also tell us we should go have a big party because life is short and we need to get all of our kicks out of it before it's over; before our time here ends.

I have a hard time believing that everything came about by some big bang; or that the earth is really millions of years old. How the earth landed just the right distance from the sun to sustain life; how it revolves around the sun at just the right distance to create our four seasons which the Bible tell us about. Then, they say that we all evolved from some lower being, and that some folks actually believe our lives might have come from one cell sitting on some rock somewhere; that that cell lived long enough, on some unknown food and water source, to split, and then to develop into some living being with a heart, lungs, body and mind. My next question, where did all those food and water supplies came from, and in just the right proportions? How did that one cell get fed long enough to develop arms and legs? What is the origin of all that would be required to make them become so many varied living beings with varied complex systems? Some are called blades of grass, or trees, or animals and, of course, people? How did some become animals, some plants and still others mankind? Why do some become male, while others become females?

Then I ask can the sun continue to burn for millions of years without burning out? Or consider the tiny element called the atom. What keeps them from imploding? The biggest question is where did all that exists come from to start with? Man has failed to come up with any valid answers to these last few questions. Many just believe that all that is was always here. That everything has just evolved to be whatever it is today. I am afraid I don't have enough faith, yes, faith, to believe there is no creator. It's impossible to believe that all could have happened by some accident or coincidence, upon coincidence, upon coincidence. The odds of all of the above happening by chance, and then the balance needed for survival of all life are far beyond any possible mathematical calculation.

When I compare all the unknowns in the last paragraph with what we read in God's Word, it is a no brainer. God's Word wins every time with every word and with every story. This along with all the discoveries man has made over time the Word of God has proven to be our best source to confirm what is real both past, present, as well as, our source for what to expect in the future. Even when we see what is happening around the Holy land today, then read what Ezekiel recorded in the Bible in the book by his name hundreds of years ago, chapters thirty eight and thirty nine are falling into place right before our eyes today. This is only one of many things recorded in the Bible in so many different places at other times, and with other writers also confirming its prophetic validity as our only true source of truth.

I know I am not in control of much. If I was, I would be in serious trouble from the start. God has all the answers to all the questions I need answered. The unknowns that are not answered in His Word are superficial. I believe He will give us the answers to all of them one day when we are with Him. His Word tells us how to live our lives, how to love one other, even how to love our enemies. I can't believe He would want us to live with no boundaries; to threaten our fellow man with no regard for their feelings or possessions; to party with no concerned about what tomorrow will bring, then to live until the end without concerns for a possible hereafter.

In John chapter one Jesus, both the Son of God and the Word, came to earth to seek and to save all who are lost. He loved us even when we are deep in our sinful life. He wants each of us to be concerned about where we, each of us, will spend our eternity. He tells us in His Word, the Holy Bible, all we have to do to be saved is to believe in the Lord Jesus Christ. To believe in Him as our Lord and Savior. To believe His Word is Truth, and further He will forgive us our sins once we ask him.

So, why would we want to live in the house of confusion, a house with no firm foundation, a place which is based upon some far-fetched theories?

We each need to determine for ourselves if God is really real. Then we need to study the Bible from cover to cover, and to see for ourselves what is real and what is not. If you haven't done that by now time is a wasting. Time is going past us very quickly. So, go For It!

Oh To Know Tomorrow

Life is like standing on one side of a high wall and not knowing what is happening on the other side. We can see what is on this side. We'll call it the here and now. Further, we can recall much of what has happened before, yesterday and even further back, however, we were not able to change a thing that was said or done back then. We can't erase a spoken word. These have become permanent records stored in our memories.

We can and should make plans for tomorrow. We should set them in concrete, however we should mold them in Jell-O. This is just another way of saying we need to be flexible as life has so many uncertainties.

Here is an example of the way things can change in an instant.

A good friend stopped one day to help his neighbor clean leaves out of her rain gutters and down spouts. The ladder she had was not the best. He fell crushing his elbow. He had surgery, when the swelling reduced a couple days later. Had he known what was about to happen, he would have gladly paid someone to do the work, or he would have gone home for his own better ladder.

We all often have our plans interrupted because of some unexpected circumstance. Most times it will changes very little other than a temporary disruption to our schedule. However, some of these changes and interruptions can be life changing.

A longtime friend, who is now gone, was in a terrible auto accident many years ago when she was twenty six years old, a wife, and mother of a young son. She broke her back and damaged her spinal column in that accident. She spent her last thirty six years paralyzed from the waist down. She gave birth to her daughter after the accident, and later spent many of her last years raising her two children as a single mother. To her credit, they both rose up to call her a blessing. She continually blessed most all who knew her.

I became acquainted with her perhaps fifteen years prior to her passing. In all those years I don't ever recall her complain about her disability, or even say a bad word about anyone.

Having children can change your life, both from the day they arrive, and all throughout your life. They do cause you to stretch, to love unconditionally, and to be ready at any given moment to answer many unanswerable questions, and then to travel many times to and fro out of your love for them. They are the only beings on this planet who can make you old and keep you young all at the same time. They are worth every effort you make, and more.

It is probably a good thing we don't know what is about to happen in our future. Can you think of all those who are dealing with a loss of a love one, or, who are very ill due to a disease or accident? To think, if we knew in advance that we were about to have a serious accident or some other life changing event, what could we do? Especially if we had no way of avoiding it. Think how we would likely agonize over anything that's unavoidable, but might be chaotically challenging, pending in our future. Possibly the time of anticipation might be harder to deal with than the actual event itself.

I don't know why we will have these problems come our way, but eventually we will all face some situation that will be very hard, and we will all one day experience our own demise.

All things considered, I believe it is so much better if we don't know what is coming our way next. We can sleep better each night knowing that it is not our place to know much, if anything, about tomorrow. Most of us do plan our schedule for tomorrow and beyond, but this planning is based upon a lot of assumptions. We assume life tomorrow will be much the same as was yesterday and to this very moment today. We also will likely assume that we will have all of our abilities and mobility, and that others around us will expect to do the things we've done in the past. Further we assume that any interruptions and time altering changes won't happen to us. These only happen to those other people.

We do need to come to realize one day when our life is over here on earth we will spend eternity somewhere. With good authority the Bible tells us we have only two choices, it's either heaven with our Creator or hell separated from Him from that time on.

The only way we can be sure we will reach heaven is to place our trust in the Lord Jesus Christ. He is our only hope, as we cannot earn our way in, nor are we good enough to qualify on our own merit. Jesus own words, "I am the Way, the Truth, and the Life, no one gets to the Father but through Me."

I encourage you to look to Our Savior for all your spiritual needs. He is the only guaranty we have available. Don't be foolish to think or let someone try to convince you that there might be some other way.

The truly amazing thing about Our Lord, even beyond His great love for each of us, is that He leaves it up to us to either accept Him or reject Him and His gift for us.

In whose hand will you place all your tomorrows? If you haven't already done this, when will you hold your hand out to Him who has control of all things? Before that fateful unknown day comes when you have no time left to make this vital decision, reach out to Him today.

Time Changes

This title has so many subjects open for discussion. Your mind may immediately go to the twice per year time changes from standard to day light savings in the spring and back again in the fall. It spring forward and fall back in the fall. It's done mainly to keep our students from traveling to and from school in the dark.

Where did the phase, "Day Light Savings" come from?

We get the same amount of hours in each day whether we are on standard or day light savings time. We cannot really save or gain day light just by moving our clocks forward or backwards.

Anyway, this subject of time changes leads us in many other directions. My first thought was about our lives. We start off as a little rosy, tender, soft human being. We are depended upon someone else for everything during our earlier years. At first we're helpless, unable to feed or dress ourselves. We couldn't walk or talk, and each time we needed something, our only method of communications was to cry out. This always leaves our care givers (parents) wondering what now? We are either hungry or wet, or sick, or anyone one of many number of needs. If only they knew which of these to check on first.

Later, as we start to grow, our abilities to better communicate comes a little step at a time. Our bodies grow and matured quickly, but we still too often leave our care givers guessing what we will want next. We all have such varying desires. One person may ask for very little, while another may ask for the world on a silver platter.

They will need wisdom to decide what is necessary and what is not. This usually leaves them questioning in search of the right answers for little ones in their charge.

None-the-less, when grown we all must forge ahead with or without a complete set of plans, but with plenty of enthusiastic energy to meet whatever might happen, or whatever comes our way.

We each have our own way of dealing with whatever comes. We will either be ready, or we will fly by the seat of our pants in our attempt to make the best or most of it. Whatever preparations we have made are sure to be inadequate; however, some preparations are better than none.

As we progress forward still more changes will come, such as growing independent away from our providers, we must learn to make our own way, provide for our own livelihood, and find out just what we will do with our life. We must then determine where we will spend our remaining days. These decision time are most often by trial and errors. We test the waters to see what works for us. We also are either a recipient or a victim of whatever comes our way. We may have some doors which we really wanted open closed to us. These include job opportunities, people who we want to share our lives with, gains and losses that are far beyond our control may dictate which direction we eventually will take. Maybe it might be college, or work in a starting job, or the Peace Corps, or the armed services. All of these may not be available to us. Our qualifications may be above what is required, or we may be limited by our abilities to meet the standard entry level.

Health issues can also be a factor in what we will do, or where we will spend our time. This too is often beyond our control. We may be the healthiest person around, or we might encounter illnesses or injuries which will affect our ability to function temporarily or permanently in various fields of work.

Later, if we marry and decide to start a family, these changes will have a major lifelong impact on us. The responsibility of raising a family, both financial and emotional are huge. One can invest great amounts of time and money for the benefit of our children. They may or may not appreciate these efforts, but your motives will likely be out of love rather than receiving that gold watch somewhere down that long challenging road.

Most of us get very little hands-on-training for the raising of children. There are few classes one can take. The modeling and examples we pick up from our parents when they were our caregivers may or may not have great value. This will depend upon how good model parents they were, or how closely we watched them in their efforts. Keep in mind they were working under that same principal of trial and error as we will be under during our own time of parenting. We have one definite advantage today with a number of how-to-books presently available. The only problem is deciding who has the right method which will work for us. Some of these books do often have parenting methods which contradict others in advice or recommendations on so many subjects.

Who has the best authority in these matters?

The steps for good parenting are modeling of their time to prepare their children for adulthood for a future time when they have their own families. Along with these parents making our own plans for their own future retirements. These will likely overlap one another. There is usually no set line in the sand when these times take place. The demands for saving for the future, while still being the primary care giver for your own offspring, can be overwhelming. These areas should be under the guidance of professional financial planning experts. Even with the above in place, the future has so many unknowns which might upset your apple carts. All the planning and plotting in the world may not be enough. We don't know what will be the cost of living for a future college student, much less, for you as a retirees which might be a ways down the road. We should start early as possible, and then try to be consistent in making these investments. With enough time and adequate contributions we will at least have a head start on all of these projected future needs.

The next subject under the heading of time changes is our attitude. We all have different dispositions, as well as, outlooks on life. We may be a type A personality who demands the best from ourselves and others. One who is willing to take certain risks to achieve set goals. One who will take the lead position and not be satisfied with mediocre accomplishments. One who is willing to work overtime to gain these set objectives?

By contrast, we might be the laid back happy go lucky person who is satisfied with just getting by. The one whose willing to work, but does not see the need to push too hard. Who is willing to let someone else take the lead by dictating all the why's, the where's, and the how's its gets done.

Over time, hopefully these two types of people will merge to some small degree. The type- A person might mellow with age, and hopefully the laid back person will see the need to be a little more aggressive in their work or leadership attitude. It is likely that these two types will never come to the same level, but will both may move closer to a more central position.

The next time and hope subject is for goals which work towards sound moral and spiritual values. These should come early in life, but too often, they come much later, or not at all. But, these two are crucial to our future hope.

At some time in our life, or towards the end of our life, we will have to deal with the fact that we will not always be living. We are all mortal human beings, and we should come to realize our days here will end. For some this comes earlier than for others. However, none of us have a set time. Like all the other events that we deal with in our life, our future is a vast unknown. No one knows what tomorrow will bring.

We should establish our belief in where we will be when our time is over based upon what we read and what others are willing to share with us. We can't see beyond today so we take the little we know, along with the information we have at our disposal and we formulate a belief that should give us some firm expectant answers.

Like the How-To books for parents, which provide some valuable information for our benefit? But which source will give us the greatest real hope?

There are some who believe that this life is all there is. They live it up like they have all that they are going to ever get in this go around. That perspective has to be almost depressing, because it has no built in hope.

Our search can vary from place to place. In this search we can read and hear of so many options. Of these, which one will address all of the needs both here and now, as well as, beyond this life?

Which one will give us direction to lead a life which will be considerate of our neighbors? Or one which will allow us to live in peace with all those who live along side of us, and at the same time, give us the hope of a wonderful future beyond this life?

The only place I've found that gives us all of the guidance and directions, as well as, the great hope for life after death is God's Holy Bible. In it there are words of correction, guidance, and a hope. Something which we could not accomplish on our own without this guide book. In it we find the words which tell us we have a savior who came to rescue us from the pit of hell. This savior paid for our passage into eternity with His own life. And all we have to do is to believe He is real and ask for His forgiveness. These written words of eternal hope and forgiveness are found nowhere else.

I encourage you to make this last subject your highest priority. Make this your goal to find these words of encouragement for yourself. I encourage you to look further into the Holy Bible for the answers you may be looking for, and there I believe you will find the hope and promise that God has freely given to all who believe that God's Son, Jesus, died so that we can live with Him beyond our life here on earth.

God Bless.

Wisdom and Truth

Wisdom is a treasure we can ask for, but may not always receive. When we ask for it for the purpose of self-gain or for prideful benefits, we may not receive it. We may get something other than we expect. However when we humbly ask for it to help deal with any circumstance that may come our way, we have a much better chance of receiving it.

Webster's definition of wisdom: 1. Insightful understanding of what is true, right and enduring. 2. Native good judgment. 3. The amassed learning of philosophers, scientists and scholars.

I like the first definition best. Truth must always be the main ingredient of wisdom put into practice. My personal definition of wisdom is knowledge put into action to accomplish the greatest good for the benefit of all in any activity.

But, what is truth?

Webster's definition: 1. Accordance with knowledge, fact or actuality. 2. The real state of affairs; fact. 3. Actuality: reality. 4. A statement that is or is accepted as being true. 5. Honesty.

I like each answer, but I feel number four to be a little weak. The statement "Is accepted as being true" leaves room for the words, "may be true."

Truth leaves no question of fact. Either something is true or it is not. If you say, "A little white lie is not really a lie." A lie is a lie whether it is fully false or only a small part of it is false. The best measure, "black is black and white is white." Neither can be mixed without giving you something other than black or white, just as mixing a lot of truth with a very little false still gives you an untruth.

In my younger years I did not realize how important truthfulness is to the integrity of a person. Without truth or honesty a person will eventually destroy the ability for others to maintain trust. I've come to realize over time that truthfulness is the key ingredient when mixed with compassion for others and a willingness to come along others in need. These, in my opinion, combined are the real measure of a person's real integrity and character.

Can one keep his or her good relationships all through life if they do not practice ongoing truthfulness? It is very unlikely. Can trust be restored once is it broken? Yes, but it will take repentance and much time to restore any broken trust.

That old profound saying is fact, "Truth is always better regardless of the consequences." But, truth spoken without compassion and concern for the feelings of others can be almost as damaging as telling a lie. While truth spoken with diplomacy will soften the blow. Always speak the truth, but always do so in love. Always considering your listener's feelings.

You are encouraged to be wise in all that you do. A big part of being wise is to always speak the truth, but with compassion and concern for the hearers.

Complain – Yes or No?

Stacey and Brad headed off to Brad's baseball practice leaving his dad, Dan, on his own for a few hours. Twelve year old Brad preferred going with his dad out on the boat, but his obligation to his team was a higher calling. His dad would understand his commitment, but his teammates would not if he failed to show up for practice.

Stacey, Brad's mother, planned to take him shopping for school clothes after practice, so Dan had all day to get out on the ocean. The cruiser was already in the water and all he needed was fuel up, and then shove off. His fishing gear was already on the board and he had packed a good, full lunch to go.

The weather report looked great and the online report last night confirmed the fish were biting. Dan could already imagine how good fried salmon or even ocean perch would taste for super. He parked his car in the short term lot, grabbed his lunch, extra water, and walked the short distance to the boat.

His excitement always ruled and getting out there to see what he could catch was the only thing on his mind. He started the engine, looked at the fuel gauge which read three quarters of a tank. That should be way more than enough for the short trip he planned for the day. He'd wait to fill up the tank next time really hoping the fuel price might drop some by then.

It didn't take him long to reach that one spot he really liked. It was only a little over a mile off shore, and just a mile and a half from where he had retrieved his boat just twenty five minutes ago.

He had a brief thought about the training course he'd taken right after he bought the cruiser. It recommended always taking someone with you whenever you went out. But, today his family had other plans, and Phil, his favorite fishing buddy, was off on vacation with his own family. So, he went against the recommended rules that day. He was on his own.

Fishing was great. He had three nice sized salmon tied off on the side. It was still an hour before he planned to stop for lunch. He remembered he had two extra gallons of bottled water stowed away. He use that stowed water first. His self-made foot long sub sandwich with extra meat and cheese, an apple and water were calling his name. He'd already planned to save the quart of ice tea he'd packed in the cold pack in with his sandwich for later in the day. He kicked back for a moment before lunch to enjoy the view of the distant coastline, and then he'd eat before starting to fish again.

Fishing had now slowed. So he leaned back content to leave his pole on his lap.

He woke up at three o'clock. He had slept for more than three hours.

He first almost panicked, and then he thought *'Oh well, not to worry, I still have about six hours of daylight, lots of time to move to another spot to fish some more before I head back to shore. I may as well move over to my second spot and try that before heading back home.'*

Dan started the engine. It purred like a gentle kitten. He headed for the other spot, which was about two miles from the coastline. He had just about reached that spot when the engine started to sputter and then it died.

'What on earth, I can't be out of fuel. It still shows three quarters of a tank. I better check to see. Maybe it just water in the fuel. I can solve that and be on my way. Oh no, the tank really is empty, but why does the gauge still read three quarters. "Lord, help me, I really need your help here."

Dan stepped back to the controls and tapped on the fuel gauge. It immediately dropped to empty. Apparently the gauge needle had stuck at three quarters. He then remembered his extra fuel can he always brought along. He started to unstrap it and realized it too was empty except for a little, maybe a half of a cup full. He was puzzled at this as he had always kept it full just for emergency times like this.

'Why? Had I forgotten to refill that last time I emptied it? Could I be so dumb to forget the most important things when we go out?

"Okay Lord, I really need some help here now. I better keep an eye out for other boats. Maybe I can get a tow? One oar is not enough to get me back to shore with this big boat. Even if I tried to row, there is no way to get back from this far out, but I'll try."

Dan wished he'd kept himself in better shape. He would have done better right out of college when he'd competed in several sports events, but today he had lost most of his stamina when he traded an active sports life for that big corner desk, and his assistant who could bring him his favorite tea. Of course, most evenings he was kicked back with the family. That hadn't kept him in training either. Now, he was in need of some extra strength and nowhere to find it.

Dan looked over in the direction of the coastline. He couldn't see it, but he could see the tall buildings at the city center. This would have to be his compass.

An hour into his rowing there were still no other boats in sight, Dan looked back towards the coastline, but now all he saw was fog. The day was wearing on and if the fog set in he could be out here for the night. He dropped the anchor but the chain never went slack. This meant the anchor was not going to hold him in place. It would slow his movement, but his boat would still drift overnight. He may lose all the distance he gained rowing, or maybe not.

Within an hour the fog bank had taken over his spot and he was ready to put on the extra layers of clothing stowed away for warmth.

He checked his ocean distress equipment. The flares, the flare gun, and water tight flashlight were all there along with the battery powered lantern. These all tested out fine.

He prayed for Stacey and Brad that they wouldn't worry. He then started thinking about all of the different scriptures that had to do with battling the sea. The disciples had more than one battle on the Sea of Galilee. Also the Apostle Paul was shipwrecked on that journey into Asia. They all came through alright with their experiences. He was confident that he too would be alright. He just needed to keep his head and look for strength to be given him.

The long, cold night passed, but the fog didn't. It was impossible to tell which way to the coastline. He could try rowing, but what direction? All that second day Dan kept watch for other boats or sounds. The water and wind have their own sounds; but nothing like the sound of an engine or the clanging and creaking sounds of a ship or boat. His food supply was running short. Stacey had bought some wrapped bars and cans of mixed nuts, but not enough to last for days. He knew the bottled water needed to be conserved in case he had to spend too many days out there. He had drunk only about a third of one gallon his first day. That was before he found out he was really in trouble.

Finally on his third day out the sun came out. Dan dressed the three salmon and laid them out to dry. Dried salmon would help fill his empty stomach. It would have been nice to have something else to round out the meal. It would have been even better if he had someone to share them with; someone to help him pass the time until he was rescued. Stacey loved to play Mexican Train Dominos. It would be wonderful to just spend time doing that with her. How he missed his family. How he missed not being able to sleep next to her in his own bed.

The dried salmon was a treat. It would have been bland at home without spices or rubs. But out here with nothing else to fill him, the salmon was magnificent.

After his meal Dan took out his binoculars to see if he could see the coastline. He had a good idea where to look, but he couldn't see anything but water. He guessed that he had drifted further out. Only God knows just how far he was from land.

On his fourth day Dan decided he should keep a diary of his time. He kept a big supply of tablets and pens in the stowed area, as

Stacey liked to write while he and Brad fished. He'd use her materials and would remember to replace these once he was back home.

"Home, how sweet that sounds."

Dan couldn't keep dwelling on home, or he wouldn't be able to concentrate on anything else. Brad would start back to school in a few days. He would miss not being there to see him off on his first day back. Time was moving on and Brad was growing too quickly. Even these few days away would make a difference, but what could he do. He could kick himself for not filling the tanks. He could have stayed home and not gone fishing by himself. He could have gone with them to Brad's practice. But, both Stacey and Brad had encouraged him to go fishing, and he had been more than willing to do just that.

On the fifth day his supply of dried salmon was running low. It was time to see if he could catch something else. After several hours and no fish, he took time to kick back. He woke thinking he heard something. When he determined the direction the noise was coming from he jumped up and headed for the supply to get the flare gun. With any good fortune he would get someone's attention. He fired one flare. It lasted only about thirty seconds before it burned out. He then fired a second. The ship was a long ways off but he needed to get their attention.

But it was all for nothing. No one responded and the ship continued until it was gone from sight. But it's in its shipping lane. Ships follow ocean currents so that's where Dan needed to be. He pulled up the anchor and started to row in that direction. Only to conclude that the current would be taking him in the wrong direction; possibly even further away from land and from home.

"Lord, I need your help here. My food supply is gone, my water supply is running low and so is my hope of rescue, well it is in your hands. I am helpless and totally at your mercy. Please be with my family. Please help them to understand that I didn't purposely dessert them. Please continue to provide for their every need in my absence."

On day six Dan caught what he thought was a small tuna. Even so, it was much bigger than all of the salmon he caught that first day. He dressed his new catch and laid it out to dry. It would be enough to last for several days. He was thankful for this provision. It was enough to fill his need for food, but what about all of his other needs? What about being rescued? What about being back with his family and providing for their needs? What about his need for fresh water?

It was late that sixth day that Dan chased a seagull away from the drying meat. "Wait, a seagull, there must be land somewhere close by? How far out do seagulls venture from land? Why can't I see land from here? Dan watched to see which way the bird flew. Was he heading back to land or was he just out scouting for food? If I headed in that direction, would it take me to land? And then, what land would it be? I can't believe I am actually talking to myself out loud. I've been out here too long. I need to find my way home. Lord, Am I complaining or am I simply asking for your help?"

That evening as darkness came on Dan was rowing towards the direction the bird had flown he noticed the big dipper in the Northern sky. He then compared it to the direction he was rowing. It was almost in the opposite direction. He was moving to the south.

He lowered his anchor and to his surprise he had slack chain. The ocean floor was closer. In the morning he would continue rowing south. With all the latest events, it was possible he was being directed to land. It would be a good thing as he was down to his last cup or two of bottled water.

The morning of day seven it was foggy, but still Dan could see the sun through the fog. It was in the east, which meant he needed to row with the sun on his left. If he continued on this course, what would he find and how long would it take to arrive?

When the fog finally lifted enough Dan finally saw it.

"Land!"

It looked like it was only a mile or two away. But after rowing all day it was still a good ways off. Dan pushed himself until it was almost fully dark. When he finally lowered the anchor it struck bottom much sooner than last night. He was making progress. He drank the last of his water, ate half of the remaining dried tuna and laid down completely exhausted from his long day of rowing. Tomorrow, if he pushed on like today, he should put his feet on solid ground for the first time in nine days.

The morning of the tenth day it was raining. Dan woke up soaked and chilled, but determined to continue on. He ate some of the last of the tuna, pulled up the anchor, and started rowing. By midafternoon he gladly let the waves carry his boat right up to the beach. The rain had stopped and the clouds were gone. He thankfully drank his fill of fresh rain water he'd gladly captured that morning. He called this drink a gift from God Himself.

The land was waiting for him.

When he felt his boat reach the beach he jumped off and felt the solid ground under his feet for the first time in a week and a half he danced around like a crazy man whooping and hollering until he realized he might not want to attract the attention of the natives until he determines if they are friendly or what?

He also had thought about what to do with the boat? Maybe he should find a good hidden place to tie off where it would be safe and could be a possible shelter for him if he needed it. He pulled the anchor out and moved it as far unto the beach as he could. He would come back after he had a look around. It appeared to be an island; but what island and were there other people living here? If there was, would they be friendly?

The first exploration attempt brought Dan to a water pond, and just above the pond was a stream coming down out of the rocks.

It looked like a spring might be the source of the water coming down. He needed fresh water even more than he needed food at this moment. He ran back to the boat and grabbed the two empty plastic jugs. He could store fresh water and have a pond to bathe in. That's when he remember the story about Mosses striking the rock and water came out. Enough water to supply God's people in the wilderness.

Around the pond he had noticed evidence of hoof prints, possibly deer or sheep or goats. Maybe this was yet another food source. Of Course, he didn't have any kind of weapon to shoot a larger animal, and then there would be the problem of storing the meat. Dried fish was one thing, but to dry cuts of deer or a sheep meat was a much larger task. It probably could be done, but it would take some planning and a larger area to set up the drying process.

"Okay Dan, one thing at a time. Water is the highest need, and then food will be next. Plus I still needed to explore the whole area and see what else is here. Still no sign of human life, but I have only seen a small part. Tomorrow will be time enough to look around more. The boat needs to be secured and I can spend the night on board and start a larger search after a good night's sleep."

He had not slept good during all the time he was lost out on the ocean. He had hoped that maybe, just knowing he now was back on land, he would rest better. But that was not the case. He was troubled about what might happen during the night. After all he didn't know about the natives, friendly or not?

Awake before sunrise Dan went back to the pond. He discovered fresh water fish were in abundance, but what variety? Also, he discovered an area on the far side of the pond where the ground looked like it was being carved up in some strange fashion. What would have caused that? Maybe wild boar? There was no sign of the pigs that morning, but he needed to be careful not to disturb them.

He had read stories of people being attacked and even killed by wild pigs.

On Dan's exploration that morning he found many types of green edible plants, wild cabbage, red turnips, wild strawberries and blackberries, asparagus, clover, dandelion, sunflowers, wild mint and wild ginger. Also, he found coconut and grapes and small red apples all in abundance. He saw many other plants that might be edible. He wasn't sure one way or the other if he should try to eat these.

What he didn't see is any sign of other human life on the island. Yes, it is an island. When he climbed to the highest point he was able to see the whole island and saw water on all sides. He looked for smoke or any other sign of human life, but did not see anything that would convince him that others lived here. He was stranded until someone came by to rescue him. On his walk back to his boat he did see the wild boar from a distance. He returned back on a route that took him far from the wild brood.

Time slipped by. Days multiplied into weeks and weeks into months. He continued to keep his daily journal of all of his activities. Some were routine daily chores while others were time s when he speared his first wild boar. Only to have the rest of the herd devour his kill before he had a chance to get even a cut of meat from his kill.

He did come back later to find that they had left the boar's bones. He broke out several teeth from the carcass and made a neckless which strung these teeth on some tree bark. His plan was to bring this home to Stacey as a gift for her to hang somewhere in their home as a reminder of his time in exile away from his family. He later decided to add one tooth for each month he was away. This became his way of keeping track of the time he spent on his island home.

Next he recorded in his journal domesticating the wild sheep and goats. He first wasn't sure he could kill one of these for food until one day he found one wounded from a fall and it died in his arms. He was just going to bury it to keep the wild boar from eating it. Then he came to the conclusion that God had given him this young sheep for him to provide food for himself. He butchered it and baked it in the same sand fire pit where he baked his first boar kill.

After that he kept his herd small by enjoying roast lamb every so often. He came to realize that the Israelis and Greeks have been eating sheep and goats for hundreds of years. He decided that he could enjoy something they had been enjoying for all these centuries. Lamb jerky soon became a part of his diet.

Dan grew tired of sleeping on the boat so he found four trees that would act as stands. He started building a raised hut. He wanted it high enough off the ground to keep the wild boar away, along with snakes and other land creatures. Over several weeks he succeeded in completing his raised hut. He carved a sign which he hung in front that read, "My Temporary Home."

He also made signs which he put out on the beaches on all sides of his island, "Man should not live alone, come visit me."

He'd built a tree stand and trained himself in spear and archery hunting. His greatest kills were the wild boar. Second were the sheep and goats he could herd and use them for meat and for milk. Over time he thinned out the wild boar population, but was never able to get them all. He never did see deer, but enjoyed herding and raising the sheep and goats.

He acquired many cooking skills. Leg of lamb and wild boar bake in a covered pit were his best accomplishments. An accomplishment was his raised hut that gave him great cover from the elements, as well as, gave him protection from all the wild boar, snakes, and whatever that might be a threat.

He also continued writing down any scripture or even parts of a scriptures as much as he could recall from memory. These and his daily journal he kept in a special wooden box he had constructed and carved his name on.

He talked to God every day just like He was right there with him. He reminded God of what He had said about Adam, "It is not good that man should live alone, I will make him a helpmate."

He reminded God that he still had a wife and son out there somewhere waiting for him to return home. They may have thought that he died out in the ocean back then, but he could only hope that they were holding out hope that he was still alive.

"God, if there is any way You can.... No, I know you created the whole world and all that is out there, You can bring me back home. I know You can. That's what I am holding out hope for. You instructed me on how to get here to my island. You showed me how to build my hut to keep me safe from any harm. Now you can find a way to get me back to my family. I will willingly give up all that You have given me here, if You will just take me back home to my wife and son."

That evening a lightning storm came up. It was fiercer than anything Dan had seen in the years he had been there. He was out securing all the things that might blow away in the storm when it happened. A bolt of lightning came down and struck Dan's hut. Fire broke out immediately. Dan had only a moment to go in and grab the box containing the scriptures and his journal. There was no way he could put out the fire and he lost his home that evening.

As he was walking back to his boat he talked to God, "How could you let this happen? I have been stranded on this island for over six years. I have missed out on six years of my son's life. My Stacey may have gone on with her life by now. I couldn't blame her. She is still young and beautiful and deserving of a life. I didn't even have Your Word to comfort me. Only these few scriptures You helped me to remember. Now, I have no home, and only that old boat that has no fuel and may not get me back home even if I had fuel. I'm about to give up God. Please help me to get through this deep valley I have been walking through."

Dan was almost back to his boat when he spotted the running lights of another boat coming towards the beach, his beach. He set his box down, and ran out into the water waving at the driver. He was still jumping up and down when the boat pulled up alongside of him.

The driver said to him in clear, concise English, "Hello, I didn't know anyone lived on this island. Are you the one who set the signal fire? If you are, I'm here to help in any way I can."

Mr. John Mellow had two cans of fuel on the back of his boat. The next morning they worked together to prime the motor on Dan's boat, they used John's jumper cables, and to their surprise the engine started right up.

John also had some motor oil as well so they changed the oil and cleaned up the mess inside the passenger area so Dan's old boat was ready to travel. He was surprised that the running lights even still worked. Dan lead the way with John following, so if there was any trouble with Dan's boat, John could always tow Dan's boat the rest of the way.

John laughed and said, "Dan, I'm pretty good barber. Would you like to have your hair cut before you head home? First, I want to take your picture with your long hair and beard so you can have that to put into your book you are going to write about your experiences. If you don't write it, then I am going to do it, using your journal, of course."

Well, Dan made it home. His few hours fishing trip turned into six years nine months and fourteen days away from home. Dan got home just in time to see Brad graduate from high school.

The only sad thing that happened before he left his island, he couldn't find the boar tooth necklace he had made for Stacey in the ashes from the lightning fire of his hut.

They all spent that whole summer together after Brad's graduation out on Dan's boat and on his island. He showed Stacey and Brad how he perfected roasting whole pigs in a pit, raising cabbage, wild potatoes, and turnips, and then they worked together to write Dan's book.

Stacey never gave up hope for Dan. When no boat had ever been found and no body was found, she simply resolved to stay in the same house and wait for her husband to come home, and "Thank God", he did finally arrive back home.

Oh! Dan's Book title is, "God's Strong Message by Fire."

Real Wood

I was in a furniture store recently looking for bedroom furniture. The store had many beautiful pieces, making it difficult deciding which set we might want to consider. The sales person gave his description of each piece. He said in most cases the construction methods are mostly equal, but the materials can vary considerably. They may all appear similar, but when you examine a piece closer it's clear that many pieces are made from something other than real wood.

I learned a whole new language regarding furniture construction. I heard words like veneer, tongue and grove, tee joint, frame joint, half joint, carcass joints, to name a few. I also learned of different types of wood and products, even plastics and cardboard are used in some of the parts of new furniture. I learned to look beyond the exterior surface and appearance. One must tip the piece up to look at the hidden materials and designs.

Since this is not a "How to Book" on how to make or even shop for furniture, I'll not go any further on the subject of furniture.

My reasons for the above information are to show others the importance of the using REAL WOOD COMPONENTS vs some lessor stable materials. Real wood in furniture making has no equal comparison. Nothing can match the quality for strength and longevity of wood, especially when quality workmanship is added to the mix.

This measurement can also be used when describing the character of a person. The symbolic term of 'REAL WOOD' in a person, someone is letting people know who that person is and how they might conducts themselves in any situation. Also how they will approach each challenge with character and integrity.

I know many wonderful people who live by this REAL WOOD approach. They've set goals for themselves to be honest and upright in everything they do. They will not let their standards be compromised.

I think of a soldier who has trained to serve his country even with his life. He is trained to be "All that he can be" within the regiments of his group or platoon or brigade. He's trained to conduct himself in such a way to protect and serve all those around him. He works from a higher calling under the authority of his duty to his country.

I think of people like the Wright Brothers and Charles Lindberg who set about to do something that had never been done before. We don't know their motives, but we do know they were willing to risk everything, even their lives, to complete their self-appointed assignments. We don't know how many attempts it took for the Wright Brothers to get their plane to lift off. Nor do we know how much planning Charles Lindberg did before his flight. But, we do know that they both were successful in their goals. We also don't know what was going through their mind just before their feat was recorded in the history books. Possibly they knew they might be honored for their accomplishments, but they knew the only way any man can fly is with the aid of a flying machine.

We conclude with the following: We are here for such a short time. Life speeds quickly by filled with trials and various activities of life. We concentrate on the things present, not noticing until we look in the mirror one certain day and see this person looking back at you shows the signs of, well you know, Age!

Somewhere we should conclude we need to add more REAL WOOD to our life. Something that will fill that ongoing void in our life. Good deeds and the gifts to charity are good, but there must be more that brings both satisfaction, justification, and sanctification.

Being mortal beings we should look for ways to achieve immortality. Men have tried for centuries to find this answer. They've spent a life time searching for the secret to eternal youth, while producing slight gains as men do live longer today than during the eighteenth, nineteenth, and twentieth centuries. However, the real answer remained still beyond our reach of so many.

We need some miraculous help to ever accomplish this. It comes only when we turn to The Lord Jesus Christ for His help, realizing we can't do this on our own. Only then can we look forward for the immortality when we finally arrive in His presence. It is not of ourselves, but it is of Him that we can be made completely whole.

Look in His Holy Word, you will find your best instructions there.

God Bless.

Cornerstone

Hal had a tough time getting his six foot eight inch frame into the little compact car Samantha was driving. They had met last weekend at the go-cart races. He was warm sitting in the sun on the bleachers that late afternoon. His golden tan gained from many outdoor summer activities on the tennis court and his weekend and evening bike rides. He was siting one row up and directly behind her. Sam, as she liked to be called, was wearing a shirt with a scripture on the back. Her shirt was the first thing he noticed. Her beautiful, sun drenched, long red hair covered most of the message. He couldn't remember how the beginning of the verse read from the address of Romans 13:11. He sat there for the longest time before he got up the nerve to ask her if he could read what else it said, "Excuse me miss, I was wondering what the scripture on the back of your shirt says. I can't read all of it because your hair covers a big part of it. Would you mind showing it to me?"

When she turned around to look at him he was smitten. Her beautiful emerald green eyes sparkled in the late afternoon sun. Her smile lit up her whole face and her smooth-as-silk complexion and the sound of her velvety voice captured Hal. After Sam quoted the scripture from memory, word for word, "And to this, knowing the time, that now it is high time to awake out of sleep; for now our salvation is nearer than when we first believed."

They visited for a short time before she invited Hal to move down next to her to watch the rest of the races. They began sharing information about themselves and before long the races were forgotten, except for the noise of the engines as they passed by. They talked for the rest of their time there. He told her where he lived and what he did for a living; where he went to church and much about his family and friends. He was surprised that Sam and her parents lived only a couple miles from his place. She went to a different church but she had graduated from the same high school as him, only three years later. She told him she is in her final year of a nursing program at the Liberty Christian University.

She was given two tickets to these go-cart races and her friend, Betsy, who was supposed to come with her, but at the last minute had a change of plan.

Sam added, "I think she had a better offer, like a date."

Then she smiled and added, "I almost decided not to come, but it felt good to do something very different, even if I have to watch these by myself. Now, I'm glad I don't have to watch them alone."

He nodded and smiled, "Sam, I too am glad you decided to come. I'm thinking of stopping at the Bixie Ice Cream shop after the races. It's one of my favorite places to stop, would you like to come. It will be my treat?"

"Oh Hal, you like Bixie's too. Yes, I'll meet you there in a few minutes. I'll call my folks and tell them I'll be a little late getting home. I'm twenty two, but they still watch for me when I go out. It's kind of sweet that they still think they need to look out for me."

Hal and Sam arrived at the ice cream shop at about the same time. While they waited in line to order Sam said, "My class load is very heavy and I have no time for a social life other than church. Even tonight, I should be home studying, but I got these tickets and haven't been anywhere for so long. Mom and Dad told me I needed a break. They said the races would be a great change of pace, and now I know they were right. They are always right, but please don't tell them that I said that."

Sam ordered one scoop of vanilla with trail mix for a topping, while Hal ordered a double scoop vanilla with crushed almonds, trail mix, and a sprinkling of cinnamon. He smiled, "I'm surprised that you didn't order something chocolate. In my past experience, and even my little sister usually orders something chocolate flavored."

After they found their table and started enjoying their treat she spoke up, "Vanilla has always been my ice cream of choice. I noticed you ordered it too. Do you like any other flavors?"

He shook his head, "No, I come from a long line of vanilla eaters. Only Gracie, my little sister, goes for something different. But, she has to buy her own, or put in a special order. All the time while I was living at home, anything other than vanilla was considered a foreign flavor in our freezer. As a matter of fact, when I got back from my tour of duty in the Navy I came home unannounced and surprised my folks by bringing two gallons of vanilla ice cream to their door step. We ate so much of it that night that I wondered if I would ever want vanilla again. But, the very next night we dug into it again."

"Oh, thanks for your service. Where did you serve?"

"Your welcome, and I served three years in the Navy. I was a land lover sailor. I never got out of California except while traveling on my leave time. When I got out, I went back to school on my GI bill funding. I took up business courses and the rest is history. I've been in mortgage banking ever since. I really enjoy helping young families get into their first home."

She nodded her head, "I guess that's why I'm looking forward to a nursing career. It will give me the opportunity to help people when they get sick. My biggest concern is where I will find just the right job. One which will allow me to keep my commitment to the Lord and do what will give Him honor."

"Well Sam, I think it's great. Helping others is what the Lord is all about. Plus, from what I hear, there is a big demand for good nurses. I read that there are places who even offer bonuses and other incentives to encourage nurses to come work for them. Is that still the case?"

"Yes, I hear that often. But, I don't want it to be just about the money. Mind you, I want it to be enough to meet my needs, but, I want it to be the right job where....how can I say it..., where

I contribute to the cause of betterment for all. We have recruiters coming in from several hospital and medical facilities on a regular basis to talk to us. So far, I have not made a commitment to anyone, but sometime this year I need to do that. It's not that I'm concerned about landing a job. It's about landing the right job if you know what I mean."

"It sounds to me like you have the best type of problem, if you want to call it that. You have people coming looking for you and offering hiring bonuses. If it was like that when I came out of school, I would call it a solution waiting to happen, not a problem to dread somewhere down the road."

"Okay Hal, maybe you're right. And maybe you sound just like my folks."

Hal became serious, "Here's the problem I see. You already told me you don't have time for a social life, but I'd like to see you again and not have to wait a whole year to do so. Is there any way I can see you again before you complete your training?"

She smiled and looked into his slate blue eyes, "Well let's see. I don't have classes on Saturdays, but I do have studying then. Maybe after several hours of studying, I might look forward to a pleasant change of pace. Just like tonight. We've spent several hours together, and it has not disrupted my study schedule too much. Well, just a little. Maybe that's a sacrifice I could make on a once a week basis. Besides, my folks would be relieved to see that I'm actually doing something other than hitting the books. So, I would be killing two birds with one stone. I think I would like to do that."

"Good, give me your phone number. I'll call you after lunch next Saturday. We'll see how you're studies are going. Then make plans that will fit around your schedule. But, wait, you do go to church tomorrow don't you?"

She shook her head, "Well, I hadn't thought of that. Do you think you could go to mine tomorrow? If it all works out, maybe

I can go with you the following Sunday." She smiled and added, "That's if we still want to hang out together by that time."

Thoughts of this conversation stayed with Hal long after they said goodnight that first Saturday evening.

Hal picked Sam up at 8:30 the next morning for church. They stayed for both Sunday school and the church service. She was able to introduce him to several of her friends before they left to grab a deli sandwich. Over lunch he told her he liked the message from the pastor. He was not used to having both a Sunday school session and church service, but, said it was good.

She responded, "That's all I have ever had, as I have been going to the same church since I was a baby. I guess I thought all churches had both every Sunday."

He came back with, "At my church we have multiple Sunday morning services, plus a Wednesday evening Bible study in place of the Sunday school."

Sam had a full class schedule on Mondays and she needed to prepare for them. Hal gave her his cell number and asked her to call any evening she finished her studies early. He promised to not keep her on the phone for long, but told her he would love to hear from her. She did call him just before ten Thursday evening. They talked for about fifteen minutes. Then he promised to call her after lunch on Saturday to see if she could go out. That's how she came to pick him up in her little compact car. He did get in, but wondered how he was going to get back out when they arrived at the bowling lanes. Bowling and a quick dinner after were their plans for that Saturday evening. He had considered asking her to go back for his car, but he didn't want to hurt her feelings.

Hal and Sam dated each weekend for the rest of her final year at Liberty. When graduation time came things changed for them. He continued working at his job, while she struggled with a decision of which job she would accept. She had offers from three different places. One hospital just thirty miles down the road, but it was for the graveyard shift five nights per week. They were not offering a bonus and the starting salary was less than the two other offers. She had interviewed with that hospital and was not sure she liked the person she would be working under. The other two offers involved relocating. One would take her just over three hundred miles away, while the other was five hundred and sixty miles away. Both were three twelve hour shifts per week, and both offered nice bonuses. The one further away was in a great location in that city. It offered the higher salary. But, both offers would require her moving and finding housing, as well as, finding a new church. She might be able to travel back home on her days off in either case. The one further away offered a $4,000.00 bonus and a much higher starting salary. She felt she needed to take this job, but the one big obstacle made her decision very difficult; her growing relationship with Hal. Under any other circumstance she would have jumped at the chance. Now she was torn between the two; take the job and possibly losing Hal, or take the night job closer to home and see him when her schedule allowed.

Her few conversations with Hal left her lacking for a decision. He had told her she should take the job she really liked. They could keep up a long distance relationship and see each other every month or two when she came home on her long weekends. Hopefully, that would have to be enough for the time being.

He was in line for a big promotion at his job, so his moving would not be in his best interest at the time. This question made her wonder just how important seeing her was to him.

Sam thought threw what they had talked about, *'Maybe Hal is not as concerned as I am about being that far away from one another. Maybe he doesn't feel for me like I feel for him? I know he cares for me, but he has never told me he is in love with me. If I don't take this job and* our relationship goes away anyway, then what? Have I lost this great once in a lifetime opportunity?'

Sam knew the great offer would not last for long. Even now they could be considering making the same offer to someone else. Someone could be working there in the job she really wanted, if she didn't make her decision immediately.

She called Hal one more time, "Hal, what do I do? Should I take that job? Give me some of your great wisdom."

Hal closed his eyes, put his hand over his forehead and leaned back in his chair, "Sam, I can't make this decision for you. All I can do is tell you it's a great opportunity. I'll be here for you when you come home for visits. I believe we can survive a long distance relationship as long as we both know we don't have to do it forever."

She shook her head and tears gathered in her eyes. The answer was clear, '*I guess my leaving is not such a big deal for him. He doesn't seem to be that broken up about my going. Maybe, if I leave he will either find he really can't live without me, or maybe he will find someone else. I guess we will have to see.*'

"Okay Hal, I guess I must take this job. I don't like being that far away from you and my folks, but if you think we can make this work, I'll tell them I can start next week."

They said goodnight and hung up. Hal sat there for the longest time with his head in his hands dwelling on their conversation, '*If she only knew how deeply I feel for her, how important she is to me, but I can't stand in her way. This is a great opportunity. If I tell her not to go, she may hate me for the rest of our lives. Maybe we should have prayed together about this before we got off the phone. I have been constantly in prayer, but maybe we should have prayed about this together.*'

Hal flew over with her to help her find a place to live. She was so glad to have this time to spend with him. They flew in early in the morning, rented a car and spent the day looking for housing. They then flew back home that same evening. She found a room with a shared bath and kitchen close to her new job. It was close enough that she could commute by bike to work on the nice days.

Sam was filled with mixed emotions for the next few days. She was excited about her new job. But she was apprehensive about leaving, moving so far away from Hal and her folks. She packed her little compact car full of her possessions, said goodbye to her parents and Hal before headed east. She promised them she would fly home every couple months, or more often when possible. Then promised to call each of them just as soon as she arrived.

Hal and Sam talked by phone almost every evening during that first year. She did come home as promised every other month during her year away. They spent that first Christmas together with her parents and New Years with his.

Hal did get his expected promotion. His new duties included managing the whole real estate lending department, and he still was somewhat involved working with families to gain financing for their homes.

On the first part of their second year in their long distance relationship Sam asked Hal why he didn't travel to see her. She was the one who always had to do the traveling. He reminded her that he didn't have a place to stay when he was there, while she could stay with her folks when she came home. Also, she got four days off each week, while he was off only on the weekends. This subject ended when she didn't have anything further to add, and they went on to talk about other things. She told him, "I always hate leaving there after my long weekends, but I have to work, and I do like my job. Who else works three days and gets four days off every week? Who else gets to do what I have always wanted to do. I get to help other people when they are in need and still get paid so well for it as well?"

It was the first week in May, during her second year over there that Hal called Sam's number two nights in a row, only to get her answering machine. He left messages both times, but it was not until the third day that she called back, "Sorry I took so long to call you back, but I've been really busy."

Sam didn't say what she had been doing on her days off. Whatever she was doing was something she choose not to share with Hal, and he didn't push her for answers even though he really wanted to.

It was a week later that she called him and said, "Hal, I've met someone here. He works at the hospital where I work. He...., I mean, I don't see any future in our long distance relationship. It's been a year and a half and I don't see any progress for us to be together. I mean get married or take the next step. Maybe it's time that we start seeing other people."

Hal looked up at the ceiling, took a deep breath before responding, "Sam, is that what you want to do?"

He could hear some hesitancy in her voice when she said, 'Y...Yes, it's not what I want to do, but it's what I feel we must do. Hal, I care for you very much, but I'm not sure that how I feel is enough. I feel like we are stuck in limbo here and can't get out. So, I'm telling you that I plan to start seeing other people and suggest you do the same. I want us to remain friends, as I value your friendship more than any other, but I still want us to have the freedom to go out with other people."

Hal's response was almost inaudible, "Sam, if that's what you feel we must do, I won't stand in your way. I will miss you so very much, but I will get through this. Goodbye Sam."

"Goodbye Hal."

'What did she mean by, "I'm not sure that how I feel is enough?"

'Doesn't she know how I feel about her? Haven't I shown her time and time again how I feel? Now she wants to break up. This is the hardest thing for me to go through.'

Hal set the phone down and leaned back with his eyes closed so the tears accumulated under his eye lids. He had put so much of himself into their long distance relationship and so had she. Now it was coming apart at the seams and there was nothing he could do to stop it, short of quitting his job and moving five hundred sixty miles east, '*Should he do that, or was it already too late?*'

Following how their last conversation went, Hal chose not to move, but he stayed in touch with Sam's parents, Frank and Bev. They were as close to him as his own parents and his little sister. They let Hal know when Sam got engaged and later when she married. At that time they told him it was time he found someone for himself. He gave them a sad smile before he said, "I don't think I could ever find anyone who could compare to Sam. She is the only one I have ever loved and now she has moved on."

SIX YEARS LATER

Frank and Bev called Hal one day at his work. Their news was both good and bad. Sam's husband, Bobby, had been killed in a head-on car accident. Sam was not in the car when it happened. The other driver's car, an SUV, had crossed over the center line. Bobby was the only fatality. The memorial was set for the upcoming Saturday and Frank wanted to know if Hal would like to come along, "Bev and I would like for you to be there. You could drive over with us, or drive over on your own, or fly in and meet us there. Let us know what you decide."

His answer, "Can I call you back this evening and let you know?"

Hal didn't get much work done the rest of that day. He spent much of it trying to decide what is the best thing for him to do, "*Oh Lord, it has been over six years. What can I say or do that might help Sam during her time of loss? Lord, show me what you would have me to do.*"

Finally, at mid-afternoon that day Hal took the rest of the day off. He drove out to his favorite spot to spend time in meditation and prayer. He knew he had to go, but what should he do beyond that? He would call Frank and Bev tonight and let them know he was flying over. Then he called first thing in the next morning to order flowers. He would fly over on his own schedule, and he could stay longer or come back sooner depending.

Bev told him they were relieved that he was going. They agreed to meet him at the airport if need be, but he thanked them and told them thanks but he already reserved a rental car there. He flew over on Friday and stayed at a Hotel close by the airport.

The memorial was much like Hal had expected. He sat with Frank and Bev and was able to talk with Sam for a short time after the service. She thanked him for coming. He told her he was here for her if she needed to talk or just needed to shoulder to lean on. She asked if she could call him later that evening. He gave her the information where he was staying and said, "Yes, you can call me any time, in fact, I still have the same cell number."

She said, "I.... I still have that. I will talk to you a little later then."

Hal rented a movie and bought some takeout food before going back to his hotel.

He watched the whole movie, and even got in a short nap before his cell phone went off just before six PM.

Sam sounded down. She said, "Mom and Dad are at my house, but they are exhausted, and are ready to retire for the night. They suggested I call you and spend some time with you. Have you eaten? There's the Uptown Eatery just down the road from where you are staying. I could meet you there in 30 minutes."

Hal arrived first and reserved a table off in a corner so they could talk privately. Sam came in just as he was being seated. Hal was able to see her clearly for the first time in more than six years. She had changed into a blouse and slacks. If possible, she was even more beautiful now than he remembered her to be.

He again told her how sorry he was to hear of her loss. She looked away for a moment before looking back at him with a steady serious pause, "Hal, can I be really straight with you?"

He looked her straight into her beautiful eyes, "Why Sam, of course you can."

Sam looked down for the longest time, then turned back at him. Her eyes narrowed as if she didn't want to share what she needed to say. But then she began. "Bobby and I have not been getting along for a long time. He was about to leave me. He told me he had found someone else and was preparing to move out at the end of this month. It was not a very Christian thing for him to do but all the same, he said he was going regardless. I believe part of our troubles is my fault. You see, I never really gave myself to him, even at the first. We lived under the same roof for almost five years, but we were two people living two different schedules and two different lives. Lives that seldom crossed the same street at the same time. I have many regrets. Things that I would do over if given the chance. One of them would be to see if we, you and I, had been more patient with our long distance relationship. Well, really me. I regret my giving up on us. I regret losing you back then. I regret not taking that job at the hospital down the road from my folks. The job here was really good at that time, but things have regressed over the years."

When Sam stopped talking for a moment Hal jumped in, "Sam, have you made any plans going forward from here?"

Sam again looked off in the distance for a time. Then looked straight into Hal's eyes, "Well, I'm planning..... Well I am going to stay with my folks for a month or two. After that, I am not sure what direction I will go from there. I am leaving my position at the hospital here and selling my house. This is just too far away from where I want to be. Do you have some thoughts on what I should do?"

Hal leaned forward and grabbed her small right hand in his big left hand. His touch triggered feelings in her that she hadn't experienced in a very long time. He held her hand with his resting on the table and looked into her beautiful emerald green eyes, "Well yes,

I do have some thoughts I would like to share with you, but I think we need to pray for God's direction to see what He wants before we get ahead of Him. We then must wait on Him before making any suggestions or changes. I must add, "I too regret what we lost years ago. I have never really gotten on with my life after we broke up. Oh, I dated a few ladies, but I never found anyone I cared for more like I cared for you. I still do have those same feelings. I have been in love with you since that first day at the go-cart races. Up until that time, I didn't believe in love at first sight."

Then he went on, "Nothing would please me more than to start up our relationship again and see what doors God opens for us. But, I believe you have gone through some things which tell me you need time to heal and to reflect. I am willing to give you that time, but I ask that as soon as you are well, you come tell me. God willing, this time we will build our relationship based upon the Cornerstone, Christ Jesus. He is the only one we can always count on."

"Oh Hal, you never once told me before that you loved me. I felt that you did, but you never told me. I will take time to heal as you suggested and I promise you, God willing, my healing will not take very long."

The Workers

I saw the bees working their way through the vines in the garden early this morning. They would stop at each blossom along their way.

Before long, more of them showed up also working their way through these vines. They seemed to ignore me as they went about their work. One by one they flew off with their special cargo joining the hundreds of fellow workers bringing home the nectar to be added together.

Back and forth those little fellows went, perhaps toiling all the day long. They all worked in such unity, not seeming to worry if other workers were doing less. Each worked with such determination and with one common goal. They all worked together first to build their hives then work to produce such a wonderful sweet substance.

I thought if only we humans could take a lesson from these worker bees. If we could work without worrying that someone else was doing less, or poorer work; if we could stay on the job until the work was done; if we could take pride in being part of a productive team. If we always did our very best at everything we do. If we are willing to admit that in our own strength we can only carry little, but with the combined efforts of many, great projects can be completed. If we too, like the worker bees, could work in such unity to create some sweet substance, or some lasting treasures.

The Golden Gate Bridge in San Francisco, and the Manhattan Bridge in New York Skyline, and all the major spans of bridges in between were not built by just one man. Each project took much planning, drafting and construction work by many hundreds, or even thousands of people. All these workers on each project had one common goal and a combined determination to accomplish the end result. Without these attributes, none of the great manmade landmarks would be here today.

This teamwork principal works the same in most sporting events, and in fund raising, and in any other worthwhile project where several people are combining their efforts. Each must feel strongly enough about some cause to contribute their all. Then, others may join in to do the same. If millions of people all do their share, multi-millions of dollars can be gathered in a fund raiser. Huge accomplishments are done with these combined efforts.

Perhaps this same unity principal could be used to help stamp out the many wrongs in our society. This unity could be used in our fight against drug abuse, and in our efforts to find cures for the numerous killer diseases. Also, this same unity could be used to create a peaceful existence in our world today. This would take a joint world wide effort from every nation. We would all have to want the same thing. We could not afford any bickering over slight differences in how this bridge of peace gets built. We would all need to commit our resources to the building of the very best bridge for this purpose; a bridge that could withstand the test of time and the weight of future generations.

Am I fooling myself in the state of things today that mankind can come to the same unity, co-operation, and joint efforts that I saw with those worker bees just this morning?

Can we get everyone to come to an agreement that we need peace in our world, and not fighting? If we can, then can we all agree on the methods used to complete our bridges of peace and accomplish our common goals for total worldwide peace?

It's not immediately clear where we can start nor if we can be successful should any one group be not fully committed to the same goals. It will also take a mutual trust established and proven over a long period of time.

Perhaps this movement towards building this bridge has to start very close to home. It means I must be up to displaying the leadership to start the movement within my own household. I must strive to promote the cause of peace through acts of sincere and loving kindness to all who live under my roof. I must then carry out these same efforts beyond the four walls of my home. These attributes must become part of my daily routine in dealing with my neighbors, my fellow workers, the grocer, the insurance man, and every other person I come in contact with. Then others must all see me as a person with total commitment to be loving, patient, respectful, considerate and trustworthy. They must see me as a source of encouragement to them. I must continue to encourage them to always look for a peaceful solution and give equal cooperation in every situation.

May I remember to be a team worker. May I show all of the above qualities and still be humble in so doing.

May God help me to always look for the most peaceful solution in every matter. My prayer is that you will chose to also go out and do likewise.

Picture This – Saved by Grace

For close to the one hundredth time your sister invited you to go to church with her and her husband. She was persistent to convert you to her way of living. To finally get her off your back you agree to go once, "Okay, I'll go if you will promise to never bug me about going again."

On the way driving over she told you to not expect to be entertained, but to expect to hear some valuable information which we all need to hear. She added, "This will help us all to see how we are to live our lives."

When you first walked in you wanted to sit way in the back in case you wanted to leave early. But your sister decided they would sit with you even though you sense they would prefer to sit closer to the front.

You're first surprised was that the music is more contemporary with an occasional old hymn mixed in to satisfy the more mature people there. You also noticed that most everyone there seems to enter in on all the songs.

Then the pastor's started his message with some scripture, reading them from the New Testament. You soon realize that his message seemed to be aimed directly at you. You start feeling uncomfortable. But not wanting to make a big show by standing up and walking out, and also not make your sister angry, you decide to hang in there.

Then pastor said something to the effect, "We are all sinners in need of forgiveness."

He also called us, including me, rotten sinners with no will power to be good.

You questioned how this man has the right to call you names. You planned to wait until this is all over. You make plans to meet this man outside to give him a piece of your mind. It's then that you realize he is also talking about himself.

He then said, "Not one of us can buy or earn our way into heaven. We don't have enough money to accomplish this, nor can we do enough good things to work our way there."

Next the pastor lists the people who will not enter heaven. He quotes first Corinthians 6: 9-10 about the unrighteous will not inherit the kingdom of God, "Neither fornicators, nor idolaters, nor adulterers, nor homosexuals, nor sodomites, nor thieves, nor covetous, nor drunkards, nor revilers, nor extortionist will inherit the kingdom of God."

Then he adds verse eleven, "And such were some of you, but you were washed, but you were sanctified, but you were justified in the name of the Lord Jesus and by the Spirit of our God."

You thought not all of these, but some, such as fornicator, idolater, and covetousness could be part of your own history. You always considered yourself as honest, not telling any major lies, only little one to enhance what others might think of you. You also did not intentionally steal anything, only borrowed a pen or pencil on occasion, then conveniently forgetting to return them.

You had always thought you were good enough in your own merit to make heaven. But verse eleven states we needed to be washed, sanctified and justified in the name of the Lord Jesus and the Spirit of our God.

Then the pastor quoted Romans 10:9 "That if you confess with your mouth the Lord Jesus and believe in your heart that God has raised Him from the dead, you will be saved."

He added, "And Romans 10:13 "For whoever calls on the name of the Lord shall be saved."

You start to wonder what else is in that Bible that you need to know! You need to get one and find out. Then you wonder if the pastor's message is recorded. You have other family members and friends who need to hear what this pastor has to say. Some of your family, like your sister, knows, but some do not, and most all of your friends don't. This valuable information could make a big difference for many of them.

Next Pastor said, "For those of you who don't take notes, or want to hear what God is saying through me today, we have this message recorded for you to purchase for just three dollars out in our book store."

You think, *"There he goes reading my mind again!"*

Next the pastor prays a prayer of thanksgiving for the good news today. He asks anyone who would like to pray for forgiveness from their sins to come forward. You think you're not going to up front unless someone else goes first. Before you could finish that thought two people step out and started forward. The next thing you know you are on your feet moving forward.

Pastor's prayer was short but covered all you thought it should cover, and at the end he said, "For the three who came forward we have a new Bible. And, we have a new believer's class available for anyone who wants to come. You can sign up for it in our church office."

You turn to your little sister, "Hey sis, thanks for not giving up on this old brother of yours."

Rough Monday

You roll out of bed on the wrong side this morning. You stubbed your big toe on the bed post, fall against the wall knocking your favorite picture onto the floor, and now have shattered broken glass all over the floor. Then you fall back onto your bed to avoid walking barefoot on the broken glass. You rubbed your big toe before trying to find an alternate escape away from the glass on the floor. It had to be a Monday, of course!

You limp out to the kitchen pantry for the broom and dust pan. Then you began to search for your slippers before returning to clean up the mess. Then when picking up some of the larger pieces of glass you cut your finger. You now have glass and blood on your floor, as well as, on the area rug beside your bed. You decided to close off your bedroom for the day and wait to clean up the rest this evening.

Your next priority was to find meds and a bandage for your wounded finger, before heading to the kitchen for a quick toast and coffee breakfast before getting ready for work. You've already decided to skip your morning shower. In the essence of time, that will have to wait until tonight after dealing with the broken glass.

It's then that you're remembered that you are out of bath soap. So you add a new picture frame along with bath soap on your to-do list.

As you finish shaving you can smell a combination of fresh coffee and burnt toast waiting for you in the kitchen. You should have eaten before shaving. If you hurry you may have time to fix another toast.

You go to your closet for clothes for your day and finish getting dressed. When you're ready except for your shoes you discover there's mud on the bottom and sides. So you need to clean them before putting them on. Well, so much for fixing more toast.

You go out back to feed the dog only to discover he has torn up that new cushion for your back porch swing. It's spread it all over the back yard. Dealing with his problem will also have to wait until after work.

On the way out the door you grab your coat, your keys and an apple to eat on the way to pick up Tom to car pool to work. It's your turn to drive.

It's then you notice the rear tire on the driver's side is flat. There's no extra time to fix it without making both you and Tom late for work, so you quickly call him to see if he'll swap drive days with you.

Fortunately, Tom says, "No problem."

He agrees to pick you up in a few minutes. If timing works well you can fix an egg and some more toast for an egg sandwich while you wait for Tom. That's when you discover you're also out of eggs. You think back, you did add them to your list, but forgot to take it when you went to the store on Saturday. So, you spread an extra thick layer of peanut butter on your toast.

On you ride to work you share your morning experiences with Tom. He's a longtime friend going back to your high school days.

He smiles and says, "Let's hope the rest of your day goes better! After all what else can get any worse than what you have already experienced."

Well, first thing Mondays are always the routine staff meeting. Surely nothing can go wrong here. Half way through the meeting your boss, a big stout man with a bald head and big nose, turns to you and puts the planning for the company picnic on you, "You did such a good job with it last year. I know you will even do better this time."

You ask him if you can temporarily give one or two of your routine tasks to a co-worker. But he doesn't feel that'll be necessary. In his opinion you should be flexible enough to take on this extra work without burdening others.

The rest of the day at work went fairly well, except for your catsup accident at lunch. Fortunately, you were able to wash the spill off your pants. That dried about half way through the first hour back at work.

The ride back home after work with Tom was uneventful.

He smiles, "Buddy, after all your problems today would you rather have stayed in bed this morning?"

After a long pause and some thought you smile back, "No way! How can one know which day the Lord will shower you with blessings, and which day He will allow you to go through the trials? Both of these are for our benefit."

That evening while you're cleaning all the Monday morning messes, and changing the flat tire, you have to wonder just what tomorrow will bring?

Is it religion or Science?

The Holy Bible tells us, 'In the beginning God Created the Heavens and the earth.' This, along with all the rest of His creation can be found in the first book in the Holy Bible. He created man and woman. This all took place within a six day period of time. God called it all very good. Then on the seventh day He rested from all His work. This was believed to have happened at least 6,000 years ago or more.

Now in contrast, some other scientific writings tell us their theory that earth, our home, which came from some unknown sources, is approximately twenty million years old, while other writings quote billions of years old. Logically, how can either of these theories be possible? Can our sun that warms and provides light to the earth, as well as, many of the other closer planets, still burn after millions, much less, billions of years? Could we humans, and all the other living species, all evolve from one tiny cell sitting on a rock somewhere? And how did that one cell survive, be fed and watered, long enough to produce other living and varied organisms? Still another question. What are the ratios of the earth being placed at just the exact distance from the heat and light source for all living beings to survive? Also what are the ratios for our having all the food and water sources needed to sustain our life here? And what are the ratios that one single cell could multiply just right amount of males and females to have the ability to reproduce offspring? Then there is the sun and moon and their functions. The sun, we have already mentioned, but then our moon being of solid form, yet has no light or function in and of itself, except to reflect the light from the sun and to magnetically control the tides here on earth. If we had no movement of tides the whole function of the earth would be completely out of balance. How were all of these things accomplished all by themselves? By some profound accidents or by some magical chance? Or, to look at it differently, was this all part of some magnificent plan designed by a higher power?

Now we go to the subject of religion. There are many different groups who call themselves this or that religion. Each have different varied beliefs, but all have at least one thing in common. They all believe in a higher power. Some groups worship the sun, the moon or some other created thing. While some others worship some man made object we call an idol. There are religions who believe in a god of hate who will control the masses by force or by the threat of force. There are still others who believe that their higher power is a God of Love. They profess that this God created all the heavens and the earth. This God being a triune God, the Father, the Son, and the Holy Spirit as part of the trinity. They believe the Son came to earth to rescue us, His people, and to die a sacrificial death on their behalf. Also to take away their sins and iniquity and to insure them a place with Him. We are told He rose from the dead. He then went back to Heaven to prepare a place for all of those who believe Him to be their loving God. He asked these believers to maintain a constant relationship with Him through their prayer and the reading and study of His Word, the Holy Bible. Thus, this relationship goes far beyond the practice of just a religion. It goes to a Father and child relationship that can be maintain only by our choice to walk with Him and talk with Him on a daily, continuous basis.

Now let's talk about science. This subject told by various scientists about many various theories regarding our origin and existence. The strongest of these is the Darwin theory. Darwin promoted the big bang idea. He told us in his writings of some big explosion. It broadcasted all these solid beings into space where they remain today. This theory has some major unknowns within it. Why didn't all these beings, planets, stars, suns and moons just continue moving further and further away from the explosion? Why are some rotating in one directions while others are turning in another? How can the spacing of each now remain in a consistent rotation around our sun which is our primary heat and light source? Then Darwin gives us no answer about the origin of these original solid materials we call planets, sun, moons, and stars. Our next question should be, "Are we correct to assume that everything must certainly have a time and a place of origin?"

But, considering all the facts, the theories, and the scientific writings, there is only one place that tells us the answer to this last question. You need to go the very first book in the Bible; the book of Genesis. It is something I quoted in part at the end of this writing. Genesis, chapter one and verse one, "In the beginning God created the Heavens and the earth."

So, you see, we can speculate all over the place, but when we search for the real truth, it is still readily available to us. All we have to do is go to the true source. I don't have enough faith to believe in the big bang or any other theory that man has come up with. I have just enough faith to believe that we have a higher power holding the atoms in place and keeping all around us a consistent motion and location allowing us all to not just survive but thrive here on earth.

Some in science scholars will try to steer us in some other obscure direction. So far, that has not upset the Hand of the One that controls it all. I believe God sent His Son to earth as a baby. He grew up sinless. He ministered to the poor, the sick, and the needy, before we hung Him on that old wooden cross where He gave up His life for the likes of us. He was laid in a borrowed tomb for three days. He then rose from the dead and spent the next 40 days, witnessed by some 500 people, before He ascended back into Heaven.

When He left He promised He would come back again for all who believe in Him as Lord and Savior that we will get to be with Him all throughout eternity. This promise is our greatest hope.

I chose to serve this God of Love, and not a god of hate, nor of any manmade idol. My future is secure in my hope of the Lord Jesus

Christ, the Son of God the Father, who one day will return for all of us, His Church, who have faith to believe He is who He said He is. I pray that all who read this have or will also receive this greatest of all gifts. His word, the Holy Bible tells us this simple yet profound truth,

"Believe on the Lord Jesus Christ and you will be saved."

To summarize all of the above, science is the study of things already in existence. I believe that religion, the personal relationship of man with the one true creator God, and His creation of all we see around us, does not need science to exist. However, science does require its interwoven connection to this one true religion and the fruits of His creation of all to exist and to be sustained. God uses sciences as tools to continue His creation through the ages. Without His creation, you and I would not be here, and there would be no one except God to reason or to question this or any other subject.

A sub answer to what came first, the chicken or the egg, is answered by the above truth. Man, the first Adam, was created fully grown, as was all of the first creatures when first created here on the earth. God created them each of their own kind, male and female. Thus, it is the reason why He commanded us to go forth and multiply. We have certainly followed that commandment to the letter.

The following are Bible scriptures giving us complete stories of all that happened during and after God's six days of creation work, and the one day He rested from His work.

Genesis 1:1 "In the beginning God created the Heavens and Earth.

Genesis 1:27 "God created man in His Own image.

Isaiah 40:26-27 "Lift up your eyes on high, and see who has created these things, who......

John 1:1 "In the beginning was the Word and the Word was with God and the Word was God."

John 1:14 – 16 "And the Word became flesh and dwelt among us and....."

Picture This – Changing Directions

We live in a time when it seems we tend to make changes in our lives more frequently than did past generations. This is more apparent when you look at the divorce rate today, as well as, how often people change jobs, and even change their occupations. This also includes how often we move from one house to another and from one town to another.

Our society, the way most of us were raised, grooms us to be less satisfied with our situation, or because of our expectations we tend to become bored with our present circumstances. Many of us are, or have become, a people needing constant entertainment. Thus some of us seem to lack the ability to find things to occupy our time on our own.

Today, our relationships, both family and friends seem to have a weaker bond than two and three generations ago. Family gatherings and activities are replaced by each member going in separate directions and having our own separate interests. Even family meals seem to be replaced with fast food stops on the run. Children are encouraged to take up as many extra activities as possible like sports and dance classes, just to name a few. This helps them develop varied interests, but does not allow other family members to share much in their experiences. These extra activities are not bad, but any one family member being over involved with too many outside events limits their time spent together with members of their own family.

A balance is one main key to making all of the above work. This is to set limits on how many activities one can juggle at a time. This reminds me of a Bible verse regarding moderation. All things are acceptable in moderation, but may not all be profitable.

I need to tell you a brief summation about a man named Joe. His life is the example of someone who fits into today's society. After his four years in the military, he has worked for four different employers during the next sixteen years. Then four different employers during the next twenty years. In those thirty six years he had seven different unrelated occupations, and was married for a total of thirty three years, but he had three different wives during those years. He now has one grown biological child and seven grown step children. Also during the last forty years of his adult life he's lived in twelve different homes.

Joe's life has been very full, but one cannot say he has had a history of stability and lasting relationships. These many changes have left behind him with a lot of baggage, to use some modern day language or terminology.

Perhaps, Joe should have set some early priorities in every part of his life. He might have made better choices to make his time more meaningful. Not just for himself but for all the lives he touched and walked away from. Beyond the structure within his schedule of activities he could have and should have created a list of priorities which would allow all those close to him to feel important in his life. A place where they sensed that he valued their presence. With his model they likely would have followed his example and done likewise for him.

The scheduling of a balance of activities for all family members, along with regular family fun times each week, would have allowed Joe's family an opportunity to express their individual differences, while still keeping the family unit as the base for each member to return home to each day. Beyond that, Joe could have structured family meals together, striking for at least two each day, along with scheduling at least one evening each week for a family fun night. Planning for these takes time and energy, but should prove to be well worth the efforts spent.

Joe's work history showed that he may not have always pursued the work of his calling. He spent years in a line of work that was possibly not to his liking. It is possible that with early and proper counseling he may have found the type of work that would have been fulfilling, rewarding, and lasting.

The same could have been said for his personal life and his relationships. With prayer, soul searching, and proper guidance he may have made better choices for who he married and in how to work at maintaining loving and lasting special relationships. All relationships take hard work. But with that effort the benefits usually follow.

There is an old saying, "You get only as much out of something as you are willing to put into it."

Maybe we all could learn something of real lasting value from reading about Joe's experiences?

Our Temporary Home

You're sitting under a shade tree at the back of your property. It's one of your favorite spots to spend relaxing time whenever you can on warm summer days. You can see the main road and all the activities happening there. People are going about their various destinations. You can also watch each of your neighbors at their places doing weeding, planting, and mowing activities. You also see a blue jay watching you as you watch him. He keeps his distance out of fear or respect, and yet, in time, even he takes a bolder stance. He ventures ever closer to your position since you show him you are apparently not a threat to him.

Then you notice a bird nest being built in the tree just above your head. Your presence probably has stopped the construction process on this nest. From your vantage point you see the intricate pattern in the work by the parent birds as they design this nest. It should safely house their young during their first days after hatching. The tiny twigs are interwoven in such a way to support each other making the nest strong. You wonder how they know to do this and how they know when it is time to have the nest ready. There is neither nest building schools for birds, nor do they have a clock or a calendar to let them know when to build this haven for their young.

Perhaps if you stay long enough the nest builders, like the blue jay, will overcome their fear of you and continue working on this building project.

Now, your mind wonders to consider all the species of birds. Each has different characteristics in their makeup, as well as, where and how they live and survive.

The beautiful eagle builds its nest on the edge of some cliff far above the ground where their young can reside safe from most predators. The parent birds feed their young meat, while many other species of birds are vegetarians feeding their young seeds and grass.

The chickadee and pheasant build their nests on the ground where they must spend most of their time defending their eggs and their young. They too are vegetarian, although they also harvest food from the insect population.

The swallows are mud dabbers and find some rock wall or some freeway overpass to attach their mud enclosure. While the sparrows and many others find a tree or any place that is both hidden and strong enough to secure their nests of straw or twigs.

The owl, a carnivore, finds some hollowed out place in a tree or wall to put their home. Their one purpose is to provide a secure place for their young where they can lay their eggs, then set on them to keep them warm until that magical moment when the little lives inside the eggs start to find their way out into this scary and threatening world.

How fascinating is this space we live in. It never fails to amaze me of all the things we see going on around us. The universe that continues to exist when the law of logic defies its existence. The sun continues to shine for thousands, not millions, of years without burning out. The moon and all the stars are held in place in the same order today as they were thousands of years ago. One plant grows from a small seed which was dead before it was planted in the ground either on purpose or by accident. All this seed needs to bring it to life is the right nourishment found in the ground and the right amount of water.

We are told that no two snowflakes are exactly the same. Just like no two people have the same exact finger prints. Our origin begins from one egg and one sperm joined together. Then they grow through multiplication of cells developing into a child with one head, ten fingers and ten toes, two arms and two legs, a complete body designed to support this precious whole person. This child is safely hidden away for the term of time needed for it to survive outside of the mother's body. It then comes forth, still in a very dependent state, yet different from every other child on the planet. Even as two twins, they each have different finger prints and individual areas, including irises of the eye and DNA, which make them different from one another.

The longer one dwells on all these truths, the more one can be convinced that all of the universe, and all it includes, was created by a magnificent master plan. To believe all this came about by chance defies logic. This is mathematically and scientifically impossible. To believe it was the result of evolution takes more faith than you or I can muster up with the brain power you or I have been given.

We should be thankful to not be in the group who denies creation. If you were there today your hope for your future would be in serious doubt.

In contrast, you can have this great hope only because of your belief in God's creation of the heavens and the earth. If you believe this, then you must also believe that all of His Word is true. He has told us to believe only in His Son for our future security. He also said to not fear him who can only destroy the body, but to fear Him who can destroy the body as well as the soul.

There are those who question the differences between creation vs evolution. Can either side provide sufficient evidence to back up their beliefs?

You can be certain and secure only in your belief of creation by The Master's Plan. This is the real reason, and is our only sure Hope for each of us to reach heaven's shores beyond our life here on earth.

A Search for Value

Are you looking for something to hold onto?

Maybe you haven't found it as yet, or perhaps you find something you think meets your needs; only to realize it falls short of your expectations. Or, it is possibly something which doesn't last; that it quickly changes or slips through your fingers.

We are each born with this mysterious void in our life; an empty place somewhere within us that causes us to continue searching for something to fill this void we feel.

Let's look at some things that are NOT the answer. It's not the need to be loved by another person, or the need to accomplish great things during our life time. It's NOT the drive most of us have to be successful. Many of us do confuse these with our need to fill the void. But we discover this vacant place takes some very special ingredient to satisfy that empty space.

Our life can be a journey packed with many new experiences and can contain a vast supply of unknowns which show up with the passing of almost every new day. No matter how much we would like to know the future not one of us knows what even the very next moment may bring, much less, what will take place tomorrow and beyond. Oh, we can speculate based upon our history up until this current time. Or based upon much of what we have scheduled and planned for our immediate future. But to know exactly what and where and how and who will affect our tomorrows is impossible for each of us to predict.

Many of us plow into our tomorrows unprepared and not expecting anything other than routine. We seem to think nothing eventful or exciting can happen to us. However when we do come face to face with the unexpected many of us might blow it. We may miss opportunities to accomplish something worthwhile, or to be able to help or come alongside of someone else that might need and want our help. We may even fail to meet our own commitments or our own expectations to accomplish those things which are our responsibility.

Before I will tell you how I found the answer to fill my void. I'll lead you through some of the areas I searched to find those special ingredient(s). I'll show you areas that so many others have tried in searching to find theirs. The list of areas to search can vary according to our own likes or dislikes. This search travels through our list of plans to be tried one by one to see if the next attempt might be the final, ultimate answer to fill our void.

I just described most of the first thirty eight years of my life. I spent much of that time and those efforts mentioned above searching here and there for that something of value. I was convinced that anything of importance had to have a price tag on it. And I found this is furthest from the truth.

My goals as a teenager and during most of my early adulthood were to be someone who would make lots of money; someone with vast responsibility and power; as well as someone others looked up to. These are not always bad things, unless they are our sole or primary motives.

My first job after finishing my four year military obligation was working in the banking industry. I assumed this was going to be the start of something big! Everyone seems to think bankers make lots of money, along with the ability to control other people's lives. In truth, bankers only handle large sums of money. They do have considerable effect on their borrowing customers, along with some influence on the investment depositor. But most bank employees make a modest income, somewhere in the middle of the average.

Frankly, I found being a banker is a thankless position. I'll give two examples of what can happen while just doing the required daily work. This was long before they came up with the point system, the credit score, to qualify borrowers for loans.

The first, a twenty two year old young man came in to borrow money for an auto loan. He had hardly any money and wanted the bank to finance 100% of his purchase. He also had no previous credit references, and was only working for a few months at a starting, low paying job. I turned him down for his loan request. He seemed to understand my reasons, but his mother did not. She paid me a visit the day after I turned her son down for the car loan. She accused me of everything short of blackballing their family's good name. I explained to her that the bank loans out money placed here by our bank depositors just like her. I was sorry but I couldn't qualify her son at this time. I further explained we loan officers have a responsibility to keep those deposits safe. We require certain levels of proven credit worthiness to qualify any person for a loan. Her son may have a good character and have a good family name. But his income and credit history were not sufficient; along with his request to borrow 100% of the purchase price. These things didn't justify approving his loan request. I further offered to reconsider his request if she would agree sign with him. She quickly refused this telling me that he still owed her some money from a personal debt and she had been unable to collect it from him. She quickly turned and left without further words.

Another circumstance with a totally different result, a young lady came in to borrow a personal loan for the purchase of new furniture. She had borrowed before for an auto loan and paid it off on a timely basis. She had several hundred dollars in her savings deposit account, she had been working full time at the same job for more than two years. She qualified for the loan and it was approved. A couple days later her father approached me. He was angry because we had caused his little girl to borrow more money. After talking with him I found out what he really was objecting to had nothing to do with me as his banker. He was unhappy because his daughter was moving into her own place and away from home. He was taking his frustrations out on his banker. He later justified my actions, but was still frustrated with the final results.

My banking career lasted through half of the nineteen sixties, all of the seventies, along with almost two years in the eighties. During the sixties and seventies a banker was fairly well regarded. By the early eighties all that changed. High loan interest rates approaching 25% made bankers look like thieves. People seemed to lose respect for their bankers during that troubling time, even though we could offer some of special depositors close to 16% interest earning for up to six months on their time deposits, called CD's or certificates of deposits.

The money I earned during my banking days never amounted to enough to accumulate any large amount. I made a good income, but it was never enough to save back much of it for my future retirement years. There was always that want for more.

It was during those years in banking I saw many people who acquired large sums of money and owned much property. Too many of these people were not any happier than the rest of us. In fact, most of them with very large cash assets seemed to be the most unhappy. Their money had not created happiness for them. In fact, it was a burden to hide it so others wouldn't try to beg, borrow or steal it from them.

It was also during those same years I acquired the shiny automobile. My first drive home was an exhilarating experience. You wanted take that chariot out often just to show off your new purchase to everyone. You looked forward to each new day so you can again show off your new, shiny machine.

Before long, something devastating happens. You parked in a store parking lot for only a few minutes when someone scrapes the side of your precious car. Your shiny chariot has been violated. A few days later a rock from a truck hits the windshield leaving a big bull's eye. Again your chariot has been assaulted. It wasn't long before the new car smell began to fade. It is replaced by a damp musty smell on rainy days and a dry dusty smell on sunny days. YOUR SHINY NEW SHOWBOAT HAD LOST MOST ALL OF ITS LUSTRE! Now, what to do to recharge your "what next" batteries. You have been eyeing that new forty inch flat screen T.V. with remote control and automatic everything. When the delivery truck backs up to your house you catch one of your neighbors peeking out their window to see your latest prize. You'll have to remember to invite them over soon to show off this addition to your collection. You spend many hours gazing at this center attraction in your living room. Even the commercials look better on the new big screen. Your car doesn't get washed as often, and the lawn mowing and yard work get put off longer. After all you spent a lot of money on this latest purchase so you cannot let it go unused.

But before long the newness also wears off. The excitement is forgotten.

Now what?

Well, the T.V. could use a neighbor. Besides, the reruns have started for the year, so why not watch what you want when you want? A new stereo video player/recorder will be just the ticket, along with several new recorded movie programs.

But, this newness too quickly fades.

Vacation time will soon be here. You have always wanted to try water skiing. Maybe a ski boat with all the extras will at last satisfy your need. The only way to find out is to own one.

But it too becomes just one more of your collection of toys. Will a motor home do it? But it will be too costly right now. You might try that one later.

Some people never finish their search. But, each new item brings only that short sprite of new excitement. Then it is back to square one with little if anything solved. Now some begin a wider search. Some try areas beyond what is considered to be acceptable, or legal or moral. All of these deviations will prove to be temporary and lacking in lasting excitement. Too often, they also cause some unwanted situations which further complicate lives.

An extra marital affair may cause a broken marriage, or at the very least a broken trust. Drug experiments may cause addictions, family problems, financial problems or worse. Too many outside activities can be rough on a family. They tend to take time away from the family and the work needed to maintain a good relationship with other family members. Even getting too involved in one's work can put these family relationships on thin ice.

It took me thirty eight years to find that the things we can buy with money do not guarantee happiness. True and sincere happiness doesn't have a price tag. True happiness in my definition is the following:

To have the love and trust of family and friends.

To know you have done the very best you can in everything you start.

To have an inner peace that comes only after you have put your whole life in the hand of your creator.

To know that there is spiritual life after death, and by faith you have received the gift of eternal life.

To have your priorities changed from the want of more and more materials goods, to the want of more and more of the things of God.

> Had I come to understand the Bible verses below earlier
> in my life, then I would have spent more of my energies on
> the things that have lasting Importance.

II Corinthians 4:18 "While we look not at the things which are seen, but at the things which are not seen: for the things which are seen are temporal, but the things which are not seen are eternal."

"But they that wait upon the Lord shall renew their strength; they shall mount up with wings as eagles; they shall run and not be weary and they shall walk and not faint." Isaiah 40:31

The search for value comes to this verse Jesus said to his disciples, "It is easier for a camel to go through the eye of a needle than for a rich man to enter into the kingdom of God."

And they were greatly astonished, saying among themselves, "Who then can be saved?"

But Jesus looked at them and answered. "With men it is impossible, but not with God; for with God all things are possible." Mark 10:25 - 27

Why place all your priorities on riches, fame, and power when these things are but temporary? They will not last and cannot be taken with us beyond death. But, remember this, the things of God are eternal.

Joshua said it best, "Choose you this day whom you will serve, but as for me and my house, we will serve the Lord." Joshua 24:15

Salvation is free, but it cost everything. The Lord wants us to give a living sacrifice, to give everything we have, even our very life to Him.

If heaven is even a fraction of what the Bible describes it to be, it will be worth it all.............Amen.

Footnote: I believe everything was planned in such fine detail. It is all part of a magnificent design by a power far above our abilities to comprehend. To believe that all that we have around us happened simply by chance takes far more faith then I have. But, who can tell? You think about that.

Part Three
Short stories + Poems + One Liners

Miracle of Life

Life is a wondrous thing. One certain cell caressed by another sparks new life. From this tiny beginning these cells begin their amazing transformation.

The tiny torso forms along with the head, the arms and legs all found in the right places. All of the vital organs are perfectly arranged for future self-sufficiency. The eyes, the ears, the nose and the mouth give evidence of the amazing progress.

With each movement gives confirmation of a precious living being is safely hidden within.

Fed by the umbilical cord to sustain this new life, the progress towards independence continues.

One day soon the warmth, darkness, and safety away from the small confines of the womb will be replaced with freedom, light and air. Even then, special extended care will be required.

This process, so complex in wondrous transformation, can only leave one with the thoughts of this miraculous life that's god's plan for all.

FREEDOM PURCHED

We rejoice not in the loss of those who gave their all in the guardianship of our freedom, but in the results gained from their sacrifice. Those lives spent, along with all who willingly served, must gain our unending gratitude for their gallant service and sacrifice.

Our freedom was purchased at immeasurable cost. It is not possible to place a value on the unselfish actions by those called to defend. They must never be forgotten, and our unwavering pledge shall be to always remember their willingness to go.

One cannot fathom all that has been accomplished on our behalf. Our vast benefits far exceed the freedoms of press and speech and religion. They include, as well, the liberty to pursue endless opportunities as the result of their great sacrifice. These wonderful gifts were given by the thousands of lives which were spent, most of whose names we know not, but whose actions we must give our utmost honor and applause.

Since we cannot affix a monetary price to our freedoms, we must strive to live our lives in such a way to give honor to all those who unconditionally gave of themselves to paved the way.

Let us remember all of these true heroes in every sense of the word in a spirit of profound gratitude. Doing daily exactly what needs to be done to pass on a continual remembrance of all those who have fallen.

It's a Beautiful Day

Our journey down this road, so frequently traveled, began at our beginning, and continues on today.

The hills and valleys, the bends and curves that are there, they expand our experiences, make us stretch, and cause us to search for strength and for direction. The rocks and potholes there make for a less than smooth passage. Yet, we must carry on as if we lack the ability to end this ride.

Most of us look forward to what is to come, while others look back to the events of yesterday. A few may seek ways to end their trip premature to the end of the road. GOD FORBID!

As for me, I look with anticipation to what will be there for me, and all the while, desire not to miss any of the little tokens of sadness and joy, of sobriety and humor, of pain and pleasure along the way. With each, may growth happen, and tolerance to others be gained. With each, may I forgive and be forgiven. With each, may I learn to love and to be loved. With each, may I come to appreciate, and in turn, gain appreciation. Through each, may I lose my foolish pride, and gain in its place a humble heart.

And, may I experience all of each long before my travels end.

WHO IS THIS GOD?

Who WAS and IS and ALWAYS WILL BE?

Who created the universe and hung the stars in place.

Who gave a name for every star.

Who created everything from nothing with just His spoken word.

Who controls the wind and brings the rain in its due season.

Who restrains the atom and rules over the ocean tides.

Who provides all of the things necessary to support all life and brings life.

Who created man in His own image and then gave him dominion over the earth.

Who knew each one of us even before we were formed in our Mother's womb.

Who gave us our ability to reason and the option to accept or reject Him.

Who gave us His written word and told us to meditate upon it day and night.

Who told us to pray without ceasing and stands ready to answer in His time.

Who knows our thoughts even before we think them and stands ready to hear.

Who can hear the prayers of the multitudes and can separate each prayer.

Who told us obedience is better than sacrifice.

Who with Him, all things are possible.

Who made a way where there was no way and made it available to all.

Who provided the only hope we need and holds out His hand to all.

Who loved each of us with such a great love and gave Himself for us.

Who told us to pray without ceasing.

Who we can know Him only in part today, but a day will come when He
has promised we will see Him face to face, and then we will fully know Him.

FLASHBACKS

Looking back, often brings fond memories.
Turn from your past learned events into present day wisdoms.
Carry who and where you were then into the here and now.
Dwell now on any wisdom from back then and there
To gain from back then to directions needed now.
Yesterday's training ground is for life today,
and today's is for your passageway into tomorrow.
What you couldn't do then, you may be able to do now.
Whoever you were effects who you've become,
then who you are now reflects who you will be future.
Dispense with all the worst, keep all the best, and then pass
All these on to whomever follows. God Bless.

IS THIS ALL THERE IS?

"Is this really all there is?"

It's a question often asked when life seems to go flat, or becomes a continuous routine where we seem to be going in circles, and is lacking any element of excitement. We might have these same feelings while going through a tremendous challenge where answers seem impossible to find; or when we can do so little for ourselves. When we might be going in the wrong direction, or even when we tried very hard and still have accomplished very little.

As younger adults we believed we can do almost anything. After all, we knew all there was to know about life. However, it doesn't take long for us find that some things are not always as easy as they first appeared. Again we may find that some of our attempts fail; or should have or could have been done differently to gain a better result.

Eventually, we may come to the conclusion that our life is not going as we once expected. That others seem to be having a better time and are having more fun. Why is this? Didn't we start off with a good plan, as well as, great expectations? But why is it not working? Are we suffering from the "Expectation vs Reality Syndrome?"

We must now start looking for a better way; a smoother road with fewer detours; a way which will bring us more ongoing satisfaction. We need to start in the right place to find a source of instructions that covers all circumstances in order to find solid information and to find out why things are working for so many others. We need to stop wandering around in this unknown and find direction that really matters. We've discovered that life is not always going to be easy and fun, but it should be fulfilling. There could be some unexpected troubles in our future. We should attempt to prepare for any of the great unknowns that may lay ahead.

Earlier, I mentioned a source of instructions, a book which gives us some guidelines. The only real manual for life is The Holy Bible. In it you will find stories about people who experienced everything possible of life's situations. It also gives us examples of what not to try and things we should avoid. In addition, it tells us The Source of our strength, as well as, the wisdom to become overcomers.

I like the song; "Put your hand in the hand of the One who stills the water. Put your hand in the hand of the One who calms the sea."

A Bible verse that speaks volumes, "I can do all things through Christ who strengthens me." Philippines 4:13

When we search for that inner strength and it fails, or when we try to go through the deep valley on our own, and we find that we just don't have what it take to finish; we can then seek the Lord's help and find the answers to our questions that come at just the right time to bring us through.

We can believe in that referenced verse, Philippines 4:13. The one true source of strength when we have no other way to overcome. He is our strength in a time of troubles. He can give you what you need, just when you need it, if you will trust only in Him.

And now know that there is lots more value to be found!

SEARCHING

I looked to the left and then to the right, and nothing that provides life changing values came into my sight.

I looked forward and likewise behind, and still no earth shaking changes did I find.

But when I bowed down and looked up, only then did I see the true source of eternal rest being made known to me.

You can do the same, you too can discover this rest which is available for all to see.

Are you a searcher, searching today, looking for beauty and peace and rest?

Then kneel down, look up and begin to pray, and you too will find **His** true promise of the very best.

It's the eternal hope each of us need. A message for all if they will simply heed.

SUMMER RAIN

As I sat in my living room one summer evening listening to the rain, I considered the wonder of it all.

Lightning flashed off in the distance, where? Only by the direction of the Heavenly Father.

Following the lightning strike a rolling thunder could be heard. This being the consequence of the explosion of the lightning bolt.

God directs the timing and place for them both.

The rain water held in the clouds too is directed to fall in a place by the hand of God. Water being heavier than air, yet it falls only after being released by His hand, and to a place and time of His choosing.

We are blessed by these gifts of rain and wind and sun. Each shares in the nourishment needed for all things to grow and flourish.

After the rain, we receive yet another blessing from the freshness of the air washed by the falling rain.

All five of our senses should be dazzled as we step outside following this gift of a summer rain.

OH, THE WONDER OF IT ALL, WHO CAN FATHOM IT.

Life is No Bowl of Jell-O

Life is no bowl of Jell-O. It is much more than that, it's like a Jell-O mold.

With all the stuff that comes our way, all the things outside of our control, and whatever our government throws at us, we have to remember where our help comes from. Our help comes from the Lord Who created the Heavens and the earth. With His help we can do the following:

We have to be able to jiggle, bounce, stretch, withstand the heat and still stay together in one mass without melting down..............

Reading assignment today if you are looking for relief from stress. Read Philippians 4: 6-7 "Be anxious for nothing, but in everything by prayer and supplication, with thanksgiving, let your requests be made known to God, and the peace of God, which surpasses all understanding, will guard your hearts and minds through Christ Jesus"

And then for extra credit, read the rest of chapter four. It's really good news to calm your mind and soul. - - - - - - - - - - - - - - - -

God bless.

TREASURES

Webster's definition of treasure: 1. An accumulated of hidden wealth, as jewels or money. 2. Something very valuable.

We each have our own idea of what these are: Most of us work hard to go out of our way to gain and to keep these.

Today many are trying to buy and sell us gold or silver or any other commodity with the hope for a short or long term gain. Some may, but some could also results in loss. We may be inclined to explore these avenues. After all, wealth can cause others to look up to us, and cause our family and friends to think we are great investors. They might even follow our examples.

Problems often follow the pursuit of wealth for the sake of just becoming wealthy. Most of us don't understand the measurement of wealth. How much is enough? Or, understand that the drive to become rich may consume all of our energy and attention, only to find the accumulation of money does not always bring happiness. Often it brings fear that others may take it away from us. And, too often, our drive to accumulate wealth allows us little time to seek real relationships and fellowships. If only we could see the narrowness of this goal that puts all of the other important areas of our life on the back burner, restricting how we interact with others.

A word picture: A man is sent to another land for a time. He is told that every penny he earned above his immediate modest needs was to be sent home. Then when he was called back home he couldn't bring anything back.

This word picture is a reminder of the instruction in Mathew chapter 6:19-21 "Do not lay up for yourselves treasures in earth, where moth and rust destroy and where thieves break in and steal; but lay up for yourselves treasures in heaven, where neither moth nor rust destroys and where thieves do not break in and steal. For where your treasure is, there your heart will be also."

Our lesson is to set your priorities for things that will last, even throughout eternity. God doesn't wants us all to be poor, however, he wants us to place His work and His will above all other pursuits.

THE LINK

Are we all connected? We do have a common bond, one that goes deeper than water. That also goes beyond being just part of the human race.

Oh, I am certain there are many of us who don't wish to claim any bond to some radicals out there. They possibly feel those rejects are too big; to small; too fat; too light; too dark; too ugly; too hypocritical; too political, or any one of possibly thousands of reasons to reject any connection.

But, "Here is that profound conjunction," <u>But</u> in looking at our family tree, and if we look back far enough into our ancestry, we will find kinship to every other person on this planet, both living and dead. We are cousins many times removed, yet still cousins. If we can look at the big picture we will see that the only logical conclusion is "Cousins."

Our great, great grandparents going back hundreds of generations were just two people starting a family. Then that family grew to extended families, and so on, until today when we have a planet population counting into the multiple billons still alive, not to mention all those who came before you and I, and who are now gone.

Some of us like to proclaim kinship to the "Rich and Famous." We like to say that, "So and So is my distance cousin. Little do we know, we can all claim, not just one or two, but, all those rich and famous as our very own kinsman. But then, so can you, and so can I do the same.

Now, what do we do with this new revelation?

What do we do with the knowledge that those noisy, obnoxious neighbors across the street, or down the road are really distant family?

We can choose to go on just as we have in the past, or we can change the way we look at them because of our newly revealed kinship. We can invite these cousins to come to dinner. We can go out of our way to help them when we see that they need it, or we can disclaim any possible ties, and avoid contact at all cost.

However, we must consider the possibility that those noisy neighbors may act the way they do because they think we are arrogant, standoffish people who think we are better than them. Or, maybe it's just that no one has told them that we are related to them. Maybe they just don't know that we are "Distant Cousins!"

From this time forward, maybe we must look at each person around us much differently than we had in the past before this family ties news became a reality.

But, there is that profound conjunction again, <u>but</u>, as for me, or is it, as for I and my house, we will open our doors to welcome in our share of "Cousins." We will make them feel loved and cared for. We will acknowledge our kinship in whatever way we can to honor all those around us. We will love our neighbors as ourselves just as we have been commanded to do; just as Jesus said in the second of the two greatest commandments has told us to do.

And now, "cousin," what will you do with this new and profound revelation?

I'LL FLY AWAY

Have you ever wanted to, "Just get away?" Just leave behind all the pressures and busyness for just a couple of days, or even a week?

Life is good, but it can also be tough. The demands that come our way can be overwhelming. We all have our own "Straw that broke the camel's back" moments. Some of us have stronger times than others, still limitations do exist for us all.

For some people stress and pressure may come from work, while others might come from home, from financial problems, or due to illness, either our own, or someone we care for. Then others it's the apprehension that comes from doing something for the very first time, the fear of the unknown.

Whatever the cause, it often take its toll on each of us, affecting our relationships, and without a doubt it can have adverse effects on our health over time. It can definitely affect our attitude.

Whatever the cause, it can be helpful to take a step back for a few days to appraise your situation, as long as you don't run away from whatever is causing your stress.

Whether our pressures and stress are work related, or a relationship that is severely threatened, or an illness or financial dilemma, just taking a few days to step back and appraise your situation may be helpful, as long as, we don't take on the attitude of running from your problems, or leaving just to get away. This will only add more fuel to the fire that may be running out of control. If possible, just step back to look at the whole picture from all sides. This just might reveal an appropriate solution, or it might show you that your past response has been to over react to the problem, turning a molehill into a mountain.

We may find that in the past we have not used our best defenses against our stress. We have many weapons that do not cause physical or emotional damage, but quite the opposite, they will relieve the pressures and ease the mind. These weapons are within each of us, some are learning to relax using stretching and breathing techniques; talking out these stress points with the people closest to your problem area; sharing your concerns with others without pointing fingers or naming blame.

The best weapon we have in our arsenal is spiritual. We can use the power of prayer for strength and for wisdom.

God's word says, "The beginning of wisdom is the fear of the Lord." He also tells us to, "Cast our cares upon Him, for He cares for us."

If we run from our problems, they will usually follow us, and show up shortly thereafter. They have usually grown in size during the trip. But, if we apply the various weapons available to us, we have a much better chance of gaining the victory.

Your assignment for today and beyond is to put your cares in the Lord's hands and see if He brings you the victory.

MARRAGE BY GOD'S DESIGN

Applying these will take time. The below scriptures can be helpful to you.

<u>ESSENTIALS SCRIPTURES</u>
    1. Be in agreement spiritually 2 Corr. 6:14-15
    A. Agree where to fellowship Mark 3:24-26
    B. Agree on tithing
    C. Agree on family devotions
    D. On serving and scheduling time for family and for serving
    2. Husband and wife relationships
    A. Treating one another Eph 5:18-24
    B. How a man treats his wife Eph 5:24-29
    C. How a wife treats her husband Eph 5:22-24
    3. Agree on child rearing Proverbs 22:6
    A. How to discipline
    B. Christian upbringing Eph 6:4
    C. Bed times for children
    D. Manner training both at Psalm 78:7-8 home and away
    E. Scheduling study and game times
    F. Scheduling family times
    G. Mutual support Eph 5:31-32
    H. Planning to be consistent
    4. On blended families
    A. Decide to have discipline be given by biological parent(s)
    B. Allow time for acceptance to happen
    C. Respect privacy
    D. Encourage all to join in for family

activities and outings
5. Agree on financial dealings I Tim 6:9-10
A. Agree on spending and saving Luke 12:43-44
B. On decisions for major purchases
C. On tithing and offerings
D. On retirement planning
E. On college expenses
F. To agree before moving forward
on any financial changes

Men, you are the pastor of your household. This is a God given position.

You, as husband and wife are equal co-leaders in your home, called to do the most important job of your life. Even though you must take these positions very seriously, the Lord wants you to make your home a very warm, loving and secure place for all who abide there.

You are encouraged to follow the instructions in Titus 2:1-8 (Pull and read)

RISEN

What can we do with a word that defies human logic?

All of us can relate that it's something we can only be called a miracle, something we've seen, or heard told by others which seems to be totally impossible. Yet it happened, with many witnesses to confirm it.

I recall one particular thing that I called a "No Way Event." It happened while I was driving in a very heavy rain storm. Visibility was very close to non-existent.

I came upon a stalled car on the bridge in my lane of traffic. It was too close to be able to stop. My only option was not to go around on the right because of a concrete side barrier. So I pulled around to the left, only to see the headlights of another car just ahead. The oncoming driver pulled as far as he could to his right, which was on my left. I somehow passed between the stalled car and the other oncoming car. Somehow we made it through that opening without touching each other.

When we were all able to stop and to regain our composure, we started to compare notes. None of us could believe that we had passed without hitting each other. We actually measured the distance between the stalled car and the left side barrier and found we each had only one inch clearance to miss one another. This is the exact width including the side mirrors of my car and theirs plus one inch between each of the three cars.

I recalled it as a miracle, an act of God, that we didn't have an accident that night.

We then cleared the roadway by pushing the stalled car beyond the bridge barrier, and instructed the driver of the stalled car to put on her emergency flasher. Then another near miracle happened within the next ten minutes. We had all three cars running and ready to go on our separate ways. It was a near miracle because none of us had any expert mechanical abilities. We were all very thankful, and also very wet.

It had almost stopped raining by the time we all moved on to our separate destinations.

I will never forget this experience. I will always wonder how we all came through without damage. I do believe someone beyond me and the other drivers was responsible for our protection.

Our title "Risen", in the context that is used, also defies our logic. Yet over five hundred people saw the risen Jesus alive over the following 40 days after He rose from the dead.

Before He ascended back into His heavenly home he promised to one day return for His church, for us who believe in Him and Lord and Savior. This report was recorded about two thousand years ago. It is still being widely shared with people all around the world. This wonderful news has effected more lives in such a miraculous

COLLECTION OF SHORT STORIES AND MORE 247

way than any other recorded or unrecorded events in the history of mankind.

This was also the amazing handiwork of our all-knowing, all loving God.

Read the verses in the Holy Bible in John 3:16 -17

WORDS

The audio sounds we speak can have such great influence on how we relate to others, as well as, what we accomplish. These various sounds, and the contrast from one word to another can be huge. If we say we love someone, vs we hate someone. How different these words affect the receiver. You can visualize the effects of praise on the recipient verses criticism. Praise is uplifting, while criticism often brings discouragement. Both children and adults can be motivated to do their best by sincere words of praise.

Being a people watcher is fun and it can also be a great learning tool. Observing what others say and do causes you to see how they make or break a relationship, or how they might finish a task and strive to accomplish anything.

Some people have such a profound ability to motivate and lead others. But success is like beauty, it is in the eyes of the beholder. Most of us can see beauty and success for what it is worth. However, some others may come out with a totally different opinion than the rest of us. This may be because most are considering the whole person or thing, while others may be looking only at appearances.

The real measure of success and beauty is in the whole. An apple pie may look delicious, but if some key ingredient is left out of the recipe, the appearance can be deceiving. It is just the same for people because looks without sound character are only a part of the real picture. Beauty alone without good character, integrity, and personality is an incomplete recipe leaving the observer wanting.

We encounter many contrasts in life. Hot or cold, light or dark, smooth or rough, a smile or a frown, happy or sad are just a few. Let's get a little personal with these in our own day. You likely learn to talk early in your life by being a people watcher and listener. Your first words were limited to just the basics to meet your needs. But as you grew in size you also grew in vocabulary as well. You'll find that you learned from your past successes and failures on how we approach anyone with these wonderful words of audible sounds.

Will I be all self-centered, or selfless?

Will I be discourteous or uncaring of other's feelings?

Will I be willing to listen to others, or will I just ignore other people's comments, and go on and on about my own little world?

Our prayers should be that we can learn how to better communicate; to hear and share in what others are experiencing; to be compassionate to other people and their needs; remembering that communication is a two way street, and everyone should get equal opportunity to share in their own way.

In the book of James in God's word says, "Be quick to hear, slow to speak and slow to wrath."

This scripture is a lesson many of us had to learn early in our lives. It works in most all situations. You are encouraged to try it for yourself.

LIFE

It's a gift. The most precious, priceless gift that transcends anything else that you and I will ever receive. It's a gift that keeps on giving, and it is of great value to even those who value spending their time and activities with us. We have no final control over this gift. Each of us has our days numbered. Oh, we can shorten the numbers of them, but we do that without being given the authority to do so. We do it assuredly with dire consequences that are bound to come both to ourselves and to the people who love and care about us.

We each receive this gift of life without asking for it. We gain it without control over how many days, weeks or years it will stay. Then we may depart from it when we may or may not be ready to do so. We are told by some around us to prepare our hearts and our minds for our going. But, all too often, this too may be one of the things that fall a victim to our own procrastination.

Our needs for preparation to depart are two-fold. We must prepare for both our physical and spiritual departure. The physical preparation requires the arrangements for instructions for all that we will leave behind. These are our financial affairs as to who will receive our earthly treasures, as well as, our burial plans. Also how and where our physical remains will be put to rest.

Our spiritual preparations are internal and vertical. This is our personal relationship, or the lack of it, with our creator. He alone was the one who brought each of us here on our first day of life and He will certainly be present in our departure.

Where we spend our eternity will depend upon our own decision which we must make while we are still alive. We determine where we will go based upon whether we believe in The Lord Jesus Christ, then our willingness to repent of all our sins. Finally our destination is determined by accepting Jesus and His offer for life with Him. Or by rejecting Him and His offer. This decision is the most profound and most personal conclusion anyone can and will make during their entire lifetime. Our life here is very short, even if we live to be over one hundred years old, it is short in comparison to the time we will spend throughout eternity.

Roman 6:23 "For the wages of sin is death, but the gift of God is eternal life in Christ Jesus our Lord."

THESE THREE TREES

These three trees were not necessarily found in the same grove, nor were they of the same variety. But, they were all grown about the same time, and they each played an important role. All were cut down and designed by the craftsman's hands, fashioned into some useful tool.

The first tree was sawed into boards to make an animal feeding trough, one which was used for this purpose for most of its existence. The second tree was also cut into boards, to be shaped and routed into materials to make a small boat for fishing or transportation.

These two objects had to have more or less fine finishing to make them useable. The trough needed only modest sanding to make it acceptable for the soft noses of animals, while the boat needed much fine sanding, along with sealing and bracing to make it water tight and strong. It was likely made by a skilled craftsman experienced in boat building.

The third tree needed little planning, nor a skilled craftsman to complete. It only needed to be cut down, and sawed into two heavy timbers, one larger and one smaller. The rough surfaces and the rugged cuts needed no extra care. They just needed to be a strong tool. It is recognized more than 2000 years later as the Old Rugged Cross used for the Lord Jesus Christ's death.

Oh! The first wooden object was a feed trough, renamed the Manger where The Baby Jesus was laid. He had humble beginning, was called the son of a carpenter, and had no place to call home, never married or fathered children. He was not born into wealth and had no great earthly possessions. He walked most everywhere, except when He rode into Jerusalem on an untamed colt. Yet His life and death, and resurrection has had a greater impact on more people's lives than any other person.

Oh! The small boat Jesus once used to give his message to the multitudes. It was just a small fishing boat until that certain day when He used it to give His message from the boat to the multitudes.

And we, like these three wooden objects, are valued not by our beginnings, or what we are made of, but, "What God choses to make of us."

God Bless.

News, What News?

If you are like me, you tend to place your priorities on what is important for the "here and now." We make our plans, and spend our time and efforts to make our lives more comfortable for now, and also in the near future. We spend money and make our schedules for today. Maybe even with consideration for another day or two beyond.

Most of us know that the rest of our lives and beyond are important, but, we often occupy ourselves by limiting only to the present. None of us knows what's in store for us down this road of life. So we convince ourselves not to plan too far ahead. Today is covered. So, why must we worry beyond?

Let's stretch. Let's think beyond today and tomorrow. Let's go beyond the immediate to consider where we might be a year from now, or beyond. We know about the unknowns in life. Our health and wealth, or the lack there of, are factors. None of us know the length or extent of our lives beyond this moment. We've seen others encounter life threating illnesses, or financially devastating situations. These are either due to poor choices or to some unexpected expenses or circumstances which were far beyond their control. These normally cannot be planned for. But, some plans and actions can be made today which can be helpful for our unknown future.

Certainly or possibly, we likely will all grow old and frail as we age. We could experience some money problems, either self-inflicted, or not. Many things that happen beyond today can change so much of our future.

People in our lives come and go. We must cultivate these relationships because their love actions are so important to us. But, we must also realize that each person we treasure may someday be gone. This too is part of life. We must show our love for each of them for as long as they are here, not just for their sake, but also for our own. These relationships are vital to our physical, mental, and spiritual wellbeing.

Now our stretch must consider what happens beyond this life. I am talking about our spiritual being. It will exist even beyond our physical life. We will each spend our eternity somewhere. This planning may not seem vital today even though it should be; considering all the unknowns we will face beyond this moment.

I have some really good news! We can plan for eternity now. We can prepare for where we spend it, where physical health and financial conditions, whatever they might be, will no longer have an effect upon us.

This plan is to establish a 'one on one relationship' with God and His Son, Jesus Christ. We then chose to allow this relationship to grow; to make this relationship number one for our life. Then to allow it to shape our character and to teach us how to interact with all those around us; to rest in the great hope and assurance that no matter what our life brings we will be given the strength and provision to get through.

Then when our physical life is over we will be living in our eternity. If we choose a relationship with God and with His Son we will have this wonderful News and His assurance ever present. Further God has told us to share this good news with all of those around us. This is His commandment to each of us as is shared in His Holy Word. Read His instructions found at the end of the book of Matthew 28: 18 - 20

News, Oh What News!

PICTURE THIS – Suppose There Fifty, or Suppose Ten

Have you ever come to the conclusion that you were not where you're supposed to be, or where you thought you were? Maybe it happened while you were driving and lost your way. You arrive at a dead end road, an awful place that makes you want to be anywhere but where you are. Or, maybe you belong to some club, organization, church, or even some political party whose agenda may have once been to your liking, but today it no longer fits who you are. It could be either because they have changed their set agenda or it is you who has changed.

Let's use the example of a political party. The Republican Party is known for its stand for lower taxes and smaller government; along with a pro-life and pro-marriage between one man and one woman. While in contrast, the Democratic Party platform now generally stands for more government programs which means higher taxes, pro-choice on abortions, and open marriages including same sex marriages. At some point most of your ideals and values fit into one or the other of these examples. You feel strongly towards one of the agendas vs. the other. The above reminds me of the Bible story of a conversation between one man, Abraham and God regarding the cities of Sodom and Gomorra. If you are unfamiliar with this story, God found both cities to be very wicked to the point that God wanted to destroy them. But Abraham pleaded with God to save the cities because his nephew, Lot and his family lived in Sodom.

Abraham's questioned God, "Suppose there are fifty righteous that live there, would you spare the cities?"

But God did not find fifty.

"If there are forty five? Then forty? Then thirty? Twenty? Then ten, would the cities be spared?"

God did not even find ten righteous people living there. However He did send two angels into the city to convince Lot to move his family out of the city before sending down the fire to destroy these two adjoining cities.

In the end Lot did leave, but without his two sons-in-law; even Lot's wife looked back and was lost. She longed to go back and she lost her life because of it.

The wickedness of the people in the two cities was so bad that God felt there was no hope for any of them, so they were destroyed.

The same method of a process of elimination can be used in yours or my situation. Oh, you may not have a conversation with God Almighty. You may not see people turn to look back and turn into a pillar of salt like Lot's wife, but you can still apply the same method used in the above conversation to see if there be fifty in your organization that agree with you; then forty, thirty, twenty or ten. If you find that you are not in the main stream of agreement, then you must decide either to stay to make the most of it; maybe even try to convince the group to move to a better position, or you could choose to leave in search of one that falls in line with your ideals and values.

Leaving a group may not be easy, neither is staying with efforts and time spent attempting to get changes made that will convince the group to conform to your liking. But whether you stay or leave, both options will come with considerable flack that may come from fellow members with whatever changes you decide upon. Decisions are not always easy, but still may be necessary.

God bless.

101 One Liners

These are an accumulation of One Liners I developed over many years of writing. They may not all fit into your life, but many should be of some help, or at least lighten your day. God Bless

1. Arrival of light always chases away darkness
2. A rope is designed to be pulled, not pushed
3. Can a cup can be half full and half empty at the same time?
4. Truth is always better regardless of the end results
5. Saving money and time usually brings gains
6. Ignoring a clock is a reminder of how time flies
7. Putting something in a space takes away what was there before
8. Wherever you go, there you are
9. Make a friend and gain an ally
10. Friendship is costly but worth the price
11. Few things that are free have great worth
12. Preventative maintenance pays dividends in the long run
13. A half hour of exercise every day is better than most medicines
14. Milk comes before meat as little comes before big
15. A person with great virtue is far better than someone only with great riches
16. Words spoken with love are far better than with anger
17. Success comes only by making the effort to get there
18. A bored mind lacks imagination
19. Belief is the acceptance of a matter by faith
20. If you hear a sound with your ears and see a site with your eyes, is it so?
21. There is a reason we each have two ears, but only one mouth
22. Words spoken softly usually receive a like response
23. Wisdom comes hard, but foolishness comes too easy

24. Feelings can sometimes be misleading, but truth is always sure

25. One picture replaces much verbal description

26. One lie usually requires a second to follow

27. Unfortunately desire for money usually exceeds the desire for integrity

28. Laughter is good for what ails you and likens as good medicine

29. Your good attitude can make someone's day

30. Be careful what you eat, as well as, what you see and what you hear

31. The worth of a good listener is more than a good talker

32. When no one is around to hear, a tree falling in the woods still makes a sound

33. We are all equal in God's sight

34. No matter what you believe, the greatest source of truth is still in God's Holy Word

35. A bridge built is usually easier to get across than a wall

36. Young man, if you must marry, look for a virtuous wife to spend your life with

37. Seek wisdom even before wealth and happiness

38. Husband listen to the counsel of your wife

39. Saturdays should be our preparation for Sundays

40. Love is still one of the most powerful words

41. At the end of each dark night daylight will come

42. Drunkenness usually promotes foolishness

43. All that we see was made by someone's design

44. One minute equals sixty seconds, just as one hour equals sixty minutes

45. A door opened reveals what is on the other side

46. A window opened lets in the heat of the day or the cool of the night

47. One hundred out of one hundred men will one day die
48. Time is short so recognize your creator and do His will
49. Walk by faith not be sight
50. On a hot day look for a shady place
51. A solid foundation is the best place to build
52. Doing a project without a plan is usually a foolish action
53. All liquids and solids are heavier than air
54. To walk a mile takes one step at a time
55. Life is short, benefit from learning something new each day
56. Children are a treasured gift from above
57. Who can know tomorrow, we have not gotten there yet
58. To know and to love is the ultimate plan from God
59. After God, the family is the center of our existence
60. Attitude is one measurement of how we interact with those around us
61. A few words spoken in error can bring destruction and separation
62. Commitment without follow through leaves all lacking
63. A book cover is only a glimpse of what is within
64. To know the whole story one must receive all the facts
65. A great purchase is only great if you get what you bargain for
66. Do the right thing even when no one is watching
67. Jesus said My door is wide open to all who desire to enter in
68. A mind is a terrible thing to starve, feed it with all the best stuff
69. A roof protects us from what falls from above
70. Life has so many benefits, don't lose it or them
71. Why crawl when you can walk, why whisper when you can speak
72. When you start a trip, be sure you have a good travel plan
73. Sow today only what you want to reap tomorrow
74. It is so much better to be right, than to be left

75. Some used to say "where's the beef," but now they say "where's the pork"
76. Spend today like there is no tomorrow, paying then for the foolishness done today
77. Your life is a wonderful gift to be cherished until the end
78. One little fly in your soup takes a small space, but makes a big difference
79. Live in truth and be free
80. Stop using words and actions which produce no profit
81. Prayer releases the hand of God
82. Grass grows even when no one is watching
83. Complete freedom is the lack of bondage
84. When all else fails, get up and get going
85. The biggest battle is always within
86. Seek just counsel
87. Seek just correction
88. The most difficult secret to keep is one's own opinion of themselves
89. Wrongs can be forgiven, but are rarely forgotten
90. Always abstain from evil and always desire to do good
91. Right is always right, but left can sometimes be wrong
92. Don't let anyone or anything take your joy away
93. Practice your walk by faith
94. Grow in knowledge of the things which really count
95. Everything means something
96. Make God's word your authority
97. Be not blind to the important things of life
98. Turn away from those things evil and seek the good
99. Look before you leap
100. Butter your bread only on the top side
101. Life is like a bowl of jello, you must wiggle and shake, but not melt down

+ 1. When all your tomorrows are secure, peace and joy reigns in all of your todays.

A favorite scripture: Jeremiah 29:11 – 12 "For I know the thoughts that I think toward you, says the Lord, thoughts of peace and not of evil, to give you a future and a hope.

Then you will call upon Me and go and pray to Me, and I will listen to you."

Thanks for reading all the way to the end. God Bless.

<u>Other Fiction Books</u>: by J. Gordon Monson

<u>Fascination With Life Series:</u>
The Longest Five Minutes Book I
The Daughter Book II
Angela The Daughter Book III
Modern Day Cowboy Book IV

<u>Survival Collection of Short Stories</u>:
Survival Collection Book I
Collection Book Survival II

<u>Sugarhill Families Series:</u>
Sugarhill Families Book I

<u>Stand Alone Books:</u>
The Bridge So Long
Captain Sam

<u>Nonfiction</u> (*new in 2021*) <u>books</u>
Daily devotional with the Inspired Word of God
WHY? Are we Crumbling from Within?

<u>Coming Soon in (2023)</u> (both fiction)
Seeking Safe Cover
Which Way To Turn

Don't miss out!

Visit the website below and you can sign up to receive emails whenever J. Gordon Monson publishes a new book. There's no charge and no obligation.

https://books2read.com/r/B-A-YEBG-STNIC

BOOKS 2 READ

Connecting independent readers to independent writers.

Did you love *Collection of Short Stories and More*? Then you should read *Sugarhill Families*[1] by J. Gordon Monson!

[2]

HAVE YOU EVER had a long running feud with anyone? Well this story wraps around one that lasted for almost three decades. The feud between Samuel Conners and Will Smithton had lasted over twenty five years. It started back in high school and just seemed to grow as time went by. It was similar to the old story about the 'Hatfields and McCoys.' If you asked most of the family members, you would get the same answer. "I don't know why or how it started." Even Samuel Conners was not sure why it existed or how this ill will could be put away. But with both families living in a small rural town and with both Samuel and Will working at the same employer, it was difficult, at times, almost next to impossible to deal with.

---

1. https://books2read.com/u/47ZMzR

2. https://books2read.com/u/47ZMzR

Also by J. Gordon Monson

Fascination With Life series
The Longest Five Minutes
Angela the Daughter II
Modern Day Cowboy

Fascination With Life Series
The Daughter

Survial Series
Survival Series Collection I (3 Short Stories)
Survival Series Collection II Three Short Stories

Standalone
Sugarhill Families
Captain Sam
The Bridge so Long
Why? Are we Crumbling From Within?
Daily Devotional with the Inspired Word of God

Collection of Short Stories and More

About the Author

The author went from telling his children bedtime stories to enlarging his work to novel-length stories offered to readers beyond his own household in 2012.

Printed in the USA
CPSIA information can be obtained
at www.ICGtesting.com
JSHW021216160823
46613JS00001B/30